D0966777

THE RING

A Selection of Recent Titles by M.J. Trow

The Kit Marlowe Series

DARK ENTRY *
SILENT COURT *
WITCH HAMMER *
SCORPIONS' NEST *
CRIMSON ROSE *
TRAITOR'S STORM *
SECRET WORLD *
ELEVENTH HOUR *
QUEEN'S PROGRESS *

The Grand & Batchelor Series

THE BLUE AND THE GREY *
THE CIRCLE *
THE ANGEL *
THE ISLAND *
THE RING *

The Peter Maxwell Series

MAXWELL'S ISLAND
MAXWELL'S CROSSING
MAXWELL'S RETURN
MAXWELL'S ACADEMY

* available from Severn House

THE RING

M.J. Trow

CRÈME de la CRIME

This first world edition published 2018
in Great Britain and in 2019 in the USA by
Crème de la Crime an imprint of
SEVERN HOUSE PUBLISHERS LTD of
Eardley House, 4 Uxbridge Street, London W8 7SY
Trade paperback edition first published
in Great Britain and the USA 2018 by
SEVERN HOUSE PUBLISHERS LTD

British Library Cataloguing in Publication Data
A CIP catalogue record for this title is available from the British Library.

ISBN-13: 978-1-78029-109-3 (cased)
ISBN-13: 978-1-78029-590-9 (trade paper)
ISBN-13: 978-1-4483-0167-6 (e-book)

All Severn House titles are printed on acid-free paper.

Severn House Publishers support the Forest Stewardship Council™ [FSC™],
the leading international forest certification organisation.
All our titles that are printed on FSC certified paper carry the FSC logo.

Typeset by Palimpsest Book Production Ltd.,
Falkirk, Stirlingshire, Scotland.
Printed and bound in Great Britain by
TJ International, Padstow, Cornwall.

ONE

I t had been a long time since William Bisgrove had seen a woman. There *had* been a couple who'd cooked and cleaned but mostly, he was used to a world of men. The chaplain, by definition, was a man and Bisgrove didn't actually know his name. The warders were men, big, beefy blokes with shoulders like wardrobes and attitudes to match. The only other man he knew was himself, counting the cockroaches in his tiny cell. Except that the annoying little buggers wouldn't keep still. He had tried common sense at first, talking to them man to man. His Sunday School teacher, back in Wookey, had told him that they were all God's creatures and surely, Bisgrove reasoned, he'd be able to get them to see sense and stand still so that he could count them. After all, seen one cockroach, seen them all.

That was before The Day. Because on The Day – and William Bisgrove didn't know what day that actually was – he had wandered away from the mailbag sewing to the latrine. There, as he heard the tinkling in the pan, he saw a sight he'd never seen before. The little window high above his head was open; only a crack, it was true, but it *was* open. All he had known for nearly five years was bars, iron and steel, brass and padlocks, leather straps and tight webbing. Now – on The Day – he could smell fresh air and see the sky. He buttoned away his privates and climbed, his laceless boots slithering on the porcelain as he hauled himself up by the pipes. He nudged the window open and saw the open courtyard far below, the roofs of the houses beyond and green fields beyond that.

William Bisgrove was not a large man. Consumption as a child had left him small and weak-lunged. He tried his head first, then his left shoulder, then his right. Suddenly, he was out on the leads, slithering his way as quietly as he could towards the main gate. He crouched in the shadows of the cupola, the gilded weathervane flashing in the sun. He heard the murmur of conversation below him and the rattle of keys. There was that bastard, the one they called Jalop, holding forth with his usual air of superiority. The little one, Minnow, was listening to his every word, lost in adoration of the senior man. Billy Inkester was there too, but since he had the brains of a louse, he might just as well have been another brick in the wall.

Bisgrove edged his way along the roof, his feet teetering on the shaky metal of the guttering. All he could see now was the sky, a cloudless blue, and he knew it must be high summer. If only he could reach the tower . . .

A bell clanged from the cupola and he braced himself. It was only feet from him and he felt as though the clapper was hammering inside both ears. He pressed himself as flat as he could. He knew what that bell meant. Prisoner on the loose. They must have missed him from the work detail now and sounded the alarm. Even a warder as dim as Inkester – and there were lots of them – recognized an open window in a latrine when they saw one. There was a scrabbling at the gates below, the grating of iron bolts and the yelp and snarl of the dogs. Whistles blew and hobnailed boots clattered on the cobbles.

Bisgrove had got out of an upstairs window; it made sense that they'd try the upper storeys and the roof first. He rolled to his left, scraping his nose on the tiles and tasting blood in his mouth. Another roll and he'd reached the tower wall. He looked down. There'd be guards on the gates but the tower had six sides. If he could just slip down in the shadow of the wall . . .

He had to try. This was his one, perhaps his only, chance of freedom; his chance to tell the world his story, about how wrong they'd all been. He hadn't done it for the money; he'd already told them that. In truth, he didn't know why he'd done it, but it wasn't for the money. And it was all for the love of Millie, really. Surely, they would understand that. He dropped over the parapet, his boots slipping on the stone. He caught the iron of the downpipe, ripping a fingernail as he did it and swung his body across. For one heart-stopping moment, his vision swam and the pipe above him doubled and tripled in his panic. The iron was almost hot to the touch and he slithered down, checking himself with each support until he could jump to the ground. His legs buckled and he lost a boot. He could hear the bells and the dogs in a mad cacophony inside. And he ran, striking out across the open ground for freedom.

Surely, they'd be on the roof by now, scanning the perimeter with their telescopes, looking out for a man on the run. William Bisgrove hadn't run anywhere for the last five years; he had almost forgotten how. His legs felt like lead and his lungs were on fire. The nearest street, where he might lose himself, seemed miles away. He could see people going about their business, little kiddies with their hoops and tops, a clergyman in a silk top hat. There were two women, shapely ones too, in those new bustles he'd heard about but never actually seen. There would come a time . . .

He ducked around a corner and instinctively changed his speed. He sauntered now rather than ran, trying not to limp in his one-booted state. It was a hot day, so the fact that he was in his shirt sleeves wouldn't draw too much attention. He looked in a shop window until he saw the shopkeeper looking back at him and thought he ought to go. He touched his cap to a passing matron then realized he had no cap and tugged his forelock instead. She ignored him just the same. By the time he'd got to the end of the street, he felt confident enough to catch the flying dice of a playing urchin, threw them back to him and patted him on the head. And he passed the sign on the end wall that pointed the way back to the building he had just left, his former home – 'This Way To Broadmoor, Hospital for the Incurably Insane'.

And since The Day, William Bisgrove had come on in the world as sweltering July had become cooler August and cooler August became changeable September. He had gone to London, where the streets, he'd heard, were paved with gold. He had acquired new boots, an overcoat and a cap. He would have to work on gloves and a scarf soon, come the winter. People had been very kind. That nice old lady pushing the perambulator had given him a shilling. The rest of her purse contents he had simply taken. He felt sure she wouldn't mind. At least, lying on the pavement where he had left her unconscious, she didn't seem to be complaining.

The soup kitchens saw him proud every day and nice people in black uniforms gave him bread and serenaded him with hymns and a tambourine. Some of the younger ones, the women that is, were really quite pretty, in a religious sort of way. Washing lines were a constant source of supply for William Bisgrove. He had never changed his combinations as often in his life.

But always, he noticed, the river drew him; and he didn't know why. Old Father Thames, brown and gliding, pulled him like an iron filing to a magnet. Upstream, as the summer died, gilded ladies with frothy parasols and crinolines were stumbling in and out of skiffs and punts, chaperoned by old dears and flirting with bright young men in striped blazers and straw boaters. William Bisgrove could have watched them for hours and sometimes did. And then he would catch sight of the Roman helmet of a park bobby and feel he should be on his way. He'd watch them again, further downstream, where the coast was clearer and he could hide in the bushes, alone and undisturbed. But in the end, they were nothing like his Millie.

Bet staggered away from her last client. He had been rougher than most, a sailor too long at sea, off a merchantman in the East India Dock. His pockets bulged with pay and they were emptier now he had met Bet. There had been a time when she still thought of herself as attractive, when she was still in service and that nice church-going Mr Melksham had deflowered her. She had only been a girl then and barely knew the taste of gin. Now, it was almost the only taste she knew. She checked herself at the door of the Britannia, looking up and down the street for undesirables.

Night came swiftly to Whitechapel and it brought near-total darkness. A gas lamp in the Abyss was as rare as hen's teeth and it wasn't always welcome. Girls of Bet's calling could use it to advertise their wares, but once they'd snared a punter, light was the last thing they needed. Punters in Whitechapel weren't choosy. Not for them the sophistication of the *poses plastiques* and the sensuality of soft lighting and softer beds. It was a case of striking a deal for fourpence; then, feet planted firmly apart, skirts up over the back and a steady grind for however many minutes the punter could last. Then, down came the skirt and the whole process began all over again.

Tonight, though, the sailor had lost his temper. Rum and years at sea had taken its toll and he had stayed as limp as a lanyard; he had taken it out on Bet, for all her techniques of persuasion. He'd hit her, slamming her head against a wall and slapping her face. So Bet had hit back the only way she knew, not with her boot or her knee, but with the slickness of her fingers. She'd lifted the sailor's wallet and it bulged with promise. She'd hurried away down the alleyways that had been her home for so long. It would be minutes before he realized his loss and by then, night and the Abyss would have swallowed her up.

She went in to the Britannia where the gaslight was green and the pipe smoke hung in wreaths over the beer-ringed tables. Irishmen sat there, the tinkers she knew well, sellers of string and beads and trinkets, men who drank for a living and prayed to the Virgin Mary. There were Mulattos, tall, dark men from the Caribbean whose ships had been routed past Liverpool to London, the greatest docks in the world, in their quest for profit. Four Chinamen sat smoking in one corner, their jabber incomprehensible, their pigtails halfway down their backs and their clogs wooden. There were no Jews in the Britannia. These were the Chosen People, the respectable ones who kept apart. When they drank, they drank together. When they prayed, they prayed behind closed doors and on the wrong day of the week. It took all sorts. And all humanity (almost) was in the Britannia that night. So was William Bisgrove.

He sat in the darkest corner and kept his head down when a copper strolled in to talk to the barman. He noticed the man's eyes darting in all directions, but it was likely, he told himself, that he was looking for somebody else entirely. Bisgrove had been on the run for nearly three months now. He had scanned the newspapers when he could scrounge a copy in the gutter or on a park bench and had read nothing about himself. That nice Dr Orange had taught him to read, in between counting cockroaches and now Bisgrove had reason to thank the man. But just because there was nothing in the newspaper, it didn't mean that the boys in blue weren't looking for him.

When he looked up again, it was to hear a scream. A dowdy woman in a black skirt, bodice and shawl was being dragged by the hair away from the bar by a rough-looking sailor, his peaked cap at a jaunty angle on his head. The accent was unplaceable and the English broken, but the altercation clearly had to do with money. A couple of chairs overturned with a crash and the Britannia's customers cleared out of the way. They were experts at this; such incidents happened most nights.

'Take it outside!' the barman bellowed and since he was already swinging a hefty-looking club, the sailor took his advice. He dragged the woman past Bisgrove and just for a moment, their eyes met. Quietly and without a word, he got up and followed the struggling pair out into the night air. He couldn't see anybody at first, then he heard another scream in a dark alley and he followed the sound. He'd been here before once, a long time ago. It was dark then too, but it was a field, not an alleyway. It was all rather vague, like a dream, but there was a man and a woman, just like now. But that was Millie, and she was different.

The sailor had forced open the woman's bodice and was helping himself to a wallet he had found there. He slapped her around the head, once, twice, then hauled up her skirts. He was just fumbling with his flies when he felt an iron grip around his head.

'I'd like you to leave this lady alone,' Bisgrove said softly. The sailor hadn't heard him creep up and he instinctively reached for the knife inside his coat. Whatever the man said, it sounded decidedly unpleasant and there was just the smallest of cracking sounds as William Bisgrove snapped his neck.

The body fell heavily to the alley floor and Bet caught her breath for the first time in what seemed like hours. She aimed a tentative kick to the sailor's head, but the man didn't groan and the man didn't move. She looked up at Bisgrove, her eyes wide, half in astonishment, half in fear. He should have been her knight errant, galloping to the aid of a lady in distress. But she didn't like the look in his eyes. She had just seen him kill a man and that left Bet in a vulnerable and lonely place.

The wallet still lay on the ground, the sailor's money that would keep Bet in gin and a doss-house bed for a month. But standing between it and her was one of the strangest men she'd ever met. He was probably thirty, with pale skin and red-rimmed eyes. His clothes didn't fit him, but that applied to many who prowled the Abyss, especially after dark. She resorted to the only weapon she had, her charms. Her bodice was already open, so she bared her breasts, jutting them out at him. Then she lifted her skirts up to her waist, opening her legs as she steadied herself against the wall.

'Feeling good natured, dearie?' She hated those words, but she had said them so often now, she knew no other way to put it.

William Bisgrove looked at the woman, offering him everything he had always wished for during his long years in his solitary cell. He bent down, picked up the sailor's knife and left the wallet where it was. 'I've got what I came for, lady,' he said.

And he was gone.

There was nothing George Crossland loved more than the early morning. True, it was cold on the river and the galley lurched heavy under the oars of just one man. But against that he could measure the silence of the dawn, the mist like writhing ghosts over the water and the sense of peace. Even the waves, lapping gently against the bow, sounded like the soft kisses of a mother on her baby's brow, somewhere between a murmur and a sigh.

George Crossland didn't get much peace at home. 'Look at her mother,' friends had warned him when he had thought of popping the question all those years ago. His Sarah was beautiful, with raven hair and a way of tilting her head that fascinated him. But that was then and he hadn't listened to his friends. Now the raven hair was thin and greying, the tilt of her head always accompanied by a barrage of questions; where was he going? Who was he going with? When would he be back? Then, there were the kids. The twins and the odd one. And they didn't come much odder than little Billy Crossland. What they all had in common however was the noise and the whine and the dribbling snot. And that peculiar smell, somewhere between a stale biscuit and something that had died behind the wainscoting. It would be a hardy person indeed who would want to drop a gentle kiss on any of the Crossland brood. Lovely Sarah had become her mother and she had bred the children from hell.

And so George lit the oil lamps in the darkness, washed in cold water from the pump and hauled on his uniform, Metropolitan Police for the use of.

He was far upstream now, watching the little eddies of dark water under his oar blades – Father Thames trying to decide which way to run. The river had its ways, difficult and meandering, still furious at the way that Joseph Bazalgette had hemmed it in downstream with his concrete embankments, burying the soft warm mud for ever as London grew into a new kind of jungle. To his right the fields lay a dull gold as the sun's early rays lit them, stretching across Chelsea to the Hospital where a few little old men in scarlet tottered around their gardens. Soon, Crossland knew, they would change into their regulation blue; the season was September and Winter Dress would come in.

To his left, the dark trees of Battersea Gardens dipped over the bank. Bazalgette's blocks had not spread this far upriver and the mud still ruled. When Crossland had first joined the River Police, there had been mudlarks along this stretch, up to their thighs in the grey-brown sludge, up to their elbows in its cold clamminess, looking for anything dropped from a passing boat. George Crossland had only a passing acquaintance with history, but he knew that men had lived along the river for centuries and men in every age were careless with their belongings. Thomas More, someone had told him, once lived somewhere along this river stretch. He had been King Henry the Eighth's right-hand man and was richer than God. He was always dropping stuff on his way home by watermen, or so the story went.

But perhaps the mud at Battersea was all played out, because there were no mudlarks here now. They'd all moved downstream towards the docks. That was where the real rubbish lay, pennies, trinkets, bonnets and shawls. All right, the clothes stank and had to be washed and dried in the sun, but they would do for the old clo' markets of Whitechapel and Spitalfields; and people couldn't afford to be too choosy these days – not if they scratched a living with the Irish in the East End.

Crossland steadied his oar as he let the galley's prow nudge the old jetty. It was still marked clearly on all the maps but no one used it now. London had grown so fast that most people

visiting Battersea Gardens went by bus or train. It was still
quicker to walk than to haggle with a pleasure-boat owner on
the river and a damned sight cheaper. He looked across to the
north bank again. A solitary copper from V Division was ambling
at the regulation speed past Turk's Row. There was no one else
about. The carters had been up for the best part of an hour now
and already hauling hay and carrying carcases for the great
markets of west London. And it would be hours before the
doxies of Chelsea tumbled out of their shabby bordellos looking
for work. For the moment, that blissful moment that George
Crossland appreciated only too well, that copper from V Division
was all alone, lost in the private thoughts inside his head.

If 'Daddy' Bliss had asked George Crossland later – and he
did – precisely at what time he had seen it, Crossland couldn't
have been sure. The River Police, alone of the Met Divisions,
had been issued with watches. Coppers on dry land, pounding
their regular beats, always had a clock somewhere in their
eyeline. St Andrew's clock was three minutes slow and St
Sepulchre's a minute and a half fast, but that was good enough.
Only on the railways were they obsessed with time. A landlocked copper could always tell the time, near as damn it. But
the river was different. In the morning, the mist made all the
clock towers invisible. The darkness of night hid them entirely
and downstream, the derricks and walls of the wharves blocked
everything. The water worked as a sounding board which
absorbed, baffled and re-echoed every sound, so the chimes
were hard to count, seeming to come from all directions at
once, their voices warped beyond all recognition.

But it must have been a little before six that Crossland saw
it, something floating white near the centre of the stream. He
couldn't make out the shape, but it was large. And he had the
oddest sensation that it shouldn't have been there, like a whale
on a beach he had once read about. The river took the object,
as Crossland knew it would, back upstream for a moment, then
down again and further out, twirling it in an eddy so the shape
was hard to fathom. Anyone who didn't know the river would
think that the white thing had a life of its own, perhaps some
huge fish coming to the surface to die; to have one last look at
London before, like the Kraken, submerging for ever. But

Crossland knew it was just the currents carrying some lifeless thing with the secret patterns that only the river knew for sure. Water, playing with its old partner-in-crime, the wind, mocking the humans who pretended that they could understand and control it.

Crossland watched the white blob slide nearer. It would pass him in a minute and something in his head told him that that would not do. He must stop its progress downstream, halt it in its journey to the sea, its attempt to beat the river at its own game. And there was something he didn't like about it, the thing dancing with the tide. As it rolled, the shape seemed somehow familiar; yet odd, because, again, it shouldn't have been there.

He wrenched the left oar around, twisting his body so that the galley moved out to the centre. Crossland steadied himself. Each of the River Police galleys had a mind of its own and Number Eight was no different. It rolled in rough water and slewed to the left, only coming into its own with a full crew on board. Against one man, it played silly buggers and many was the morning that carters on their way along the banks or gentlemen out for a morning ride heard George Crossland talking to Number Eight in decidedly unfriendly – and unprofessional – terms.

Number Eight rocked a little as he stood up; then steadied itself as it sensed the rising unease in Crossland himself. His brain and chest were pounding, his mouth hanging open in disbelief. As his oar-blade caught it and he held it fast to Number Eight's ribbed, wet side, he knew exactly what the white thing was. It was the left side of what had once been a human being, sliced neatly at the hip and below the breast. There was no arm. No head. No legs. It was pale and curved, like the carcases hanging outside the butchers' shops or in the meat market at Spitalfields or Smithfield.

In the sudden chill of the morning, Constable George Crossland of the River Police had found a body.

TWO

Mrs Rackstraw, as she would tell anyone who would listen, was not a nosy woman. Her neighbours could do exactly as they liked, and she would scarcely notice a thing. If the brazen hussy across the road was fool enough to let her fancy man out of the side door in the grey light of dawn while her husband was away on business, then that was her own affair; quite literally, Mrs Rackstraw would tell the baker's boy with a disapproving sniff. If the bailiffs called more frequently two doors down than any delivery boy, then that, too, was none of Mrs Rackstraw's business; they had carted off a rather nice Sheraton desk last time, she told the charwoman in hushed tones.

But what she would admit to, without demur or condition, was that she would look out for her two young gentlemen to her dying day. As her eyes clouded over with the film of death, they would nevertheless be peeled to watch for danger. So she noticed the man outside straight away, from her vantage point behind the drawing-room curtains. It was true that 'danger' was not the first thing that she thought when she saw him. Scrawny, yes. Furtive, certainly. Even underhand. But unless he had the skill to hide an extremely large, heavy and sharp weapon under his coat, he would be little danger, even to a household of women, as they were until the young gentlemen came home. Mrs Rackstraw, though not at all fat, was tall and rangy. The char, finishing off the rough in the kitchen, was seventeen stone at a conservative estimate and had a nasty temper. The between maid – a bone of contention between Mrs Rackstraw and the men who erroneously assumed themselves to be her employers – was small and timid but had once proved to an overly forward butcher's lad that she had a vicious bite. So they would all be safe enough. But the man's behaviour was plenty to arouse Mrs Rackstraw's suspicion. She had been watching him for a while and his movements had taken on the rhythm of a sinister pavane.

She had noticed him first as a shadow under the porch of the house across the way. Surely, she had thought, the hussy hadn't got herself *another* fancy man? But no; the shadow had peeled itself from the wall and crossed the road, jinking and jittering around the cabs and carts which trundled through Alsatia all day long. On reaching the pavement on the other side and so close to the wall beneath her window that she could see the nap on his hat, he waited, looking up at the front door almost longingly. Then he walked a few yards to the left, then stopped and turned, walking the same distance to the right and, looking up at the house again, almost met her eyes. She ducked behind the curtain and when she looked again, he was at the bottom of the steps, looking now right, now left.

She stepped away from the window and made her way to the door. The daft girl she had employed as a between maid – young gentlemen of her calibre, she had told them, should not just have a housekeeper; what would people say? The younger, the apple of her eye, if she had been forced to the point, had said that people would say how sensible of them to save money by not having a between maid, but his remark had fallen for once on deaf ears – the daft girl sometimes opened the door when the knocker sounded; more often she didn't. Time and again, Mrs Rackstraw had hauled her out of the coal cellar where she was hiding, her hands over her ears. Time and again, she had told her that it was her job to answer the door, to take a message, to put visitors in the drawing room, whatever was appropriate. But poor Maisie was not one who could appreciate the subtleties of choices that complex and she preferred to hide.

So Mrs Rackstraw straightened her apron, patted her hair and waited, hands folded, inside the door, ready to whip it open as soon as the knocker hit the wood.

Nothing.

Puzzled, she went back to the window and peered out. And there he was again, on the pavement. Ten feet one way, ten feet back. Up the steps. Down the steps. Ten feet one way, ten feet back. She began to feel quite giddy, but wouldn't relinquish her post. Danger. Or if not danger, then at the very least an escaped lunatic and if everything she had read in the penny press was true, people like that could have the strength of ten.

The clock in the hall struck twelve. Twelve and a half; she made a note to herself to remember to call the clockmaker around the corner in the Strand to come and check it over. It had never been quite the same since a client of the young gentlemen had gone berserk and set about it with a knobkerrie under the impression it was his mother-in-law. She had said from the start that the man was as mad as a bloater, but they would have it they were the experts and look where it had got them. But twelve or twelve and a half; they would be back for their dinner any minute and they could deal with the lunatic themselves. She took herself off back to the kitchen, to make sure that Maisie had remembered to move the stew over onto the hot plate. September could be treacherous, and her young gentlemen would be ready for something hot.

The lunatic was on his ten feet to the left when Matthew Grand and James Batchelor came swinging around the corner from their office in the Strand. They had had a good morning. Not only had the Duke of Buccleuch paid his bill – finally – but they had also discovered who had been stealing the lead off the roof of St Andrew Undershaft, so had had the blessing of the Bishop of London. Money would be nice, but the wheels of Christendom grind slow, they knew; they could look forward to that sometime in the next decade, probably, but the good wishes of a bishop were as good as money in the bank. Almost.

'So, James,' Grand said, bounding up the steps two at a time. 'I believe I had ten shillings on it being chops for lunch.'

James Batchelor smiled a slow smile. 'It's as good as mine, Matthew,' he said, smugly. 'It's Tuesday. It's never chops on Tuesday; it's stew or my name is Guillermo Fazackerley.'

Grand turned the doorknob and pushed open the door, releasing a savoury waft of stewed beef. Without another word, he passed a folded banknote behind him to Batchelor, who followed him into the house, laughing.

The lunatic turned at the end of his ten-foot march and looked after them, need and hunger in his red-rimmed eyes.

*   *   *

The stew was, as always, magnificent. Mrs Rackstraw was not perfect, Grand and Batchelor would be the first to admit, but her cooking skills were never in doubt. Grand was still having trouble coming to terms with cow-heel pie, but that was more a failing of English cuisine than the woman herself, so he was prepared to let that one go.

'Is that lunatic still outside?' the housekeeper demanded, spooning out seconds.

'Lunatic?' Batchelor paused in mid-slurp to check.

'Yes. Lunatic.' Sometimes, she wondered how they made a living as detectives at all; they noticed nothing, not even when it was under their noses. 'You can't miss him. About so high,' she held out a hand at about her own head height, 'scrawny-looking. Pale. Derby hat. Brown coat.'

They both looked at her and shook their heads.

'He's been there most of the morning.'

Two identical shrugs.

She sighed and put down her ladle with a splash. 'You can't have missed him.' She sounded almost plaintive, not her usual confident self at all. 'About so high . . .'

The dining-room door opened, and Maisie's red-tipped nose came around it. 'Mrs Rackstraw,' she murmured, resolutely refusing to look at either Grand or Batchelor. Her mother had told her without mincing words what happened to girls who looked directly at gentlemen. She had stopped listening in detail when the litany had reached the drawers, but it hadn't sounded nice at all.

'Yes, Maisie?' The woman rounded on her like a cobra. 'What is it? How many times have I told you to knock first?'

The girl retreated and slammed the door behind her. The three people in the dining room waited patiently. This had happened before.

A timid knock came from the other side of the door.

'Come in,' said Mrs Rackstraw, barely containing her irritation.

The dining-room door opened and Maisie's red-tipped nose came around it. 'Mrs Rackstraw,' she murmured, 'there's a gentleman at the kitchen door, wants to speak to . . .' and her voice died away. Her mother had been unspecific, but she preferred not to use gentlemen's names in case it brought on a Fate Worse Than Death.

'Who?' Matthew Grand said kindly. Maisie nearly died on the spot.

Mrs Rackstraw strode to the door. 'I'll go and see, shall I?' she said, bustling Maisie out in front of her. 'It's probably the lunatic.' And with that, she was gone.

It was the lunatic, but even Mrs Rackstraw, predisposed to see madness seeping from every pore, had to admit that, closer to, he seemed a little less mad, a little more simply upset. He was waiting in the doorway to the kitchen, the way being barred by the char, a woman who could stop – and, so the rumour ran, actually had done so – a runaway horse by the simple expedient of planting her feet firmly and not budging an inch. He looked even smaller and more woebegone when dwarfed by Mrs Gooding; but as that applied to most people, that was little guide. His clothes, Mrs Rackstraw decided on a cursory glance, were good if a little out of date, but as her fashion interest had last been piqued in 1854, that might not have been a very pertinent observation. After a moment, she decided he was fit to be allowed into the house and edged Mrs Gooding aside.

'Would you care to step this way, sir?' she said. 'It is unusual for us to have visitors to the back door.' She didn't mean to remonstrate with someone who might yet turn out to be a gentleman, but these things were important; an Alsatia address was after all, when push came to shove, an Alsatia address. That part of London was going up in the world.

He looked both ways and leaned in to whisper out of the corner of his mouth. 'I didn't want to be seen,' he said.

Mrs Rackstraw drew herself up and sniffed. In that case, he would have done well to have dispensed with the marching up and down outside the house, but it wasn't her place to say so. 'Name?'

'Umm . . .' the man looked back and forth again. 'I'd rather not say.'

She looked at him with contempt. So he *was* a lunatic, after all. 'I can't show you in to see my gentlemen without a name, sir,' she said, firmly.

'Smith.'

'Really?' She looked down her nose at him. She and Mr

Rackstraw, may he rest in peace, had once had a memorable holiday in Ramsgate as Mr and Mrs Smith, before they had tied the knot. No one had believed it then and she didn't believe it now.

'Well . . . Wellington-Smith, to be accurate.'

As they had just passed the boot-room on the kitchen side of the green baize, she was unimpressed by his flight of fancy. However, it gave her something to say as, having crossed the black and white tiled hall, she flung open the door to the drawing room and showed him in.

'Mr Wellington-Smith,' she said, almost keeping the snort of derision from her voice.

Neither Grand nor Batchelor was feeling very amiable, having been dragged away from their meal without benefit of dessert. Stew was always followed, as night follows day, by treacle sponge and Matthew Grand had learned to love it like an Englishman born and bred. Never mind; a lunatic needn't take up too much eating time. Grand stepped forward and grabbed the man's hand and pumped it up and down in a friendly fashion. 'Mr Wellington-Smith,' he said and led him to a chair. 'How may Mr Batchelor and I help you?' He felt he should make something clear. 'We do have consulting rooms, you know. Just round the corner, in the Strand.'

'Yes,' Wellington-Smith said. 'I do know. But . . . this matter is extremely sensitive.'

Batchelor slipped a knowing wink to Grand. Sensitive was their stock-in-trade, but if every wife who wanted her husband followed or every husband who wanted to find out where his wife went on alternate Tuesdays came round to the house, it would be like Piccadilly Circus.

'Now you're here,' Batchelor said, 'you can speak freely. We guarantee confidentiality at Batchelor and Grand.'

'At Grand and Batchelor,' Grand affirmed, 'we promise not to share any information. Except,' and he paused, 'where we discover that a crime has been committed. In that case, we must report it to the police.'

Wellington-Smith leapt up with a strange cry. 'The police!' He turned pale. 'The police? I can't involve the police! She's as good as dead if I involve the police!'

Grand and Batchelor looked at each other with wide eyes. This was clearly not a case of a missing poodle, an unreliable business partner or a neighbour whose horse had been eating the hedge.

Grand was first to speak. 'Dead? Who is as good as dead?'

Wellington-Smith grabbed his hat and made for the door. 'I had no idea you worked with the police,' he muttered. 'I was led to believe you were confidential enquiry agents.'

Grand was more familiar with Mrs Rackstraw's rather profligate placing of occasional tables and got to the door first and stood in front of it. 'Totally confidential,' he assured the man. 'We have to say the bit about the police because . . . well, it has happened from time to time that a crime has been discovered as a side issue, one might say, of our enquiries.'

'Like the dog thing, that time,' Batchelor chipped in.

'Indeed. Indeed, the dog thing. So, you can see,' Grand said, though Wellington-Smith was still trying to dodge round him to the door, 'it is sometimes our duty to inform the police, but only if there is a crime tangential to our enquires.'

Wellington-Smith, looking mutinous, went back to his seat and stowed his hat on the floor. 'I really can't tell the police,' he said. 'They said they would kill her if I went to the police.'

'Kidnapping,' Batchelor said, nodding.

Wellington-Smith bridled. 'Who said anything about kidnapping?' he said, his voice shrill with nervous tension.

'No one,' Batchelor said. 'But as a rule, the only people who threaten to kill anyone if you go to the police are kidnappers.' He looked across at Grand. 'You'll correct me if I'm wrong . . .'

'No,' Grand said. 'Kidnappers. The only choice, really.'

Wellington-Smith was mollified but still sat looking down at his hands in an agony of indecision.

'If you tell us your problem,' Grand prompted, 'and you don't want our help, we promise we won't do anything with the information.'

'Including going to the police?'

'Including that.' Grand wanted to move this conversation along; the afternoon was going to be tedious enough without this drawing information out as if it was an impacted tooth.

Wellington-Smith relaxed a little into his chair and began his story with little preamble. 'My name, as you may have guessed, is not Wellington-Smith.'

Batchelor, who had already written the name on the outside of his new client notepad crossed it out and tried not to look too annoyed.

'My name is Byng. Selwyn Byng. You may have heard of me?'

Grand and Batchelor tried to look both intelligent and noncommittal – they had never heard the name before in any context.

'My family are timber importers, with warehouses down the Thames. Sillitoe, Byng and Son, Finest Siberian Timber.' He looked from one to the other but saw no sign of recognition. 'Never mind. I am "Son" you might say, also Selwyn, after my grandfather, who started the business. My father runs it now and I work for . . .' he swallowed the word, 'alongside him. And of course, all of it will be mine one day.'

'And your son's,' Batchelor said, pleasantly.

Byng gave vent to a bloodcurdling howl that made Grand almost lose his stew. 'Ah, the pain that gives me, Mr Batchelor. If only I will one day be the proud father of a boy to bear the proud name of Byng.'

There seemed little to be said by way of small talk following this outburst and so the enquiry agents waited for him to gather himself together and continue his tale.

'I married less than two years ago, Emilia, the daughter of old Josiah Westmoreland.' He paused but decided that these two knew nothing of the great importers of London and explained without waiting to be asked. 'Westmoreland tea importers are one of the primary companies in the field; one day, their name will ring alongside such greats as Tetley, but for now, they do well enough. They wholesale tea to workhouses, hospitals and lunatic asylums, a sadly growing market, though not for Westmoreland of course.' He forced a laugh. 'Emilia and I were scarcely married before Josiah passed away.' He lowered his eyes and seemed to take a pause to recover himself. 'Tragic,' he muttered. 'Tragic.'

'I think I remember that,' Grand said. 'Wasn't he crushed by a falling bale of tea?' Batchelor looked at him aghast. This was where the gulf of the Atlantic sometimes showed itself – 'crushed' was perhaps not the best word to use when speaking of a man's father-in-law's sad demise. Although even he could see that 'passed away' was not perhaps the most appropriate way of describing a death by crushing. There was such a thing as being a tad too genteel.

'Indeed, Mr Grand,' Byng said at last. 'Crushed is the word. He was unrecognizable, save for his half-hunter, which was still going.' He foraged in his waistcoat pocket and fished out a watch. 'This very one.'

Batchelor felt a little better – it was a touch ghoulish to carry around a watch prised from the crushed solar plexus of a loved one, so perhaps he hadn't minded the word after all.

'Emilia was of course devastated and so, although the patter of tiny feet had been her overwhelming wish, she felt that, as she was in mourning, it would be inappropriate. So we . . .' he looked up and seemed to change his mind. 'So we decided to wait a while.' His smile grew forced. 'Abstinence does no one any harm, gentlemen, no harm at all. However, to make things easier, Emilia has been staying with her aunt, Jane Moriarty, in Eastbourne for the last two months. This week, it will be a year since the accident and so, to our mutual delight, she was due to get home on Monday. Imagine my joy as I went to meet her at the station.'

It was a tricky pause in the conversation, but it seemed time for a small interjection. Batchelor leapt into the breach. 'It must have been a wonderful moment.' His brain was whirling. Had she arrived looking rather more with child than a year's abstinence could explain? Had she arrived with an actual child? Not arrived at all? Arrived on the arm of . . . the possibilities seemed practically endless.

'Her train came and went and so did the next three but, alas, no Emilia.'

Batchelor tried not to look smug, but it didn't seem much of a puzzle, particularly one which was especially sensitive.

'What did arrive, eventually, was an urchin carrying a note. This note.' Byng delved into his pocket and brought out an envelope, folded in two. He handed it to Grand, who spread it out on the table at his elbow and read it through. It didn't take long; the note had been made up of letters cut from a newspaper and was a mixture of whole words and individual letters. Batchelor, looking over his partner's shoulder, thought he recognized the typeface of the *Telegraph*.

There was no salutation. The note began, 'We've got yur wif. If you wunt to see her again, you must pay fiv thousand pund. We'll let you know were to leve it. Wait for our next leter. You'll get it at your house. No plice or she dies.'

The two enquiry agents read it through several times and then sat down again, facing their client. 'Have you had another letter yet?' Grand asked.

Byng shook his head.

Batchelor held out his hand for the letter. He wanted to give it another look through – though not an expert in ransom notes, there was something about this one that seemed a little strange to him and he needed to work out what.

'Could it be a prank?' Grand asked.

'A *prank*?' Byng was horrified. 'Who would do such a thing?'

'Mrs Byng, perhaps?' Grand was treading on very sensitive ground.

Selwyn Byng drew himself up and looked down his nose at Grand. He was American, so he could perhaps be excused. 'My wife,' he announced coldly, 'does not have a sense of humour. Of any kind. Really; she would be most distressed.'

Grand, rather more of a man of the world than Batchelor, suddenly felt deeply sorry for Selwyn Byng. He appeared to be married to a nightmare in human form; a woman who would rather stay with an aunt in Eastbourne than sleep with her husband and who also had no sense of humour. What would be the point of being married to her at all?

'She has her position to consider. She is, after all, heiress to a considerable tea fortune.'

Ah.

'Although of course, not until she is thirty-five. Her father had very strong views on the capacity of the fair sex to manage money and business and so, rather than put such a terrible burden on his only child, he set up a trust for her, until she should be of sufficient maturity to cope.'

'How old is your wife now, Mr Byng, if I might ask?'

Batchelor had stopped re-reading the ransom note and looked up.

'Twenty-two.'

'So she has a while to wait until she needs to take up the reins of the business,' Grand observed.

'Thirteen years, yes,' Byng agreed. 'But she takes it very seriously already, believe me, gentlemen. A tea empire is not something that you can wear lightly.'

The ex-journalist in James Batchelor winced at the grim metaphor but he moved on. 'I don't think that this note is a prank anyway. For one thing, it isn't even slightly funny. For another, it has been made by someone who is trying just a little too hard to be convincing. A joker wouldn't take the effort.'

'What do you mean?' Byng asked.

'Well, the spelling is a little random,' Batchelor said. 'Simple words, such as "wife" are misspelled. But more difficult ones, such as "thousand" are correct. Besides that, the grammar is right; I've seen worse grammar than this turned in as copy on a very reputable paper.' Batchelor's *Telegraph* days were never far away.

'So, what does that mean?' Byng was confused.

'I think,' Grand said, looking his colleague in the eye, 'I think it means, Mr Byng, that you should go home and wait for the next letter. And we'll be right behind you.'

THREE

'I don't see any pickles, Brandon.' Daddy Bliss was examining the plate in front of him.

'Sorry, Inspector.' Constable Brandon bobbed next to the man. 'I didn't have a chance to get to the market today.'

Bliss looked up at the lad. As spotty and stupid as any other rookie he had encountered in the River Police, Brandon couldn't even find a decent pickle when a man's life might well depend upon it. 'Do you intend to make a career in the constabulary service, lad?' he asked.

'Yessir!' Brandon stood as near to attention as he could under the cramped deck of the *Royalist*, the River Police's floating station on the Thames.

Bliss slid back his chair, letting his girth fill the open space. He was suddenly looking at Brandon in a new light. 'Can you actually *row*?' He squinted at him, taking in the soft fingers, the scrawny arms under the blue serge.

'Twenty laps on the Serpentine, Inspector.' Brandon was proud of that.

'Serpentine, my arse,' Bliss grunted. 'This is the *River*, boy. Its fogs'll give you consumption and its currents'll pull your arms out of their sockets if you let 'em. We'll have to toughen you up if you intend to make a go of things around here.'

There was shouting on the deck and the clatter of galoshed boots on the stairs that came down into the mess quarters.

'Don't you knock, Constable?' Bliss was tearing apart a hunk of bread while Brandon, anxious to stay in the service, was busy brewing the tea.

'Sorry, sir.' George Crossland stood there, river weed trailing from his boots. 'Something's come up.'

'Funny, isn't it?' Bliss grunted, 'how things always come up when I'm having my lunch – Mother of God; what's that?'

Crossland held the white thing in both hands, as though he

was offering the inspector dessert. 'It's a body, sir. Or part of one. Left side, I'd say. No distinguishing features.'

'Take it up top, man. God knows what it'll do to my Stilton. Double up, damn you.'

Crossland clattered back up the stairs again, onto the *Royalist*'s deck. It took a lot to rattle Daddy Bliss, yet he was clearly rattled and Crossland was secretly glad of that. He was glad that it wasn't just him who had been nauseated by carrying a piece of a person with him. The river threw up all manner of things, from dead dogs rolling in the currents to suicides, unable to stand the mortal world any longer and flinging themselves into the dark and deadly water. But somehow, a *section* of a cadaver was worse than anything. For a start, it had to be the result of a murder. Even the most determined suicide couldn't carve themselves up into convenient sections.

'Murder, then.' Daddy Bliss had broken off from his lunch, sans pickles as it was, and was looking down at the part torso now. Bliss's kneeling days were over – if a man of his weight had ever had them – and he left that sort of work to his underlings, the six Water Babies who patrolled the river above and below Westminster Bridge.

'Looks that way, sir.' George Crossland was a careful copper. He had worked under Daddy Bliss for five years now. Appear too smart and he'd assume you wanted his job so you'd find yourself in L Division checking the horse troughs come morning. Appear too dim and you'd find yourself looking for Mary Annes along their murky half mile around the arches of the Adelphi. There was a happy balance whereby you stayed in the Abode of Bliss and George Crossland knew exactly how to achieve that.

'Where did you find it?'

'Battersea, Inspector,' Crossland said, steeling himself to turn the battered thing this way, then that. 'Centre stream but veering to the south bank.'

'Moving downriver?' Bliss was looking for any telltale marks on the skin.

'I'd say so, sir, yes.'

Bliss sucked his teeth. George Crossland was a good copper, perhaps the best of the Water Babies and the inspector trusted the man's judgement. 'What's your best guess, then?' he asked, giving the thing another poke. 'Man or woman?'

Crossland shrugged. 'Has to be one or the other, doesn't it?' He was talking to himself really.

'So they tell me,' the inspector nodded. And to be fair, a man in his position had got out more than most.

'Woman, sir.'

'Why?'

'Softness,' Crossland said. 'Paleness. A certain gentleness about it, one way or another.'

Bliss scowled at his constable. That was all he needed, with a woman's part on his desk, a poet. 'Where did she go in, d'you think?' he asked.

'If I *had* to stick my neck out, sir . . .'

'You do,' Bliss assured him.

'The Wandle, that'd be my guess.'

Bliss leaned back on the *Royalist*'s rail, spreading his arms along the weathered timbers. Both men knew that the Wandle was a tributary of the Thames, a fast-flowing stream that ran, sometimes underground, from Croydon to Battersea. If Crossland was right, if somebody had dumped the partial cadaver somewhere along the Wandle banks, that was scarcely any help at all.

'All right,' Bliss said. 'That'll have to do for now. But of course, the *real* question – and this might take a while – is where is the rest of her?'

The two men looked down at the body part, pale and still on the deck. Crossland was thinking sadly about how she – he couldn't help thinking of it as 'she' – had once lived, breathed, laughed and, he hoped, loved. He glanced at his boss who was looking thoughtful. Who would have supposed that the old man had a sensitive side?

Bliss looked up at the constable and pushed the ribcage to one side. 'Bread and Stilton, George?' he said, rubbing his hands together in anticipation.

Grand and Batchelor were not right behind Selwyn Byng, in any accepted sense of the phrase. He had jinked like a startled horse at the very suggestion and had given vent to another of his bizarre cries. He couldn't put his dear Emilia in such peril as to have two well-known enquiry agents accompany him home. He couldn't even allow them to visit under cover of darkness for now; he would much rather keep their connections to the simple expedient of him visiting them, by way of the back door. Mrs Rackstraw would be outraged but she would have to learn to accept it. Selwyn Byng was a gentleman in his own right and married to an heiress; perhaps they could encourage her to think that he was an eccentric millionaire or something similar. Eccentricity could cover a multitude of sins. Meanwhile, though, they had a list of things to do. They needed to visit the timber and the tea warehouses along the Thames and also the aunt in Eastbourne.

'I used to have an aunt in Eastbourne,' James Batchelor said.

'Used to?' Grand didn't really want to know, but it was polite to ask.

'Yes. She was a housekeeper to an old gentleman. He died and . . .' Batchelor coughed and became incredibly interested in a thread on his cuff.

'And . . .?'

'Oh, nothing. Just a bit of unpleasantness about the will, that kind of thing.' Having met Grand's family, Batchelor didn't really know why he felt embarrassed, but he did. His auntie had disappeared shortly after the whole debacle, gone to Australia, so the family said.

Grand could recognize a brick wall when he met one and obligingly changed the subject as far as he was able. 'So . . . what station for Eastbourne?'

'Victoria, as far as I remember. We only visited Auntie once.' Batchelor didn't see that it was necessary to say they visited her in the local gaol.

Grand consulted his pocket watch. 'Do we have time to get there today?'

Batchelor hesitated for several reasons. Firstly, he had no idea. But secondly, and rather more importantly, he thought it would be polite to warn the lady in question that they would be visiting. Her niece had, after all, gone missing and to all intents and purposes from her care. True, she was not a child but she had clearly been sheltered all her life by her family and

if the aunt was as sensitive a blossom as the niece, having them
suddenly turn up on her doorstep would not be pleasant. 'Should
we write first?' he suggested.

'Write?' Grand was sometimes exasperated by the English.
'Write? She might well be the writer of this note. Her niece
might be tied up in her basement. Why should we write?'

Batchelor shrugged. 'It just seems polite.'

'We're not writing, James.' Grand was adamant. 'If you don't
want to call on her late, I understand that. But we can't warn
her we're arriving. If she is in cahoots with the letter writer,
she would have time to hide things, hide *Emilia*, if she has her
stashed somewhere. No; we'll compromise. We'll set off today
but visit her tomorrow. Mid-morning. Around eleven; is that
when maiden aunts are ready to receive visitors?'

'I still think . . .'

'Is it?' Grand didn't often put his foot down, but Batchelor
had learned to recognize those rare occasions.

'Yes. Eleven would be perfectly in order.'

'Wonderful. We won't need much – just an overnight bag.'
Grand went over to the fireplace and tugged on the bell-pull.
'I'd better tell . . .'

With a crash, the door was flung back and Mrs Rackstraw
stood there. Either she had a turn of speed that neither man had
suspected or she had been listening outside the door. 'Yes?' she
said, with ill-concealed irritation.

'Mrs Rackstraw,' Grand said, in his most ingratiating tones.
'We're off to . . .'

'Eastbourne. Yes. Very treacherous, the coast, at this time of
year. I've put some woollen vests out on your beds. You'll have
time to change before the cab gets here.' She folded her arms
and leaned back, looking at them over the formidable prow of
her nose. 'Is this to do with the lunatic?'

'He isn't a lunatic, Mrs Ra . . .'

'Are you suggesting I don't know a lunatic when I see one?'
she demanded. 'With at least two on the loose, I'd be surprised
if he wasn't one.'

'Two?' Grand blinked.

'Bloke called Bisgrove – I was reading about it only the other
day. Walked out of Broadmoor cool as you please.' A thought

suddenly occurred to her. 'You don't think he's the one hanging around outside, is he?' She looked towards the window as if she thought he might be lurking behind the curtain.

'No, Mrs Rackstraw.' Batchelor felt it was important to make that clear. 'And lunacy isn't catching, you know.'

'Tchah!' Mrs Rackstraw was staggered by the man's naivety. Really, he shouldn't be out on his own. 'Believe that if you want, Mr Batchelor, but I have reasons to know you're wrong. Anyhow, I can't stay here talking all afternoon. I have things to do even if you don't.' And she spun on her heel and was gone. 'Don't forget the wool,' she called over her shoulder as she went to the front door to summon a cab.

'Tell me something, James,' Grand asked as they made for the stairs. '*We* employ *her*, is that right?'

'When I know for sure, Matthew,' Batchelor said, 'you'll be the first to know, I promise.'

The wool next to their skin was itchy, but they were glad of it as the wind from the sea cut straight through their clothes. They had found a very poorly drawn street map at the W H Smith's at Eastbourne Station and after much turning it round and round and finding that it had been printed upside down, they succeeded in finding Maple Avenue. Part of the reason for the difficulty they had was that there were no maples and a street less like an avenue it would have been hard to find. It wound, narrow and sunless, behind the promenade and the houses seemed to be a mixture of stately semi-mansions gone to seed and small villas, built on a shoestring and already showing signs of the inevitable depredations of the sea air.

Number Twelve was one of the latter sort, but with a neat garden flanking the path to the front door and fresh paint on the woodwork. The windows sparkled and the net curtains behind the glass were crisp and white. Emilia Byng's aunt might not be rich, but she was clearly a lady who liked things nice. Grand rapped on the door with the bright brass knocker shaped like the Lincoln Imp. He had hardly let go of it when the door was swung open and a little old lady stood there, looking as though she had just stepped out of a bandbox. Her multitude of frills, which she wore from the top of her head to the edge of her petticoat just showing beneath her skirt, were starched so stiffly they almost crackled. Her eyes sparkled, and her lips were parted in a smile, which faded when she saw her visitors.

'I'm sorry,' she said, recovering quickly. 'I was expecting someone else.'

'Emilia?' Grand asked.

'Why, however did you know?' the old lady gasped, stepping back. Her hand flew to her throat. 'Don't tell me there's bad news?' She looked closely at Grand. 'Are you foreign?' She raised her voice slightly, as all nicely brought up maiden ladies do when speaking to foreigners, dogs, children and the indigent.

'No, no, nothing like that,' Batchelor reassured her. 'But we would like to ask you some questions about your niece, if we may? Could we come in?'

It suddenly seemed to dawn on the woman that the neighbours could well be watching and of course, that would never do. She stepped aside and ushered them in, closing the door swiftly behind them, against prying eyes.

The room into which they were taken was as frilly as its owner. Every shelf, every table – and Mrs Rackstraw would have been struck dumb with envy at the profusion – had its own edging; crocheted, tatted, goffered and crimped, there was not a sharp corner in the place. It was like being invited to sit down in the crib of an extraordinarily pampered baby.

Their hostess sat across from them on a low chair, designed originally for nursing or possibly spinning. Her neat little feet were together on the hearth rug and just peeked out from beneath her petticoat edge. Her bright little eyes peered up anxiously into first Grand's face, then Batchelor's. She decided to concentrate on Batchelor; the other one, the foreigner, was a little shifty, in her opinion. Besides, she had never really taken to blond men, after The Incident in the Winter Gardens that time. 'Have you really no news of Emilia?' she asked, plaintively.

'I'm afraid not, Miss Moriarty,' Batchelor said. The foreigner had felt the chill coming from the little woman and decided to leave it to his partner. Batchelor had handed the woman their calling card but she had only the vaguest notion as to what 'enquiry agent' meant. 'Mr Byng has approached us to look into her disappearance.' It was best at this stage to keep things general. He didn't know how much the woman knew.

'Mr Byng?'

The enquiry agents flashed a look between them. Could it be that the whole thing was a put-up job, or was this old dear as mad as a cake?

'Her husband.'

'Oh, I see. I always think of his father as Mr Byng and Selwyn as . . . well,' she tinkled a laugh, 'Selwyn.'

'Do you know Mr Byng senior?' Grand risked a question.

'Yes,' she sniffed. 'I am afraid that I do. Not at all a . . .' she gave it serious thought. 'Not at all a *generous* gentleman. He pays Selwyn, of course, but refuses to hand over the business to him. He can't bear to hand over the reins, you see. Selwyn, to my mind, is perfectly ready to take over. Emilia is full of his praises and I must say that, love her though I do as though she was my own daughter, Emilia can be a very difficult girl to please. She has been the same since the cradle and I don't see her changing now.'

'So,' Batchelor tried to get the conversation back to somewhere he could recognize, 'we have been asked by her husband to look into Mrs Byng's disappearance.'

'Mrs Byng?' The bright eyes looked from one man to the other, the mouth set in a position that made it clear that she was trying her best to understand. 'Surely, Selwyn's mother hasn't disappeared. She has after all been dead these . . . oh. Silly me. You mean Emilia.' They nodded and Grand tried his level best to prevent a quizzical eyebrow from rising up his forehead. 'She is still a little girl to me, you see.'

'We're looking into her disappearance.' Batchelor really couldn't go through all that again.

Miss Moriarty took a shuddering breath. 'You must excuse me, gentlemen, if I seem a little distrait, but I haven't had a wink of sleep since the telegram came to tell me that poor, dear Emilia did not return to London. I cannot imagine where she might have gone.'

This seemed to clarify the situation somewhat; the woman clearly knew nothing about the ransom demand. She seemed to have regained the flow of the narrative, though, so they let her carry on.

A light blush swept over her maidenly cheek. 'Are you aware of the . . . circumstances . . . of her visit here?' She looked down and twisted a ring around her finger.

'Yes,' Batchelor told her. How to put it so that she didn't get even more embarrassed and clam up altogether?

'She and her husband needed to stay apart,' Grand offered. He preferred to call a spade a shovel. 'Newlyweds and all, not wanting to have relations while she was in mourning. Sounds a little cockamamie to me, but I know you do things differently here.'

Miss Moriarty closed her eyes and clamped her lips together until the shock receded. Foreigners; whatever were they for? Eventually, in a pained voice, she continued, speaking to Batchelor only. 'My niece has been very beautifully brought up,' she said. 'My sister, her late mother, was of even finer sensibilities than myself and I think I won't need to assure you that I am a very sensitive woman.' She waited for Batchelor's understanding nod before going on. 'She married quite young. She and Selwyn became engaged to be married when she was just eighteen, and she had never and will never look at another man.' Her eyes flashed and, if looks could kill, Grand would have been so much carrion on the hand-pegged hearth rug. 'So, if your minds, your *filthy* minds are thinking that she has gone off with another man, you can think again!'

She seemed to be in a bit of a tizzy, so Batchelor was quick to deny any such belief.

'That's all right then. She didn't confide in me, of course. As an unmarried lady, it would have been inappropriate in the extreme. Not that I didn't have offers, dearie me, no. But I could never find a man to live up to my requirements. There was a curate once but . . . well, let's say he began to have doubts and I could not continue with a man like that. Where was I?' She looked desperately at Batchelor; she had completely lost the thread and hoped he might have the end of it.

'Confide. Unmarried. Inappropriate.'

'Thank you.' She let a dazzling smile creep through and for a moment, Grand and Batchelor felt sorry for the doubting curate and what he had missed. 'She told me no details, of course, but I gathered from her suitably veiled conversation that Selwyn was very . . .' she fanned herself with her hand, '. . . ardent, and she returned his ardour in a way that had surprised her. So, after some time of trying to . . . abstain . . .' This time, she had to pause and press a perfectly laundered and frilled handkerchief to her lips. 'Young man,' she said to Batchelor, 'could you just tug on the bell pull? I really must have a sip of something.'

Batchelor pulled on the cord and a maid appeared almost with the speed of Mrs Rackstraw. She was all but invisible beneath a swathe of frilled apron, but seemed bright enough and rushed to a corner cupboard when she saw her mistress, lolling pale and distressed on her chair. She poured a brandy that would fell a docker and Miss Moriarty swallowed it in one without a blink.

The maid turned to the enquiry agents who were looking at the maiden lady with some respect.

'The mistress takes these turns,' she said, a touch aggressively. 'Her medicine is the only thing what will bring her round.' She looked anxiously at Miss Moriarty, who had by now a rather better colour and was looking less limp. 'Madam,' she said, anxiously, taking one small, white hand and chafing it between her work-worn palms. 'Should you not go to bed for the rest of the day? You know how your turns can tire you?'

'No, no, Enid. I can continue. These gentlemen are here to help us find poor, dear Miss Emilia. Pass them the portrait.'

The maid bobbed a curtsey at Grand and Batchelor. 'Oh, sirs,' she said, 'if only you can find them safe.' And, with her own rather more plebeian hankie pressed to her eyes, she stuffed a miniature into Batchelor's hand and ran from the room. The painted face was pretty, with a curved mouth, grey eyes and a mass of golden hair. But Matthew Grand and James Batchelor were not enquiry agents for nothing; something else had caught their collective attention.

'Them?' they said, in concert.

'Pardon?' Miss Moriarty had allowed herself a little swoon and had missed the last few minutes.

'Your maid said "them"?' Grand said.

Miss Moriarty bridled. 'A perfectly correct word and, if I may venture, used correctly, if it was Enid speaking. Her grammar is immaculate. I taught her myself.'

'No, no,' Batchelor was quick to interject. 'My colleague meant no criticism. He is merely pointing out that she said "them". "I hope you can find *them* safe" was what she said.'

'A worthy wish, surely.' The brandy had given Miss Moriarty a slightly hectic look around the eyes.

'Indeed. But who is "them"?' Batchelor reran the sentence. Is them? Are them? Was them?

But Miss Moriarty had got the general gist, grammar notwith-standing. 'Why, Emilia and Molly, of course.'

'Molly?' Grand made a mental note to try and avoid choral speaking. It didn't help and made him feel a fool.

'Molly Edwards, Emilia's maid. I saw them both off from the station. In fact, I have been wondering why you are speaking to me when surely, Molly would be the one to ask.'

Batchelor could foresee the end of the conversation already, but he had to say the next sentence. 'We haven't heard about Molly until now,' he said.

Miss Moriarty clutched her hands together at her breast. 'Then . . . has Molly disappeared also?'

The two men were at a loss to answer. Slowly, uncertainly, they nodded their heads. And, as Batchelor had predicted, Miss Moriarty slid gently to the floor, beyond the aid of brandy.

'Shall we see ourselves out?' Grand asked.

Batchelor nodded, giving the bell pull a quick tug as they made for the door.

FOUR

Thomas Fisher had been struggling with this scene for quite a while. As an amateur student of architecture, the Naval College at Greenwich fascinated him, its Queen Anne corners and subtleties of brick and stone. As an amateur artist, he had to contend with the light; and that, of course, changed from day to day and even during the course of each day. The early morning was hopeless. There was too much mist along the river's curve and it played merry hell with his water-colours. This was Sunday, so the river traffic would be less and the combination of late morning and the foreshore of the south bank offered the best combination for him.

He anchored his easel carefully, wedging the feet with stones and planted his rubber waders just so, his coat tucked under him on the canvas campaign chair. Today, he would concentrate on the turrets that stood sharp and clear against the leaden sky, etching in the wrought-iron flags on the smooth surface of his canvas. He'd handle the clouds later. They were too fleeting to catch in reality and, as an artist, he was allowed some licence.

He was sitting there, sketching, the paintbrush clamped between his teeth, when something bobbed towards him in the water. If somebody had asked him then what he thought it was, he would have guessed that it was a partially decomposed sheep. Except that, as an amateur artist, he knew perfectly well that sheep didn't have arms – at least, not in the conventional sense – and this object clearly did. On an impulse of curiosity, he laid the brush on the easel tray and clambered to his feet. The south bank's mud, grey and oozing, was heavy going but he managed and, reaching out, was able to prod the flotsam with a stick. The prod sent the thing twisting in the water and it floated to his feet. It was a shoulder, the flesh grey and flabby and the bone at the end of the arm, just above the elbow, had been sawn neatly through. It was then that Thomas Fisher heard the church bell of St Nicholas, Deptford, toll. It was actually ringing for morning service, but it seemed to him that it tolled for the dead.

Grand and Batchelor picked up their luggage at their hotel and made their way to the station.

'That didn't go too badly,' Batchelor ventured.

'Whatever are you talking about, James?' Grand snapped. He had been treated like something the cat had dragged in by a mad old toper and was not feeling in the best of spirits. 'It was probably one of the least helpful mornings I have ever spent and I speak as one who once interviewed an East End laundress for three hours before discovering she only spoke Cantonese.'

'We found out about the maid,' Batchelor pointed out.

'Yes. And where does that get us, may I ask? Either, the maid came back on her own and Byng didn't think it worth mentioning. Or the maid *didn't* come back and he didn't think it worth mentioning. Or he didn't know she was supposed to be coming back and—'

'Yes, all right, Matthew. I do know what you mean. But what *I* mean is that we have at least discovered she exists. We can ask Byng about her and it will change the whole picture. It might even be the maid who is behind all this. How many times have we known a crime committed by a disgruntled employee? Hmm?'

Grand looked up and counted on his fingers. Eventually, he spoke. 'None.'

'There was that . . . I concede that they might not have been disgruntled. But a lot of them have been employees.'

'You might just as well say that they had heads. Or feet. Almost everyone is an employee in some shape or form. No, I think this maid thing will turn out to be a bit of a red herring. She probably had some days off owing or something. If they had been down in Eastbourne for months, that's a lot of Sunday afternoons she would be owed.'

'She would have had time off down there.'

'Not if she had a follower in London. Why would she waste time off so far from home?'

'You're being difficult on purpose. We found out that Selwyn and Emilia are in love. From someone other than Selwyn, that is.'

'I'll let you have that one.' Grand was never grumpy for long.

'We learned that his father is a bit of a tartar. I wish we'd asked whether he and Emilia got on.'

'Fathers-in-law don't kidnap daughters-in-law just because they don't like them,' Grand said. 'It's a rather extreme reaction, isn't it? Surely the simplest way is just not to ask them over for Thanksgiving.'

'Christmas.'

'Christmas, yes.' Grand had been in England a long time, but while it is not that difficult to take the boy out of Boston, it isn't always easy to take all the Boston out of the boy. 'I suppose it could just be him, if his business is in trouble . . .' He shook his head. 'No, no, that's ridiculous. Forget I even said that.' Grand's own father was a businessman known to be pretty ruthless and he was the benchmark by which his son measured everyone. And there was nothing in God's green earth that would induce Andrew Grand to sink so low.

'Miss Moriarty doesn't seem to be very well off,' Batchelor ventured. 'That street isn't smart and she only seems to have the one maid. She opened the door to us herself, don't forget.'

'That was because she thought it might be Emilia. And all those frills don't come cheap. But what's your point?'

'Well, that if she is Emilia's aunt and not too wealthy, perhaps this trust fund, this tea thing, isn't worth much. So perhaps it's all a case of mistaken identity.'

Grand knew about trust funds. His kept Grand and Batchelor, Confidential Enquiry Agents, afloat, with some to spare. They were usually complicated things, but the obvious answer in this case was in the relationship. 'Miss Moriarty is Emilia's mother's sister,' he said. 'So there may be no money on that side. It's true that mostly these families marry more money, but it could have been for love. Why not? It does happen.'

'I hadn't thought of that.'

The train arrived in a hurricane of steam and cinders. They clambered aboard into an empty carriage. The train's arrival had broken their thought processes and it was a while before either of them could encapsulate what they needed to do next.

'We need to ask Selwyn Byng about the maid,' Grand said, taking the words out of Batchelor's mouth.

'We'll make a note to ask him when he comes round next. Speaking of which, this is most unsatisfactory, you know. We must get round to his house next time; how can we catch who is sending these notes if we can't see them being delivered?'

'True. But if it's just the postman, we won't be any further forward. If he is still nervous about us being seen at his home, we will have to follow him. But it won't be tonight; I'm out.'

'Really?' Grand and Batchelor didn't live in each other's pockets but the American hadn't mentioned he was going anywhere. It was unusual for him to go out when in the middle of a case.

'Yes. I told you, didn't I?' Grand looked a little furtive.

'No.' Batchelor knew how to answer a question so as to leave no room for shilly-shallying.

Grand tried a boyish laugh. 'Lady Caroline, you remember, one of the friends of the—'

'Hush!' Batchelor put his finger to his lips. 'These compartments are made of matchwood. You never know who may be listening.'

Grand nodded and leaned forward, dropping his voice, to the chagrin of the eavesdropping vicar just behind his head through the wall. 'Lady Caroline?'

Batchelor nodded.

'She has a box at the Gaiety and we're going to see the latest show there. I doubt I'll be late . . .'

Batchelor raised an eyebrow.

'But in any event, I'll see you at breakfast.'

And to close any further conversation, Grand leaned back and tipped his hat over his eyes. And soon, the feigned snores were genuine and half of Grand and Batchelor, Confidential Enquiry Agents, No Job Too Small, The Strand, London, slept.

Batchelor looked at him across the carriage. So, Lady Caroline, eh? He hadn't seen that one coming. But it was probably only a matter of time. Handsome, tall, with a brave military background and more importantly a substantial trust fund and inheritance from his uncle, Matthew Grand was a catch, no matter how you looked at it. Batchelor smiled to himself; if he was lucky, he might get the friend of the lady in question. He racked his brain; was Lady Caroline the one with the friend with the wall eye? He sincerely hoped not. With a chuckle, he leaned back too and only woke as the whistle of the train told them they were approaching Victoria Station.

James Batchelor was first down to breakfast the next morning and almost immediately wished he had stayed in bed. Sunday was always difficult chez Grand and Batchelor. Mrs Rackstraw had been brought up in a God-fearing household and didn't really hold with young gentlemen of their calibre not going to church. But she had stopped mentioning it as it was clearly having no effect. Had they been asked, both Grand and Batchelor would have preferred the constant nagging; her frozen silence and the way the boiled eggs bounced in their cups as she slammed them down on the table was infinitely worse. She was in a more disapproving mood than usual this fine Sunday morning.

'You were late in last night,' she remarked, crashing the butter dish down just out of Batchelor's reach.

'Yes. I met some friends as I was on my way from the station and Mr Grand had an appointment.'

The housekeeper's sniff was so loud it made Batchelor's ears pop and a small skitter of soot came down the chimney. 'It was a long appointment,' she remarked to the gas mantle. 'He's not home yet.'

'Well, you know how it is for us, Mrs Rackstraw. The case has to take priority over our own comfort.' Batchelor tapped the top of his egg and peeled back the shell. A perfect three-minuter, as always. Being furious happily had no effect on Mrs Rackstraw's culinary skills.

'A case.' Her voice sounded like the last nail going into a coffin. 'If you say so, of course, Mr Batchelor. He was in full fig, I can tell you that. White tie. Cape. Topper. Oh, yes; very natty.'

'Erm . . . plain clothes, Mrs Rackstraw. Blending in, do you see?'

Maisie crept in with a coffee pot. Batchelor began to feel quite overcrowded. 'I just bought this in, m'm,' she whispered. 'A fresh pot for Mr Grand.'

Mrs Rackstraw narrowed her eyes. There was no doubt about it, the girl would have to go. She didn't have the brains God gave sheep. 'Mr Grand isn't in, Maisie,' she said, coldly.

Maisie looked even more confused than usual. She knew she wasn't to argue with Mrs Rackstraw, but there was also the fact that she had promised her mother never to tell a lie. Raising her voice until it was almost audible, she said, 'Yes, m'm. He's in his room. I just went in to make up the fire and air it out and he was just waking up.' She didn't add that he looked like some magnificent Greek god, rising up out of the pillows with his golden hair all anyhow and his blue eyes all sleepy.

Just as Mrs Rackstraw was preparing some vicious response, the door opened again and the Greek god in question swanned in, neat and tidy in a silk robe and a smile.

'Morning all,' he said, sitting opposite Batchelor and smiling at Maisie as she proffered her coffee pot. 'Lovely day for the time of year.'

Batchelor smiled back. There was nothing like spending the night with one of the aristocracy for making an American just that little bit more English.

'I'll get your egg,' Mrs Rackstraw said and exited with as much of a flounce as her position allowed her.

Maisie lingered over the coffee and looked desperately between the two men. She had to speak to them, though it went against every fibre of her being. 'That lunatic was round again yesterday,' she muttered to the toast. 'He left a message.'

'Really? What?'

'I don't know,' she told the sugar. 'He left it with Mrs Rackstraw.'

'Thank you, Maisie,' Grand said and patted her on the hand, making her heart turn over. 'Don't worry; we won't let her know you told us.'

He was as kind as he was beautiful. She positively floated back to the kitchen and even being told to scour out the chamber pots couldn't dent the rose-coloured cloud in which she was swathed.

'So,' Batchelor said, when she had gone. 'A message from the lunatic. I think we need to speak to Mrs R.'

'It does make you wonder how many other messages haven't

reached us over the years,' Grand agreed. 'I had no idea she was deciding who got through to us.'

'Perhaps it's just this once,' Batchelor said, always ready to see the best in everyone.

The door opened and the housekeeper appeared with Grand's eggs. He waited until they were safely down in front of him and the woman had stepped back before he spoke. 'We had a bit of a long day yesterday, Mrs Rackstraw,' he said, mildly, swiping the top off an egg in the way that he knew set her teeth on edge. 'Were there any messages at all?'

In anyone with skin less grey than the housekeeper's, a blush would have swept up from throat to hairline. She didn't stir, but a small muscle jumped in her temple. 'I'd have to check,' she said, coldly.

'Check?' Batchelor asked. 'With whom?'

'Maisie may have taken a message,' she said, but there was little conviction in it. 'You know how she is.'

'Yes. Indeed we do. I wonder, though,' Grand said with a smile, a dripping soldier halfway to his mouth, 'if you could go and check with her now. We have an important case on at the moment and really can't afford to miss a single trick.'

She stood there, immobile, her hands folded at the front of her apron.

'So if you could go now,' Batchelor continued, 'that would be absolutely splendid.' He always tended to go a bit upper crust when he felt ill at ease and managing Mrs Rackstraw could make the bravest soul feel edgy.

With a snort that could strip paint, she left the room, not neglecting to slam the door.

'I hope Maisie will be all right,' Batchelor said anxiously.

'Maisie can stand it,' Grand said, foraging in his egg for the last bits. It was his second breakfast – Lady Caroline always breakfasted in bed and liked to share – but he was as hungry as a hunter this morning, for some reason. 'She wouldn't be comfortable if she had an easy life, poor little scrap. I hope a handsome butcher's boy or similar carries her away soon; she needs to be loved.'

Batchelor looked at him in amazement. Could he really not see that the girl worshipped the ground he walked on? He was about to tell him, when the girl herself walked in, eyes on the ground and a crumpled piece of paper in her hand.

'Mrs Rackstraw says to give you this,' she murmured, 'and to say that I had thrown it away.' She paused and then raised her head, looking at them properly for the first time. 'But I never.' Her eyes were full of tears.

'We understand, Maisie,' Batchelor said, kindly. 'Just dry your tears and blow your nose and give yourself a minute. As long as we have it now, that's the main thing.'

'Here,' Grand rummaged in the pocket of his robe and handed her a snow-white handkerchief. 'Use this.'

She tucked it in her bodice as though it were some kind of relic – that she laundered and ironed it and its fellows every Monday meant nothing; this had come from the hand of the beloved and would be hidden for at least a while until Mrs Rackstraw noticed it was gone on one of her periodic linen counts. 'Thank you, sir,' she bobbed to Batchelor and then to Grand. 'Thank you.' And she scuttled out.

Batchelor opened the note. At least the envelope showed no signs of being steamed open; Mrs Rackstraw obviously didn't think anything from a lunatic could be worth reading. There were several sheets of paper in the envelope and he moved aside the marmalade to make room to spread them out.

'"Sirs,"' he read, '"I came hoping to see you but your house-keeper tells me you are out. I have received the enclosed. It came while I was out at my place of business and my man did not notice who brought it. It was pushed through the door. I will attend you on Sunday at 11 in the morning, hoping it will be convenient. Yrs SB."' He passed it to Grand, who looked at it closely.

'It's written on our notepaper and—' he glanced across – 'it's in one of our envelopes, so he obviously hoped to find us in.'

'As opposed to . . .'

'Deliberately timing his visit to find us out. He is definitely having second thoughts. He is a frightened man.'

Batchelor shrugged. 'Perhaps. The note is a bit terse, though.'

'You'd hardly expect him to talk about the weather, surely? What's in the other one?'

Batchelor spread it out so they could both see it.

'Hav you got the fiv thousand punds yet? If you havnt, you shuld get it because without it, yull never see your wif again. Next leter will tell you were to leve it.'

'Same spelling errors,' Batchelor pointed out. 'Easy words misspelled, hard ones correct.'

'And still cut out of the *Telegraph*, by the look of it,' Grand agreed. 'Did you happen to notice what newspaper Miss Moriarty takes?'

'It can't be her!' Even after all he had seen since working with Grand, Batchelor still had problems with little old ladies as perpetrators of crime. Grand had seen little old ladies in the Wilderness, cuter and older than Miss Moriarty, skewering Yankees with pitchforks when they looked at them funny; he had no illusions about the breed at all.

'Even so – make a note to find out.' Grand felt at his midriff for his watch and remembered he was in his pyjamas. 'What time is it, James?'

'About ten, I think.' Batchelor couldn't remember hearing the clock, but the bells of a London Sunday were clamouring from all quarters, so it had to be about that. 'What time did you get in, by the way?'

Grand grinned. 'A gentleman never tells,' he said. 'It was good enough for me that Mrs Rackstraw didn't catch me. I'll go and get dressed, though. I think we need to be waiting for Mr Selwyn Byng this time, before he can get turned away at the kitchen door.'

'Good idea. Is that coffee house down the road open on a Sunday?'

'No. But the kosher restaurant is – we can take him there for a drink and a sandwich, perhaps.' Grand missed his salt beef sandwiches; when would the English learn how to eat? 'If we wait one at each end of the road, we won't miss him.' Grabbing a final slice of toast, he got up and went over to the door. 'Oh, by the way. Lady Caroline has a friend who would like to meet you.'

'What's wrong with her?'

'James! I'm shocked!'

'Cast in the eye? One leg shorter than the other?'

'She is very lovely, as it happens. But, if you're not interested . . .'

'We'll see.'

With a grin, Grand went out and the next thing Batchelor heard was him singing as he went up the stairs. 'Peas, peas, peas, peas, eating goober peas . . .' Not one of the current favourites on the Halls, but catchy enough, he supposed. He swirled the coffee pot and poured out the dregs; it was not tea, but it was hottish and wettish and it would do. Working on a Sunday – he hadn't expected that when he left Fleet Street, that was sure.

Jack Sandal didn't do Sundays. All round him, on both sides of the river, the bells called the faithful to church. He'd gone once, when his dad had dragged him along, but some annoying old biddy with loose and clattering china teeth had told him all about some bloke called Saint Paul and Jack had nearly fallen asleep. For all of his ten years, Jack had had to shift for himself. His dad had died, not long, as it turned out, after the old biddy and St Paul and that left Jack as the only man of the house. His mum and his sisters earned their bread as washerwomen, breaking their backs every day, up to their elbows in suds. As for Jack, he was up to his elbows in river mud today, as he was every day. And he had to be careful. For the last three years of his young life, the parish of Stepney, where the Sandals lived, had appointed what they called a Truant Officer, a kid-catcher with a mean streak a mile wide who could drag innocent, God-unaware lads like Jack off to the hell that was the new National School. Unfortunately for the kid-catcher, Jack Sandal knew the man's mournful face and Dundreary whiskers at a hundred yards; he even recognized his footsteps. So there was very little chance of Jack Sandal ever learning to read and write; but still, you couldn't be too careful.

Jack knew Duke's Shore at Limehouse like the back of his own hand. Ben Carpenter worked the stretch downstream and the pair had been mates for months. But there was no sign of Ben today. Maybe he'd been dragged to church. Maybe but no; it was Sunday and the kid-catcher didn't work on Sundays. He'd turn up later.

Jack watched the river's edge, the meeting of dry and wet worlds that few people had experience of. The lightermen and stevedores knew the river all right. They understood its moods, its tides, its currents, its winds. But they didn't know the water's edge, not like Jack. He'd take the bread his mum had cut for him early in the morning and a handful of jellied eels from old Eli's stall on the way. At dinner time – half past twelve by the church clocks clanging across the city, St Anne's closest to his ear – he'd wash the ooze from his hands in the cleansing river and sit under a jetty to eat the lot. It didn't take him long. The bread wasn't exactly fresh and he noticed that old Eli's eel portions were getting smaller by the day. Soon, Jack hoped, he'd be able to make enough money at the mudlarking game to supplement his dinner with some ale.

The boy's eyes were everywhere. You never knew whether that floating material might be pure silk that some lady had lost upstream in places he'd only ever heard about, like Henley, where the toffs held their regattas. The gold braid on a sculler's lost cap could keep Jack in jellied eels for a week. And who knew what treasure might lie in the rocky mud at Limehouse below the breweries and the wharves? This part of the river had been trading for centuries and all kinds of goodies might have been dropped. Unlike Jack, Ben Carpenter *had* been to school sometimes and he had told his friend about the history he had learned, how some bloke called Brutus had founded the city of London and that Julius Caesar himself, the greatest ancient Greek of all time, had built the Tower of London just upstream. Then there was that King John, the worst king in the world. He had lost his jewels somewhere or other, but it was bound to be in London. All the kings who ever ruled, Ben's teacher had told him, lived in London. So it all made sense.

Jack was back at work now, his food eaten, his knapsack containing the day's finds – two old keys, rusty and useless; half a comb; a length of hemp like the hangman used; and what appeared to be a handkerchief with writing on it. Still, it was early days, and the mellow, grey September day wasn't over yet.

The bag came creeping towards him on the ebb tide, the colour of the sky. It looked like linen, discoloured here and there and of course saturated with the Thames. Jack reached out and caught it. It danced away on a sudden current, eddying around in a tight whorl and he scrabbled for it. There was no Ben to catch it on the lower reaches, so if he wasn't careful, he might lose this for good. Experience told him that the bag must be empty; otherwise it wouldn't be floating. Even so, if there was fancy embroidery on it, once dried out and washed, any old clo' dealer might give Jack a penny for it.

He checked his balance. A mouthful of old Father Thames was not something that Jack relished, and he'd had plenty of experience of that. Planting his feet apart, the cold water swirling around his hips, he lunged and got it. Holding the bag in both hands, he looked down. It wasn't a bag at all. It was some sort of mask. It had eyeholes without eyes, and it had eyelashes too. The lips were still there, cut and notched though they were. The mask felt peculiar, like . . . and it was a while before Jack could place it . . . like skin. And slowly, as the hairs rose on the back of his neck, Jack Sandal, mudlark, realized that he was holding in his hands the skull-less head of a woman.

FIVE

Selwyn Byng was ludicrously easy to spot. He wore his Derby hat low on his forehead and his coat buttoned up to the neck, the collar turned up to hide the bottom half of his face. Grand couldn't help but smile; all he needed was a large sign on his back saying, 'I am on the way to a clandestine meeting' and the picture would have been complete. He let him pass him and signalled to Batchelor, waiting at the entrance to the mews which led behind their house. A pincer movement would do the trick and they could merely fall into step with the man and no one would know that they weren't just acquaintances bumping into each other all by accident.

'Mr Byng,' Grand muttered and the man jumped as though shot. 'Just keep walking and my colleague will join us in a moment. We'll go to the kosher restaurant along the way; they know us there and will give us a nice quiet table at the back.'

'But . . .' Byng was looking round like a man possessed. 'What if . . . they see us? Emilia . . .'

Grand looked around ostentatiously. There wasn't a soul in the street, except for Algernon, the blind crossing sweeper at the far end where it met the Strand. Grand had often wondered how that worked but it seemed to; after all, Algernon had been there ever since he had moved to Alsatia and he seemed to be unscathed. 'We're quite safe, Mr Byng, but I think you might create less of a stir if you walk upright, turn down your collar and push your hat back a tad.'

Reluctantly, Byng did as he was told.

'There,' Grand said, clapping him on the back. 'Now we look a lot more like old friends out for a stroll and a lot less like a mountebank and his zany.' It was a shame that Batchelor was too far away to hear that – he would have been so proud.

As they passed the mews, Batchelor stepped out and shook Byng by the hand. 'Hello, old chap,' he said. 'I haven't seen you for ages.' Batchelor had often longed to tread the boards.

'How is the little woman?' And he fell into step on Byng's other side and between them, they got him to the restaurant without him falling in a dead faint or letting rip with one of his strange cries. He looked from one to the other constantly and had anyone been interested enough to guess what was going on, they would probably have concluded that he owed Grand and Batchelor money. Which, in a way, since Friday, he did.

The shutters were just being rolled up when they got to the door and the proprietor turned round ready to send the men away; his fires had been banked since the Sabbath and he needed a while to get everything going again. But when he saw who it was, he was effusive in his welcome. No one appreciated his salt-beef like Matthew Grand.

'Gentlemen, gentlemen, come in, come in. A nice table in the window?'

'Thanks, Isaac, not this time. Can you put us somewhere quiet, at the back?'

'Of course, of course. But . . .' Isaac saw the fear in Byng's eyes, 'there will be no violence, I hope.'

'Violence?' Batchelor was puzzled. This man had known them for years. Then he looked at Byng's expression and understood. 'No, Isaac. He isn't scared of *us*. It's some other people he's avoiding!'

The restaurateur smiled and ushered them in. 'In that case, let me show you into my private dining room?'

'You've got a private dining room?' Grand was a little miffed that he hadn't been shown into it before. 'Why am I only just finding out about this?'

'You've never had a man ready to faint with you before,' the owner said, shrugging. 'It's bad for business, men lying on the floor. People will wonder what it was he ate. *Was it the fish?* they will ask. *Was it the chicken?*'

Byng was sagging heavily on Grand's shoulder now and he could quite see Isaac's point of view. Between them, the three men got him into the private room and closed the door, with a bottle of brandy on their side of it.

'Come on, now, Mr Byng, snap out of it.' James Batchelor was a kind man, often too kind for his own good. But this lily-livered behaviour was beginning to get on his nerves. He didn't believe that the writer of the ransom note was watching and following Selwyn Byng every minute of every day. In a deserted street such as they had just walked along, he would have to be invisible. And although he had seen some sights in his time working alongside Matthew Grand, an invisible person had never turned out to be the miscreant.

'Yes, come on, Selwyn. We may call you Selwyn, I presume?'

Grand had chosen the right way to snap the man out of his fugue. 'I would much rather you didn't,' he said coldly, sitting up straight and adjusting the hang of his rather outdated coat. 'I would prefer to keep things formal, if you don't mind, gentlemen.'

'That suits me,' Grand said. 'And since this is to be business-like, may I present you with our bill to date?'

Batchelor was surprised. Although it was good to be paid, he had never seen Grand so quick off the mark.

Byng opened the envelope. 'I say!' he said. 'This is a bit steep, isn't it?' He prodded the paper. 'What are these extras?'

Grand leaned over. 'Fares. Hotel. Food. We went down to see Miss Moriarty in Eastbourne, for example. Mr Batchelor here went along the river to see the warehouses of which you spoke.'

Byng gibbered briefly and then folded the bill savagely and thrust it into his coat. 'I will pass this to my man of business. But I hope, since you have brought the matter up, that you didn't divulge anything of this heinous crime to either my poor aunt-in-law or anyone at the warehouse.'

'No,' Grand said, 'we didn't. Miss Moriarty was helpful up to a point, but she got quite distressed about a collateral matter. The warehouses were closed. But before we get on to the second letter, we must ask you something.'

'Which is?' Byng's eyes were narrowed and he looked suspicious.

'Why didn't you tell us about Emilia's maid?'

'Her maid?' Byng swivelled his head frantically from side to side. 'What about her maid?'

'That's what we are asking, I think,' Batchelor said. 'You told us that your wife didn't appear at the station, but you didn't mention the maid.'

Byng got to his feet. 'I've made a mistake,' he said. 'I don't think you are up to the job. I will thank you to return my correspondence and I will be on my way.'

Batchelor pulled him down and he sat with a bump. 'I think our question is quite reasonable, Mr Byng. If the maid turned up or if she didn't is very relevant to the case. If she turned up, where is she? If she didn't, she may still be with your wife, in which case the whole situation is a little more complex. So . . . did she turn up or not?'

'Well . . . not, I suppose.'

Grand's eyes widened. 'You *suppose*? How long has she been with your wife?'

'Since before we were married.'

'So you would recognize her in a crowd.'

'Of course.'

'So . . .' Grand was getting a few goosebumps as this strange man sat there, oblivious to the world outside his blinkered view. 'So . . . did she arrive or not?'

Byng put his head down in his arms and howled his peculiar wail of distress. The door flew open and the owner stood in the doorway.

'I thought you said no violence!' he said, brandishing the chair leg he kept beside the register for just this eventuality.

Grand and Batchelor held up their arms to show they were not touching the man. Isaac's eyebrows almost disappeared into his hair. 'A lunatic?' he asked. 'You have brought a lunatic into my restaurant?'

'He's upset,' mouthed Batchelor. 'We'll make him be quiet.'

'Make sure you do,' the restaurateur said. 'He's curdling my *sufganiyot*.' That went without saying.

Grand patted and then bashed Byng on the back. 'Hush up, now. This won't get us anywhere except thrown out into the street. What's the matter now?'

Byng straightened up and blew his nose thoroughly and wiped his eyes. 'I was late,' he said. 'I was late for the train, so I don't know if Molly came up from Eastbourne.'

'And you don't know if your wife did, either.' Batchelor was not a happy man.

Byng shook his head.

'So she may have been taken in London?' Grand asked.

'Yes, I suppose she may.'

Grand sighed and lolled back in his chair. 'Do you think, Mr Byng, that it is possible that your wife, angry at you not meeting the train when you were supposed to be so excited to see her, went off, perhaps to a friend's house and that between them, they have concocted this note – these notes, sorry – to make you suffer?'

'Emilia wouldn't be so unkind.' Byng shook his head, adamant.

'I have never had the pleasure of being married,' Grand said, 'but I freely admit to you, Mr Byng, that I have had my share of female companionship.' He threw a glance to Batchelor which killed the incipient snort at birth. 'And my experience in that respect has taught me that you can never, never *ever* be sure of what a woman will do when slighted.'

Byng was outraged. 'I would never slight Emilia,' he said. 'I worship the very ground upon which she walks. I would die rather than upset her . . .'

'And yet,' Batchelor remarked, evenly, 'you failed to meet her train.'

Byng hung his head. 'I . . . my father had given me a task to do which took me longer than I expected . . .'

'So you stayed at work rather than meet the train. Had this happened before?'

Byng drew himself up. 'Business is important. It puts food on the table . . .'

Grand leaned forward, his arms on the table, and looked Byng in the eye. 'So, long story cut short, Mr Byng, you failed to meet your wife, not for the first time. And this time, it was a meeting which was devoutly wished by you both. Miss Moriarty described you as "ardent" . . .'

Byng slapped the table in annoyance.

'Her word, Mr Byng, not mine. Or perhaps, I should say, your wife's word. She, also according to Miss Moriarty, was just as ardent and could barely wait until she was back in your bed. Actually, to be fair, that isn't exactly what Miss Moriarty said, but it is the gist. So, picture the scene, Mr Byng. Your wife, eager and ardent, gets on the train in Eastbourne and travels north to London. Perhaps she gets more . . . excited . . .

with every mile. She gets to Victoria Station, ready to fling
herself into your arms. She leaps down from the train, her maid
behind her with the luggage and – what's this? No husband,
ardent as she, with arms wide with passion. Not even a message.
She sends the maid home to her family for a much-needed
holiday. She puts her luggage in a cab and goes . . . where?
She has no family, so it will be to a friend, or even a hotel.'

Byng was silent, looking down at the table top with its crisp
linen cover.

'Well,' Batchelor said, slapping his hands on the table and
getting up. 'I think that's all to be said for a while. Mr Byng,
we'll leave you to find out from your wife's friends whether
they have her visiting. Don't worry about embarrassing yourself
– believe me, if she is with one of them, they all know of your
shortcomings by now. And if you find that she is with one, let
us know. If she isn't, let us know. But until then, I think I am
right in saying, am I not, Matthew, this is goodbye.'

Selwyn Byng sat like a dead man at the table as Grand and
Batchelor showed themselves out. Isaac met them at the door.

'Is your friend . . .?' he looked towards the door to the back
room.

'Leave him for a bit,' Grand said. 'He's had a bit of a shock.
The brandy's on us – just put it on the tab.'

'No sufganiyot?'

The paperboy was late that morning. As a result of that, Mrs
Rackstraw had not only told him his future, she'd also cuffed
him around the ear. As a result of that, he was even later to his
next port of call. So by the time James Batchelor got hold of
The Times, he was on his third cup of tea and Matthew Grand
was draining the last of his coffee.

'What news on the Rialto, James?' Grand was peering out
of the window, trying to guess the weather, that good old English
pastime.

Batchelor still winced a little inwardly when his American
associate came out with the lines of the greatest English bard
but he'd never said anything and by now, nearly eight years into
their business partnership, the moment had gone. 'Looks like
Gladstone's reconsidering the match tax again.' He was scanning

the headlines, holding the paper to the window to help him decipher the tiny font.

'Ex luce, lucellum,' Grand murmured.

Batchelor translated in his head. Out of light, profit. 'We're very erudite this morning, Matthew.' He lowered the paper in salute.

'I read it in the *Telegraph* the other day,' Grand was man enough to admit. 'May have to cut back on the old cigars if Gladeye gets his way.'

'I wouldn't worry,' Batchelor said. 'If the Old Man's Licensing Bill goes through, he'll be out of a job by Thursday and Dizzie is bound to reverse everything he's done.'

'We'll make Americans of you cusses yet,' Grand chuckled.

'Ask Mrs R. for some more toast, would you, Matthew? I could eat a horse this morning.'

'Be careful what you wish for,' Grand said. And Batchelor swept on to the Finance Section, always a rich source of clientage. He didn't notice the small print headed 'Suspected Murder'.

By that afternoon, Dr Felix Kempster was already hard at work. He had his private practice in Lockington Street, but his role as police surgeon to V Division kept him pretty busy. Today, he was at his most creative, at the request of Daddy Bliss, who hovered at his elbow now. He had known Bliss for years and the men had a grudging respect for each other. Kempster knew that the fat inspector kept most things to himself and woe betide the hapless copper who tried to muscle in on his manor. Bliss knew that Kempster was a misfit, an artist and an adventurer trapped in the bloodied apron of a surgeon. Today, in Kempster's laboratory, this was a marriage made in Heaven.

The doctor had placed a butcher's block on the table and had shaved off its corners. Then he had taken the skin mask that little Jack Sandal had found and stretched it over the frame. The fit wasn't good, so Kempster played God, not for the first time and pulled it off again, using a file on the smooth oak to fashion a head. He had to guess the jut of the chin and the shape of the nose and more than an hour passed before he had finished. Kempster was able to dissociate himself from death – he had done that since medical school – and to forget that he was trying to reassemble what once had been the head of a human being. In his imagination that Monday, he was Michelangelo chipping away the Carrera marble to sculpt his Moses or his David and the huge man waiting patiently alongside him was one of the great genius's apprentices.

He stretched the skin again and stood back. It wasn't – couldn't be – a work of art. And he suddenly snapped out of his Florentine daydream and looked reality in the face. He peered closer, passing his magnifying glass across the distorted features.

'Well, doctor?' This was something of a red-letter day; Daddy Bliss had not said anything for over an hour.

'I don't know how far I would care to extrapolate,' Kempster murmured, still looking at the folds of grey skin.

'Doctor,' Bliss sighed. He was not a man exactly known for his patience. 'I've got a quarter of a body and a shoulder which may or may not belong to this head. I'd like to know who this was before the rest turns up.'

'You think there'll be more?' Kempster asked.

'I'd stake my pension on it. Extrapolate away.'

'Very well.' Kempster straightened, only now realizing how his back ached. 'We're looking at a woman. Probably over forty.'

'What makes you think that?'

'Look,' the doctor said, pointing to the upper lip. What we in the profession call a feminine moustache. You don't get that in young people. She'd be naturally dark.'

Bliss could tell that from the portions of hair that still clung to the scalp at the back of the block.

'And that's peculiar,' Kempster said.

'What is?'

'Notice these hairs, behind the ears?'

There was nothing left of the ears, but Bliss could approximate.

'They've been cut short.' The doctor lifted a few with his tweezers. 'Do you want my diagnosis?'

'Fire away.'

'Our head is that of a middle-aged woman who sees herself as over the hill. The water has had an effect, of course, but I'd say she'd been in the river for three days, perhaps more. She cut her hair because it was thinning – she may have had alopecia

– and wore a wig. As for the removal of the head,' he pointed to the edge of skin below the chin, 'that was done with some precision. Surgeon's scalpel followed by a fine-toothed saw.'

Bliss frowned. 'Are you saying the murderer is a doctor, doctor?'

'I'm saying no such thing,' Kempster said. 'No one who took the Hippocratic oath could carry out butchery like this. I'm talking about implements, not people.'

'What bothers me,' Bliss said, 'is that the papers have already got hold of it. When I find out who talked to *The Times*, I'll have his bollocks in the rowlocks as we say on the river. You've come out with a theory of sorts, Dr Kempster and you're an educated man working with evidence. Can you imagine the lunacy that's about to be unleashed? Every other madman in London is going to claim this woman is his mother, auntie or downstairs maid. And the other madmen will claim they killed her.'

'But you need to find out who she was?'

'Of course,' Bliss conceded.

'Can I suggest a photograph, then?'

'Of this?'

Kempster nodded.

'The papers'll never publish it. It would upset the fine ladies over their breakfast tables. Anyway, as I understand it, the cost is prohibitive.'

'Leaflets, then,' the doctor suggested. 'The Met can stick 'em up on walls and other vantage points.'

'The Met, doctor?' Bliss frowned. 'Are you suggesting I farm this out to other Divisions?' He was horrified.

Kempster turned to face the man. 'You said this face was found at Limehouse?'

Bliss nodded.

'What about the other body parts?'

'Torso near Battersea Park; shoulder off Greenwich.'

'There you are,' Kempster shrugged. 'That's two miles as the crow flies. Covers more than one Division, does it not?'

'It only covers one Division, doctor. Mine. This one belongs to the River Police. When you say "photograph", who did you have in mind?'

'Probably Sergeant Ballantyne, V Division.'

Bliss nodded. 'Yes,' he said. 'That's all right. As long as it stays with us. I'll sort it.' He looked at the tragic head again, the features scarred and ill-fitting on the block, the eyes blank and oaken, the ragged lips hanging open. He turned to go. 'Of course,' he said, 'while we're still extrapolating, the short hair could have another explanation.'

'Oh? What's that?'

'Our lady of the river could have been a recent guest of Her Majesty. The first thing they do with a stretch in a women's prison is to shave off their hair. It was a nice day when I came in here. Think I'll take a little cab ride up to Holloway.'

While Sergeant Ballantyne of V Division steeled himself to set up his tripod and photograph the head, other portions of the dead woman were coming to light. On the Thursday, the thighs turned up, one at Blackwall Point; the other at Woolwich Dockyard. The next day, an embarrassment of riches, as though the murderer was taunting the River Police with the multiplicity of finds. Somebody's cocker spaniel, splashing on the foreshore near the Royal Arsenal, came bouncing back to its less than enchanted owner with a pelvis. An arm was jammed into the slime-weeded stanchions of the Albert Bridge; the other one bobbed in the brackish water of White Hart Docks, near Vauxhall. And the sluice gates of Wandsworth Distillery produced a lower leg, giving rise to rather unpleasant jokes about the effect their beer had on people by the distillery workers.

When all the pieces had been brought in, dried and roughly assembled in Dr Kempster's mortuary, he had most of a person lying on the slab in front of him and he could give Daddy Bliss a clearer picture of the victim. He had been right about the head; the woman was perhaps forty, though she may have been younger. The pubic hair of the pelvis matched the colour of the short crop on the scalp and the 'feminine' moustache that he had noted earlier. There were no feet, but Kempster estimated that the dead woman had been about five foot three inches tall. She was not a virgin and had given birth. The condition of the breasts and nipples led him to believe that, at some time, she had suckled a child. And there, as so often in Kempster's grisly profession, his enquiries came to an abrupt full stop.

SIX

'**M**an cannot live by bread alone' the homily painted on the workhouse wall had told him. As September lengthened into shorter days and the nights brought a vicious chill, William Bisgrove had been forced to admit himself. He was of no fixed abode, he told them, his West Country accent a risk in betraying his background. He told the Overseer of the Poor that he couldn't read, told them his name was Bickstaff and he made his mark. Picking oakum and sewing mail bags was not that different from Broadmoor, but there was no one here to strap him to a chair and dunk him in cold water to clear, as they had told him, the pathways to his brain. Above all, there was no electric current to shoot through his body, making him jerk like a puppet and dance like a marionette.

And so, for William Bickstaff, né Bisgrove, the workhouse would do; until the river called him again and he could look for his lost love.

Mrs Rackstraw had had what for her was a relaxing week. True, she had had to deal with the mountain of laundry that any Monday brought; how two young men of moderate habit made so much washing, she couldn't imagine. It was like working for a family of ten. But it kept Maisie on an even keel; for some reason, the girl seemed to positively enjoy washing out smalls and ironing shirts, if the silly grin on her face was anything to go by.

Tuesday had been a particular highlight. She had been looking for an excuse to bite the butcher's boy's head off for some time now, a feud sparked by an inadequate delivery of mince some years before, and Tuesday brought a perfect excuse with some lamb chops she wouldn't give to a dog. She boxed his ears and sent him on his way, his head ringing. She went through the rest of the day humming happily under her breath and made a cake so light it would make an angel weep for joy. Grand

and Batchelor never knew because the whole thing was eaten at the kitchen table, with a few ribald anecdotes from Mrs Gooding on the literal shortcomings of Mr Gooding.

Wednesday had brought a slight retrenchment of Mrs Rackstraw's good mood, but she perked up in the afternoon when she discovered to her delight that the grocer had charged her twice for a delivery of Garibaldis. She had donned her bonnet and tied it with unusual determination under her chin and set off to give battle. The man had quailed when she went into the shop; he had been adding a penny a pound on sugar for about a year and thought his day had come. He was so delighted to find it was a simple biscuit discrepancy that not only did he capitulate at once, he gave her a bag of only slightly broken Nice and she returned home vindicated.

Thursday was her afternoon off and she went to visit her married niece, living in two rooms over an undertaker's in Bermondsey. She took with her the only slightly broken Nice, a gift which, lacking only a vowel, she thought particularly pertinent. She chuckled over the pun as she clung to the rail and bounced about on the wooden seat on the omnibus over Waterloo Bridge. She came back late, smelling slightly of pine shavings and embalming fluid and went straight to bed.

Friday began well enough, but soon took a turn for the worst.

'The lunatic's back,' she announced as she brought in the toast.

'The lunatic?' A week is a long time in the enquiry agent business and Grand was at a loss.

'That lunatic from last week. I thought you'd given him his marching orders.'

Batchelor took a slice of toast and buttered it thoughtfully. 'I certainly thought we'd seen the last of him,' he said. 'Perhaps he's come to tell us he has found his wife.'

'Or to pay the bill,' Grand added. Neither of them had any hopes of getting any money out of Selwyn Byng, but hope could still spring eternal.

Batchelor added a load of marmalade and cut his toast into quarters. 'Give us a minute to finish this, Mrs Rackstraw, then show him up.'

'I shall do no such thing,' she said, bridling. 'A lunatic in my kitchen, indeed. I'll put him in the drawing room and tell him he can wait. There's nothing worth taking in there.'

Batchelor forbore to mention his grandmother's collection of cranberry glass – it wasn't to everyone's taste, perhaps, but who knew with lunatics?

'All right, Mrs Rackstraw,' Grand said. 'We won't be long.'

When the woman had slammed her way out and they heard the baize door flap close, Grand spoke for them both.

'I didn't think we'd see him again, did you?'

Batchelor wiped his fingers on his napkin and looked thoughtful. 'He didn't seem the kind of man who would come and tell us the outcome, I agree. He would just find out where she was, grovel, and then put it all behind him. He certainly wouldn't come and tell us we were right . . .' The alternative hung in the air.

'So . . . you think he's come to tell us we're wrong?' Grand said, doubtfully.

Batchelor had no chance to answer. They heard the baize door open and Mrs Rackstraw telling the lunatic in no uncertain terms to wait in the drawing room until her gentlemen were free.

'She has her uses, doesn't she?' Grand said. 'Despite the drawbacks . . .'

The door to the dining room flew open and Selwyn Byng hurtled in, Mrs Rackstraw in his wake. She grabbed for his flying coat-tails but he foiled her by the simple expedient of tripping over the rug and measuring his length at Grand's feet.

'I'm so sorry,' Mrs Rackstraw said, hauling him upright with one wiry arm. 'He got away from me. Hold him here and I'll send Maisie out to fetch someone from the asylum.'

Byng hung limply from her grip, all fight gone out of him. He had a package in his hand, roughly wrapped but indisputably bloodstained. Without drawing attention to it, Grand said smoothly, 'Perhaps if you would bring another cup, Mrs Rackstraw, we'll talk to Mr Byng over coffee, as he's here.'

The housekeeper looked from her young gentlemen to the sorry-looking specimen in her grasp and unceremoniously let go. Byng sagged at the knees but managed to find a seat at the table without actually falling over. With one of her very best snorts, she left the room, sending Maisie back with a cup; one from the second-best service, with a chip in the saucer and a crack in the handle. It was pure foolishness to trust the best china to a lunatic.

While they waited, the enquiry agents looked at their erstwhile client. The days since they had seen him last had not treated him kindly. Weaselly from the outset, he had lost more weight and the shirt collar, noticeably grubby and creased, hung a little loosely on his neck. He had dark circles under his eyes and he had shaved in what could only be called a cursory fashion; a sprout of whisker adorned one corner of his mouth. He slumped in the chair and waited to be given food and drink, like a sulky child.

He sipped the coffee and sat, the gory parcel next to his plate where some toast, spread and cut by Batchelor, got cold and leathery.

'Do you have news, Mr Byng?' Grand asked at last.

The man turned haggard eyes to him and then to Batchelor. He didn't speak, but pushed the parcel into the middle of the table.

'May I . . . open it?' Batchelor asked.

Byng shrugged and took another sip of coffee, watching them over the rim of his cup.

Using a clean knife from the sideboard, Batchelor teased open the parcel and revealed a finger, neatly removed at the third joint, still wearing a ring. The fingernail was neatly cut and discreetly polished and, despite being a disarticulated body part, caused little horror in the men around the table. Grand had seen far worse when he was little more than a boy, on the battlefields of Shiloh and Chickamauga. Batchelor had developed a thicker skin than he had thought possible in his years as an enquiry agent and Selwyn Byng, who might be expected to be horrified, had lived with it now for over twenty-four hours and had become inured to it.

There were clearly many questions to ask but Batchelor got in first. 'Is this your . . . wife's?' Of the difficult questions he had asked in his life, this ranked up there with the best of them.

Byng nodded.

'You're sure?' Grand checked. It seemed to him that it was a small enough piece to be so sure about.

Byng spoke for the first time. 'Yes,' he said, dully. 'It is my wife's finger.' He sounded as if he had been practising this statement for a while. It came without inflection or emotion. 'It's her ring. I haven't looked, but if you care to, you will see that two initial Es are entwined inside, in a heart. It . . .' and his voice broke a little, '. . . it is Emilia's own design.'

Grand and Batchelor looked at the finger, lying there amongst the crumbs and detritus of their breakfast. Neither really wanted to touch it; it would be a matter of who would blink first.

Batchelor saved them both from a gory task. 'I think the best thing to do would be to take it to a doctor to be examined. A police surgeon, for preference.'

Byng came alive. 'No police! No police!'

'No, not the police,' Batchelor reassured him, re-wrapping the finger and adding a napkin for good measure. 'A police surgeon. And I happen to know one; I used to get details from him after inquests in my newspaper days. Dr Kempster; Felix, I think his name is. He lives out in Battersea – I'm sure he'd be pleased to help.'

'I'm still not—'

'Mr Byng.' Grand spoke firmly but kindly. 'This is another matter now. We need to know whether . . .' he paused. How did you put it when the finger's husband was sitting there? '. . . whether the finger was removed when your wife was still alive.'

Byng replied with one of his visceral howls. Down in the kitchen, Mrs Rackstraw chose a sharp knife and tucked it into the waistband of her apron. Lunatics; no good would come of it.

'Please, Mr Byng.' Grand reached out and grabbed the man's wrist. 'Believe me, although you don't want to think of her in pain, it is far better than the alternative, surely! Dr—'

'Kempster,' Batchelor chimed in.

'Dr Kempster will be able to tell us what we need to know. Do you have anyone at home?'

'Just the staff.' Byng was calm again now, but it was a thin veneer.

'What about your father? Could you go and stay with him?'

Byng's eyes sprang open. 'My father! What day is this?'

'Friday.' The two forgave him for losing track; it wasn't every day a man got his wife's dismembered finger in a parcel.

'I must . . . I must get to the warehouse.'

'Not today, surely.' A work ethic was all very fine and dandy, but Grand felt sure that this was an occasion where a man would be allowed a bit of furlough.

'I . . . I haven't told my father about my bit of trouble,' Byng said. 'He . . . let's just say he isn't a very emotional man. He couldn't understand why I wanted to marry Emilia in the first place. She is an heiress, true, but not for many years. He had another girl in mind, one who had already come into her trust. But . . . from the first time I saw her, Emilia was the only one for me. And now . . .' Suddenly, he turned on Grand. 'This is your fault! If you had looked for her . . .' and again he collapsed in a storm of weeping.

'Mr Byng,' Grand said, severely. He couldn't help feeling that he was speaking to a recalcitrant horse. 'Did you have a third note?'

'No.'

'Then how is this our fault? We had no clues, you lied to us – if with that you felt we could possibly find your wife, I am afraid you have a sadly erroneous view of what enquiry agents can do. We might as well have gone door to door, knocking and asking if they had Mrs Selwyn Byng stashed in their base-ment. I think you'll agree that that is a question unlikely to be answered in the affirmative.'

Byng shrugged but didn't answer. He had found someone to blame other than himself and for now, that was enough.

'Her captors have racked up their demands in the most cruel way, but it isn't anyone's fault but theirs. What I suggest is that you go home and get some rest, but if you insist on going to work today, then get a shave on the way.' He looked at the man, assessingly. 'You are much the same size as James. He will lend you a clean collar.'

'Will I?' Batchelor was affronted. He was very particular about his collars.

'Of course you will.' With a glare, Batchelor went to get one. 'We must have your address now, Mr Byng; we need to tell you how we get on with Dr Kempster.' He fished out a small notepad from his pocket and pushed it across with a stub of pencil. 'Write it down for me and we will come and let you know as soon as we know anything. It will probably not be today. The doctor may want to do . . . tests. But if you could arrange to be at home tomorrow, we will wait on you then.'

'I can't just . . .'

'This isn't a case of "just", Mr Byng. This is your wife's life. Be at home tomorrow. We'll see you then.'

An Indian summer came suddenly to London that late September and the streets of Whitechapel were dumb in the heat. Piles of clothes, black and patched, lay on the street corners and the narrow pavements, the cobbles were slick with grease and the walls crawled with cockroaches.

William Bisgrove gave up counting these because there were just far too many of them. He had carried the banner for the past three nights, settling down with the homeless and hopeless who infested this end of the Metropolis. In the end, the mortuary of the workhouse had got him down; that and the increasingly nosy questions the Overseers asked. He walked out one morning and never went back. Irish tinkers' carts creaked and wobbled over the iron-hard ground and the great drayhorses that serviced the parish's innumerable pubs and off-licences snorted and sweated in the sun. They lashed the flies with their tails and tossed their heads as the harnesses jingled and they champed their bits.

He saw the poster stuck to a crumbling wall along Baker's Row, the huge block of the workhouse to his left. 'Have You Seen This Woman?' it asked below a photograph of a ghoul, hideous, eyeless and open-mouthed. 'Believed to be in her thirties or forties, 5ft 2ins tall, dark hair.' He looked at it for a long time, twisting his head to left and right to try to make sense of the ghastly face. How could anyone miss a woman who looked like that? Then he heard the heavy tread of the hob-nailed boots of H Division and made himself scarce.

'Can I help you, sir?' Constable Gosling was on gangplank duty that Friday morning. It looked like rain over Limehouse; but then, it always looked like rain over Limehouse.

The ferret-faced man on the quayside squinted up at him. 'Is this the *Royalist*?' he asked.

Since the word was painted in large gilt letters on the boat's prow only feet from where he stood, Gosling couldn't really understand the man's confusion. 'It is, sir,' the constable said.

'The police station?'

'That's the one, sir.' Tom Gosling was the oldest of Daddy Bliss's Water Babies; he saw himself as more of a Water Toddler, really. And Bliss had long ago instilled the notion in his men that the general public were terminally stupid. That and the notion that politeness was the punctuality of policemen. So Tom Gosling was endlessly patient, understanding and sarcastic, all in one. 'On account of it says "Thames Police Station" on the side.'

The ferret-faced man bared his teeth, yellow and curved. 'I don't think I care for your tone,' he said. 'It may have escaped your notice, Constable, but I pay your wages.'

'Thank you, sir.' Gosling touched the peak of his cap. 'Eternally grateful. What can I do for you today, specifically, to earn my crust?'

'You can tell me how *this* sort of thing is allowed to happen in this great country of ours, in the beating heart of the greatest city in the world.' He held out a canvas bag, dripping water from its bottom.

Gosling looked at it. 'You'll have to be a little more precise, I'm afraid, sir,' he said.

'Look inside, man,' the ferret said. 'If you dare.'

Gosling frowned at him, then squared his shoulders. He peered inside. 'It's a sheep, sir,' he said.

'Don't be ridiculous!' the ferret snapped. 'I read the papers, you know. I know what's going on. Some maniac is butchering women and dumping parts of them in the river here. I am an angler of some repute and I found this portion not two hours ago.'

'Where, sir?' Gosling asked.

'What does it matter?' the ferret wanted to know.

'It might be very germane, if we are to trace who is dumping sheep in the Thames, sir.'

'Will you stop with this sheep nonsense?' the angling ferret almost screamed. His voice carried to the canal barges where the women were hanging out their washing, anxiously searching the skies. 'Who's in charge here?'

'Inspector Bliss, sir,' the constable told him.

'Take me to him.'

'What, now, sir?'

'Of course, now. I don't have to make an appointment, do I?'

'I think you'll find it's a waste of time, sir.'

The ferret scowled, taking two steps nearer to Gosling. 'A waste of time to see your superior? Would you like me to tell him that?'

'You must tell him as you see fit, sir,' Gosling said. 'This way.'

He led the ferret, still holding his bag at arm's length, up the slope of the gangplank and onto the deck of the *Royalist*. The ferret picked his way around the blocks, tackles and piles of hemp to a little door that led down to the Abode of Bliss.

'Mind your head, sir,' Gosling said and smiled just a little as he heard a thud and a whimper as the ferret misjudged the height. A large man in a black patrol jacket, braided in regulation Metropolitan Police pattern, sat at a table poring over charts and maps of the river.

'This gentleman has bought . . .'

'. . . what was a human being,' the ferret cut Gosling off, 'that I caught with my rod and line not two hours ago.'

Bliss peered up at the man over his rimless glasses. '*Not* two hours ago? How long ago was it, then?'

'Are you trying to be funny?' the ferret asked. 'It's a figure of speech.'

'What is?'

The ferret blinked. He had only come here to do his public duty, having had the shock of a lifetime and so far, all he had met was stupidity and off-handedness. 'Who are you?' he asked.

'Inspector Harold Bliss, River Police,' Bliss told him, taking off his glasses and placing them on his charts. He made no attempt to get up. 'And you?'

'My name is Allen. Colin Allen.'

'Delighted, Mr Allen,' Bliss said, unsmiling. He lapsed into general practitioner mode. 'What seems to be the trouble?'

Allen slammed his grisly load down on Bliss's charts. The inspector, unhurried and unruffled, opened the top and peered inside. 'I'm afraid it's my turn to ask the question now, sir,' he said. 'Are you trying to be funny?'

'What do you mean?' Allen frowned.

'That's not a figure of speech, Mr Allen, it's a direct question. *That*,' he pointed to the bag, 'is a portion of ovine anatomy, viz and to wit, a sheep, hind quarters. Very nice with spuds and carrots. Thank you for bringing this to our attention. Can you see yourself out?'

'A sheep?' Allen repeated, bewildered. He flicked a glance at Gosling, standing smugly to attention at his elbow. 'That's what he said.'

'Well, two of us can't be wrong, can we, sir? It takes years of training for a River Policeman to reach our state of high alert and readiness. In future,' Bliss got up slowly, looming over the ferret, 'should there be one, when a Constable of the River Police tells you that an object is a sheep, you can assume it is a sheep. Do we understand each other?'

'I was only doing my duty,' Allen whined.

'Very commendable, sir. Now, bugger off before I do you for wasting police time.'

'I shall take this further.' Allen stood his ground.

'You can take it where the . . .' but his precise directions were drowned out by the sudden blast of a ship's horn on the river outside and Allen didn't catch what he said. It was just as well, because that *would* have given him something to complain about.

SEVEN

Felix Kempster had a huge practice, but his income didn't reflect it. Most of his patients hadn't two ha'pence to bless themselves with, but a sick person was a sick person and he had never been known to turn anyone from his door. The police surgeon post was really all that kept starvation at bay but that wasn't the only reason he loved it. If he had had his time all over again, he would have worked in a laboratory somewhere, well away from the dropsy and the quinsy and the croup. So when his wife put her head around his consulting room door and told him there were two gentlemen outside with a finger in a napkin, he didn't hesitate.

'If anyone comes in, Nancy,' he said, jumping up, 'you know what to do.'

The woman sighed and nodded. The rules were simple. Laudanum for dropsy. Ipecac for quinsy. Honey and vinegar for croup. The bottles weren't labelled with those names, but that was what they contained and if it only worked in nine out of ten cases, well, it was better than none at all.

Kempster bounded out into the hall. He had been up to his armpits in body parts for the last week, but nevertheless, another was always welcome.

'I know you, don't I?' he said to Batchelor. 'Spinster, isn't it? The *Examiner*.'

'Batchelor,' said Batchelor. 'The *Telegraph*. But close enough. How are you, Dr Kempster?'

'Bearing up, you know. Bearing up. Now, Nancy tells me you have a finger.'

'May I introduce my partner, Matthew Grand?' Batchelor said. 'We have a business in the Strand. Enquiry Agents.'

Kempster looked impressed. From cub reporter sniffing around inquests to enquiry agent with his own business sounded quite a step up to him. 'Hello.' He shook hands enthusiastically. 'Pleased to meet you, Mr Grand.'

'Pleased to meet you, too, doctor.' Grand laid on the accent as he always did when being introduced. It gave them something to talk about and he was making a small collection of the clichés people came out with. Kempster did not disappoint.

'You're not from around here, are you?' he said, peering.

'No. I'm from—'

'No. Don't tell me, don't tell me.' He looked at Batchelor. 'I make a bit of a study of accents, as you may remember, Batchelor. Now . . .' he held up his hand as Grand opened his mouth to put him out of his misery. 'I have it. Leicester.'

'Nope.' The American laid it on even thicker.

'Ooh, perhaps a bit far west. Lincolnshire, then, I would bet my stethoscope on it. Place in Lincolnshire! There. I wager I am correct!'

'No. Washington. And Boston.'

'Ah. Close, then. We'll call that a draw, shall we?'

Grand exchanged a glance with Batchelor. If this was an expert, then he didn't have high hopes.

'We have this finger we'd like you to have a look at, Dr Kempster,' Batchelor said, proffering his napkin.

'Ah, yes, the finger.' The doctor held out his hand. 'Do you think it has a link with the rest of the body?'

Either the agents had missed something or this expert had certainly lost contact with reality altogether.

'Rest of the body?' Grand ventured.

'Yes.' Kempster was heading for the stairs to the cellar. 'The one we have been fishing – well, I say "we", of course, but by that I mean the River Police and various civilians – fishing out of the Thames for the past week.'

'Um – I don't think we knew about that,' Batchelor said. If the finger were connected, then something had gone horribly wrong with this case and from some time before they had been engaged.

'It's been in all the papers,' Kempster pointed out. 'We've been appealing to the general public to come in to try and identify the woman.'

'So, you know it's a woman, then?' Batchelor said, glancing at Grand.

'Oh, definitely. If for no other reason, the very well-developed breasts would give the game away. We even have a face . . . but let me show you.' He lit the gas mantle on the wall and the whole macabre collection sprang into pallid life. Laid out on a table, in the right order but not quite touching, were ten body parts in total, making up almost a complete corpse, minus the hands and feet. The head, if that was what it could be called, stood upright on a table just to one side. 'I see you are admiring my work on the head,' Kempster said. 'I like to think it is groundbreaking.' He took them over to where the skin mask stood, stretched over its oak block. 'It is far from perfect, of course, but I like to think that a relative or close friend would recognize her.'

Grand and Batchelor were not sure; but as neither of them had ever seen the skin of a loved one stretched over some wood, they couldn't really tell. It was certainly painstaking, they could see that much.

'But, let me see the finger, gentlemen.' Kempster cleared an area on his workbench and laid the napkin-wrapped bundle carefully on it. He unrolled it using tweezers. The finger lay there, pink and delicate and it didn't take an expert to see that it had little in common with the body parts lying within arm's reach.

'The first thing I would say,' Kempster told them, 'is that this is unlikely to come from our dead woman from the river. I doubt it was removed more than a day to a day and a half ago and these body parts began to turn up a week ago; last Friday, in fact. So, that's our first problem. Next, the age. Although I would grant you that it is as yet beyond science to age a person from a finger alone, I would say that this digit is that of a young woman. The fingernail has been well kept and the ring is expensive. Our river body is not of the same age or class. I would say that twenty years separate the ages of these women; if I were to guess at a connection, the best that I could manage would be that they are mother and daughter; our river body has borne and suckled at least one child.'

'I don't want to put words in your mouth, doctor,' Batchelor said, 'but I think so far your conclusions about the finger are right. We believe it to be that of a young woman of a leisured class, aged twenty-two.'

'I see nothing to contradict that,' Kempster said. 'Have you examined the ring?'

Neither Grand nor Batchelor wanted to admit to being too squeamish, so shook their heads.

'Very sensible. Where a crime has been committed, the less interference, the better. I constantly try to teach that to the police of V Division, but usually to no avail. By the time I am called, the body has usually been mauled about dreadfully; the keen constable tries to see if life is extinct and tries to sit them up, even get them walking. The lazy ones just want to tidy up their patch and commandeer the nearest coster's barrow to bring it round to this house. Either way, I rarely see a crime scene unsullied.' He sighed. 'Detection will get nowhere while the police are involved, I fear.' He brightened up. 'But you have been as careful as possible, so well done!' He beamed at them. 'You have even kept the original wrapping. I assume that this was sent as a warning or similar. We see a lot of that around this neck of the woods – Italians, mostly.' He prodded the finger thoughtfully. 'Not usually the finger of a young and genteel lady, though. I can't think of anyone who would do something so terrible. Daddy would know.'

Grand and Batchelor were surprised to hear Kempster refer to his father in such a way; he seemed so professional otherwise.

He read their faces. 'No, no, goodness me, not my father. He's a retired rural dean in Wiltshire. No, I mean Inspector Bliss of the River Police. Everyone calls him "Daddy" – we've all forgotten why. You should see him later. It seems too much of a coincidence that you have a severed body part while we have such a substantial collection.' While he was talking, he had removed the ring, again using tweezers. He held it under a magnifying glass held above the bench in a caliper attached to a wooden rod screwed to the desk. Dr Kempster was the mother of invention.

Grand leaned in. 'Yes,' he said, straightening up. 'The entwined "E". It's Emilia Byng's ring all right. And presumably, her finger. Say, Dr Kempster, can you tell us if it was taken off before or after death?'

'That's a really good question,' Kempster said, turning back to the finger. 'It does appear to have bled freely – see how pale the nail is – and the edge is a little inflamed. If I were to be asked to answer on oath, I would have to say I couldn't tell, but between you and me, I would say that the woman was alive when this finger was removed.'

'That's good,' Batchelor said.

'Really? It would have been exquisitely painful.'

'We believe this to be the finger of a missing woman – her husband is a client of ours. So, we would rather she were alive than otherwise.'

'She would need medical attention for this wound,' Kempster pointed out. 'Even though it is neatly done, she would need stitches at the very least. But tell me, you say "husband"; of long-standing?'

'Over a year.'

'I would have expected more of a groove under the ring. I don't believe the finger has been immersed in water, otherwise there would be what we call "washerwoman's skin" on the fingertips. And yet, the ring has left hardly a mark.'

'That does prove something we have wondered,' Batchelor said. 'We think that the two had been estranged, but by all accounts, they were excited to be back together when she set off to come home last week. So perhaps she had taken the ring off.'

'That would make sense,' Grand agreed. 'The husband had certainly behaved like an asshole.'

Kempster bridled. Even for Lincolnshire, that was rather ripe language.

'I think you should bring him in to see the body I have here,' Kempster said. 'Though the odds are very much against there being any link, we really should leave no stone unturned.' Almost suiting the action to the words, he slipped the paper from under the finger. 'Oh, now that *is* disappointing! I was hoping for an address. I make something of a study of handwriting, but the paper is blank.'

'We know it was delivered by hand,' Grand said.

'Even so, most people, even when delivering a finger, add some kind of salutation. Still, there is no second-guessing a criminal mind, I suppose.'

The three men stood there, staring down at the finger, mute as only a disarticulated digit can be. The door at the top of the stairs opened and the silhouette of Nancy Kempster appeared.

'Felix, have you finished down there?' she called. 'Mrs Farthing is in labour.' A high-pitched voice behind her added something. 'Giving birth right now, her husband says.'

'I'll be right up,' Kempster called. Then, to Grand and Batchelor, 'I must go. Amy Farthing has had seven children, two of them twins, but to hear her husband on the subject you would think she was a complete novice. May I keep the finger for a while? I may be able to find out more.'

'Be our guest,' Batchelor said. He and Grand would be glad to be out of this charnel house and back into the air of Battersea – it may not be the freshest in the world, but at least it didn't smell of formaldehyde and decay.

It took a sustained walk in the stiffish breeze from the river until either of them felt fit to mix with anyone. The smell of the corpse clung to their coats as if they had hugged her. Finding themselves along the river bank, it seemed a good time to visit the warehouses – tea and timber – which loomed so large in the case they found themselves back in. They had other cases, to be sure, but none had presented them, that day or ever, with a finger. Deceived spouses could get very nasty, but thus far had never resorted to lopping off bits of each other; and if they did, it was not likely to be a digit.

'Shall we divide and conquer?' Grand asked, sniffing his sleeve doubtfully.

'Why not?' Batchelor said. 'Tea or timber?'

Grand rummaged in his pocket for a florin and tossed it in the air. Covering it with his hand, he said, 'Heads or tails?'

'Tails.'

'Tails it is, so; tea or timber?'

Batchelor gave it some thought. Both were likely to be in a more fragrant setting than Kempster's laboratory. 'Timber.' Too late, he remembered that the timber warehouse was also likely to be loud. Huge tree trunks being lugged around versus soft sacks of whispering tea leaves. Damn!

'Good choice,' Grand smiled. They were standing near to the

Limehouse Pier and the huge walls of Byng's timber warehouse loomed over them. The tea warehouse was downstream and on the other bank by the Garden Stairs at Greenwich, so Grand stepped carefully down the steps, slippery with weed and general river detritus, to hail a water taxi. Since Kempster's mortuary, he was watching very carefully where he put his feet.

'Boat, guv'nor?' The voice came from below the parapet of the lowest step. The tide was low and the mudbanks across the Thames gleamed slick in the September sun. The smell was enough to overwhelm any memory of the cadaver and Grand stepped gingerly aboard. 'I just need to go across to the Westmoreland tea warehouse. It's just across the way there, look.'

The cabbie knew where it was. Hadn't his old man been a lighterman on this very stretch of river – and *his* old man before that – helping themselves to other people's property left carelessly lying about on the ocean-rigged steamers? He feathered his oars to keep his skiff still while Grand got comfortable in the stern. The boatman had spotted the foreign accent straight away and saw an opportunity to earn a bit more than a quick scull across the river could bring in. 'Visiting, are you, guv,nor?' he asked, all Cockney sparrer and charm. 'I could take you a nice scenic route, show you where they found all them women, you know, the chopped up ones . . .'

The cabbie couldn't know he was talking to probably the last man in London who wanted to know more about the body parts. So he was a little startled by Grand's reply, which cut few corners and made it abundantly clear as to how very much he didn't want to see the sights. It was a long time since the waterman had heard any new words, but he heard a few that morning, all the way from West Point.

'Right you are, then, guv'nor.' There seemed little else to say. 'I'll get you across in two shakes of a lamb's tail.' And he bent to the oars and, dodging the bigger traffic making its way into the city from Tilbury, sliding expertly across the narrows, he deposited Grand on the opposite bank, in the shadow of the tea warehouse.

He walked round to the land side, expecting a small office, perhaps, or even a shop. Many of the importers sold their wares

directly to the public from such shops, which also gave wholesalers a chance to try out the goods. But Westmoreland Teas
presented a dour, blank face to the street and he walked along
it, looking for an alleyway, perhaps, or a wicket gate. He was
about to give up and retrace his steps when he saw a small hut,
almost leaning on the wall. In it, an old man was hunched,
eating a sandwich that Grand didn't want to know too much
about. It was about two inches thick and something nameless
was oozing out of one side and daubing the old man's cheek.
Grand tapped politely on the door and the man jumped a mile.

'What d'you want to do that for?' he screeched. 'You could've
choked me. What do you want?'

It seemed rather an over-reaction and Grand couldn't help
thinking that the old man was perhaps not the best advertisement for tea, that most genteel of drinks. 'I'm looking for the
entrance to Westmoreland Teas,' he said, politely.

'Waddya asking me for?' the old man said, taking another
huge bite of his sandwich, which now made itself known as
containing tripe.

'Well,' Grand waved an arm, 'you seem to be attached to the
building . . .'

'Attached? Attached? I ain't attached. I just lean, kind of
thing. No, I'm here to watch the 'ole.'

Grand looked around. 'Hole?'

'Well, it's not here at present. But they often digs an 'ole
and when they do, it needs watching, see. So I sits here and
watches it.'

'I see.' Grand felt an urgent need to cut this conversation
short. 'So . . . Westmoreland Teas?'

'Rahnda corner.'

Grand silently translated in his head. 'Round this next corner?'
He pointed ahead.

'Nah.' The old man pointed back the way he had come.
'Back to the corner. Rahnd that corner. Then rahnd the next
corner. Faces onto the river, don't it?'

Cursing the waterman under his breath, Grand retraced his
steps, leaving the hole-watcher to his sandwich. The way back
seemed substantially longer than the way there, but he was soon
facing a small door, half glazed with knobbly glass so it was

impossible to see in. On a small plaque beside the door, 'Westmoreland Tea Importers. Please Knock and Enter' had been engraved, but constant polishing had almost worn it away. Batchelor tapped the glass and pushed the door open. It swung easily and he stepped inside, onto tiles slightly gritty with spilled tea. A man in a brown coat was sweeping the floor and collecting the piles of dust and tea leaves into a cardboard box, labelled 'Westmoreland Breakfast; economy tea for the discerning'. When he saw Grand, he hurriedly kicked the box under the counter which stretched halfway across the room and turned to him with an ingratiating smile.

'Good morning, sir. Or is it afternoon? In any event, welcome to Westmoreland Tea Importers.' This looked like a live one; they didn't often get top-notch buyers these days at Westmoreland and this one was well dressed and looked a bit of a toff.

'Thank you,' Grand said. 'It's hard to find the way in, isn't it?'

Oh, praise be, the man with the broom could scarcely contain himself. A foreign buyer. The old gentlemen will be so pleased. Aloud, he said, 'I'm sorry, sir. We do have a board, with an arrow, but the urchins round here will keep taking it. I didn't realize it had gone again. I'll get someone onto it at once.' He banged his hand down on a bell on the counter and was rewarded with an injured 'dung' sound.

'While he's about it, he can mend the bell as well, perhaps.' Grand was beginning to think that he had wandered into rehearsals for a panto.

'Ha ha, that's a good one, sir, yes indeed. He can. But now you are here, sir, how can I assist?'

'Well, I'm not sure, really,' Grand said. 'I really need to speak to someone in authority. Um – it is quite confidential . . .'

The man in the brown coat was outraged. 'You can trust me with anything, sir. I am the general factotum here, I work both here "out front" as you might say and also in the offices. Don't be confused by this garb, sir – I was just doing a bit of sweeping up.'

'Blending the economy Breakfast,' Grand remarked.

'I can see you like to have your little joke, sir. Just tidying up. So you can ask me anything, sir, and it won't go an inch further.'

'I need to speak to the people who look after Mrs Byng's trust fund.' Grand was suddenly tired of beating around the bush.

The man started visibly. 'May I ask why, sir?'

'No. Unless you are one of them, of course, in which case I would be delighted to share the information with you when everyone is assembled.' The man's speech patterns were catching and Grand gave himself a mental shake. 'So just get the cusses together and we'll talk.'

'I'm not sure whether Mr Teddy and Mr Micah are in, sir.' The sweeper-up was playing for time and they both knew it.

'Shall we go and look?' Grand was still polite but was letting his claws show, like a kitten playing with a child. The man took the hint.

'Just let me divest myself of this coat, sir, and I can take you to their offices. But, as I say, they may not—'

'Be in. I know. Let's risk it, shall we?'

The man led Grand through a warren of passageways then out into a huge warehouse, where bales and bags of various tea leaves awaited shipment to wholesalers, grocers and the various institutions catered to by Westmoreland Teas. To say it was a hive of industry would be a lie, but compared to what he had seen so far, Grand considered it quite crowded. Women stood to one side of the vast space, spreading out leaves onto drying tables and men on the other man-handled the enormous bales. Grand could easily see how Emilia Byng's father had been killed by one falling from one of the huge pulleys overhead. The smell of dusty tea was overwhelming and Grand sneezed violently. His guide turned round with a laugh.

'It gets most people like that to start with, sir,' he said. 'You get used to it eventually.'

Grand sneezed again and about a dozen voices said, 'Bless you!'

'It took me about five years, but not everyone is as quick.' The man darted down a side corridor and clattered up a flight of rickety steps. He pointed to a door. 'Mr Micah is in here, if he's in. And Mr Teddy is in here.' He pointed to the next door.

'If he's in.'

'Indeed. Oh, can I have your name, sir? Just to introduce, you know.'

'Grand. Matthew Grand.'

'Thank you.' He flung open the nearest door and shouted, 'A Mr Grand for you, Mr Micah.' He turned back to Grand. 'He is in. In you go. I'll send Mr Teddy in, if he's in.'

Grand went through the door into the office, which was lit by the low embers of a neglected fire and a single gas mantle. An old, old man sat behind the desk; he was alive, that much was clear from the bright eyes glittering below a tall, bald dome of a forehead. But he seemed to be composed of tea; everything about him was the same dusty, brownish olive of the leaves downstairs, including the teeth he now bared in a welcoming smile.

'Mr Grand.' The voice was low and mellow and Grand was totally taken by surprise. He had expected, from this desiccated and tea-stained tumble of clothes and cranium, something weak and scratchy; even a little demented and confused. But this man was clearly in possession of all his marbles so, at least from that side of things, he ought to be able to get what he came for; if Mr Micah would tell him.

'Hello, Mr . . .'

The man's smile broadened. 'I suppose that idiot manager called me Mr Micah. And my brother Mr Teddy?'

Grand nodded.

'I suppose you can't blame him – we are both Mr Westmoreland and it would get confusing.'

Grand was now very confused. If there were still Mr Westmorelands, why was Emilia an heiress to the whole tea empire?

'I see you are wondering who we are; our poor cousin's sad death caused quite a stir and you possibly remember it.'

Grand smiled. There was no reason to question this man; he seemed to be able to guess the next question all by himself. The door behind Grand opened and another man came in, as tea-coloured as the first but with a wild shock of white hair instead of a gleaming dome.

'This is my brother, the younger by three minutes.' The elder Mr Westmoreland chuckled. 'We don't look much like twins now, I agree with you, Mr Grand, but you should have seen us when we were children; like two peas in a pod, eh, Teddy?'

Teddy Westmoreland bared an identical set of teeth in an identical smile. 'Peas,' he agreed. Unlike his brother, he was a man of few words.

'But you are not here to see how twins look in their dotage, Mr Grand,' Micah Westmoreland told him. 'Nor to order tea, I'll warrant.'

'No.' Grand felt it was time to actually take part in what was fast becoming a one way conversation. 'I'm here on behalf of . . . a client . . . to ask some questions about the trust fund of Mrs Emilia Byng.'

The twins smiled in unison, shaking their heads regretfully. 'Unless your client is Emilia, Mr Grand, and unless you have written authority signed by her, then I am afraid we can't help you,' Micah said.

'Help you,' echoed his brother.

'This is very difficult,' Grand said. 'Has Mr Byng not been in touch, then?'

The twins looked briefly at each other; Grand wondered if Lewis Carroll had ever met them. 'We are not in touch with Mr Byng,' Micah said. Teddy just shook his head.

Grand was between a rock and a hard place. He could hardly just get up and go, but on the other hand, he couldn't really tell these two old gents what was going on, if Byng hadn't.

'Can we talk generally?' he said.

'Ah,' Teddy said, suddenly coming to independent life. 'No names, no pack drill, eh?' He had been the company's representative in India for some years and had a rather martial cast to his character sometimes, to the chagrin of his brother, who had been no further east than Kent.

'That's right. If I just . . . remark about some things and you . . .'

'. . . remark back!' Micah clapped his hands. 'This could be fun. But,' and he frowned, gathering the expanse of his forehead down over his bright eyes for a moment, 'we decide what to tell you, Mr Grand. At all times.'

'Of course.' Grand smiled and they all settled down for a good old chinwag.

'Tea?' Teddy suddenly asked.

Grand was puzzled for a moment, then saw the kettle singing

quietly to itself on the hob. He hated tea as much as the next Bostonian, but he nodded politely and hoped it would be drinkable and not Westmoreland's Breakfast Economy.

While Teddy busied himself with warming the pot and generally being mother, Grand began. 'First of all, how big is Mrs Byng's trust fund?'

'Good mercy of heaven!' Micah almost sat up straight in his agitation. 'Cut to the chase, Mr Grand, why don't you? I can't answer that but suffice to say, substantial. Although the old firm isn't what it was, the total of the trust is spread over several different investments and is doing very well.'

'Could it stand the removal of five thousand pounds, for example?' Grand asked.

A wheezing sound indicated that both men were laughing. 'Is that a week, Mr Grand, or just one payment? Because the answer to either would be "yes".'

Teddy came back to the desk with the teapot and Micah opened a drawer and extracted milk, sugar and cups. Teddy nudged Micah and muttered, 'five thousand pounds' to their mutual hilarity.

Grand made a note in his little book – it seemed to him that this meant that the person holding Emilia Byng and sending bits of her to her husband had no idea of how large the pot was in which he was dipping so shallowly. Anyone in the know would have asked for far more. He asked his next question. 'Can she . . . extract any funds?'

'When she's thirty-five,' Micah said and shut his mouth with a snap.

'Sugar?' Teddy said, his hand poised with some exquisite little silver nips over the bowl.

'Er . . . yes. One, please.' Grand had no idea whether he took sugar in tea; this would be a learning curve all round.

'Excellent.' Teddy dropped the small lump in and stirred it carefully. He handed over the cup to Grand and the twins leaned forward to watch him take a sip.

Grand was ready to force down the dreadful brew, but found his nose, his mouth, his entire brain suffused in a joy of meadows, of sunshine, of fleeting citrus and fugitive honey-drenched flowers. He looked up over the rim of his cup, his eyes wide with amazement.

'He likes it!' Teddy said, nudging Micah.

'Of course he does,' Micah said, kindly. 'Your blends are legendary, Teddy.'

'Oh, now.' Teddy looked down, blushing.

'This is . . . wonderful.' Grand didn't want to waste good drinking time on talk. 'What is it?'

'It doesn't have a name as yet,' Teddy said. 'I only perfected it yesterday. But if I may, I will name it after you. "Westmoreland's Grand Blend".' He smiled at Grand. 'It sounds good, don't you think? I will pack you up a couple of pounds before you go.'

Grand gathered his thoughts, but the teacup kept drawing him back. 'Thirty-five?' he said, at last. 'And not a moment sooner?'

'Not a single moment,' Micah said firmly. 'Even if we wanted to, we couldn't. Neither Teddy, nor I, nor the business itself could manage to advance it. The only way the trust can be touched earlier than her thirty-fifth birthday is if she should decease and then, of course, it would go to her heir, her husband as things stand.' The twins looked downcast. 'But she is only a girl and as far as we know, in good health. So,' Micah's beam was back in place. 'Thirty-five it is; another thirteen years.'

Grand made another note in his book and drained his cup. 'Thank you so much,' he said, standing up and shaking hands with them both. 'The tea was a revelation and I have all the information I need; thank you for being so helpful.'

'Not at all, not at all.' Micah hadn't moved from the spot and didn't now. 'Teddy will show you out, via the blending room for your Grand Blend. Do come and visit us again – and with news of Emilia if you can. We miss her since she . . . well, we miss her. Goodbye, Mr Grand.'

EIGHT

Messrs Sillitoe, Byng and Son's Timber Warehouse stretched as far as Batchelor could see. It was one of those vast, anonymous blocks that fringed the river along Trinidad Street, where the Chinamen walked, its walls punctuated with derricks, pulleys and cranes that hauled the swaying catches from the ocean freighters to be stacked in vast piles inside the cavernous holding hall. From there, huge draught horses carried the timber to the goods yards where they were loaded onto rolling stock and monkey boats to begin their journey to every part of the country, via rail and water. The sawing and the turning would come later, as the middle classes bought their sideboards, their gate-leg tables and jardinière stands, their fireplace surrounds and their beds. At the end of the timber's journey, the giant trees may even find themselves in vestas in gentlemen's pockets, tipped red with sulphur and phosphorus and enough to gladden the heart of an old prime minister, still anxious to gain some profit from light.

'No, no,' the ancient retainer was saying as Batchelor sneezed his way across the threshold. 'Old Mr Sillitoe passed away some years ago, but Mr Byng is such a kindly soul, he couldn't bear to take his name down from the roof or off of the stationery. Er . . . it was Mr Byng the elder you wanted to see, sir?'

'Yes.' Batchelor blew his nose. His eyes were swimming and his throat prickled.

The ancient retainer chuckled. 'That'll be the Russian fir, sir,' he said. 'We're all used to it now, of course, but it still comes as a bit of a trial to them as hasn't encountered it before. Trees in here aren't the same as them growing in the parks, you see.'

Batchelor sneezed again and followed the old man up a flight of stone steps, past windows that let out into the warehouse. The noise there was terrifying, like the seventh circle of hell, as timbers crashed and chains rattled. Each movement was accompanied by the frantic yells of the warehousemen, screaming above the row in an incomprehensible language that Batchelor scarcely recognized. At an ornate oak door, the retainer paused. 'May I say what your visit is in connection with, sir?'

'That's confidential, I'm afraid,' Batchelor told him, 'between me and Mr Byng.'

'Quite. Quite.'

The old man pushed the door and ushered Batchelor into a comfortable waiting room. There was a plush carpet and around the walls were panels of every conceivable type of tree – sequoias, redwoods, black tupelo and ginkgo bilobas – all of them available from Messrs Sillitoe, Byng and Son, Timber Importers. But that wasn't what caught Batchelor's eye. In the far corner of the waiting room, a young lady sat in front of a machine on a table. It had a piece of paper in the top and she was hesitantly poking the keys below it with one finger.

'Is that a typewriting machine?' he asked.

'Please, sir,' the retainer took his arm to hurry him along. 'No disturbing the staff. Miss Plunkett is doing her best, but personally, I don't see what's wrong with a quill pen.'

'Quite. Quite.' It was Batchelor's turn to say it this time. He had to agree with the old boy. He had been reading about these inventions of a printer's devil for weeks now but he had never actually seen one. He honestly couldn't see how Fleet Street could manage. With that speed of printing, the very idea of a deadline would be out of the window.

The retainer rapped on a second door, just as ornate as the first and there was a gruff grunt from beyond it.

'Mr Batchelor, sir,' the retainer announced as though the enquiry agent was being shown into Buckingham Palace's throne room. The presence at the far end of this cavernous office didn't get up from behind his rosewood desk. At first glance, he looked even older than the retainer, but his eyes were bright, even mischievous and his jaw firm.

'Mr Byng,' Batchelor said. 'Good of you to see me at such short notice.'

'Make that no notice at all,' Byng grunted. 'What do you want?'

'It's a rather delicate matter, sir,' Batchelor said, 'of a personal nature.' He glanced at the retainer.

'Leave us, Todmorden,' Byng said.

The retainer half bowed and shuffled out of the room.

'Well?' Byng waited until the door had closed.

'It's about your son, sir.'

'Selwyn?' The old man's eyes narrowed and his flowing Dundrearies twitched. 'What about him?'

'I'll come to the point, sir, if I may.'

'I wish you would,' Byng sighed. 'It may be something of a cliché, young man, but time is money. Especially mine.'

'I am an enquiry agent, sir.' Batchelor passed his card across the desk and could barely reach the man's hand. Byng read it and frowned. '"Grand and Batchelor",' he read. '"Enquiry Agents".' He raised his eyebrows. 'Not too bad an address. Which one are you, again?'

'Batchelor, sir.'

The old man snorted. 'Junior partner, eh?'

'No, sir. Mr Grand and I are equals.'

'How quaint. So . . . the purpose of your visit?'

'Well, obviously, sir, it's about the kidnap.'

'The what?'

Batchelor blinked. For a moment he wondered if the old boy hadn't heard him, but seconds later, it was clear that he had. 'What kidnap? Who's been kidnapped?'

'Emilia, sir. Your daughter-in-law.'

'Poppycock!' the elder Byng snapped. 'I saw her only the other day. Oh, she's not right for Selwyn, of course; but then, he isn't right for her. I knew that this would end in tears.'

'Not a happy marriage?' Dislike the work though he did, much of Grand and Batchelor's bread and butter came from their evidence before the divorce courts. He was used to asking questions like that.

'You have *met* my son, I assume?' Byng asked. 'In person, I mean, not through some correspondence course?'

'Yes, sir,' Batchelor assured him. 'I have.'

'Well, there you are.' Byng leaned back in his chair, clasping his fingers across his sprigged waistcoat. 'How could anybody be happy with a man like that?'

'Believe me, sir, when I say that your daughter-in-law's kidnap is real enough.'

'How do you know?'

'The kidnapper sent her finger to your son through the post.'

'Good God!' The elder Byng sat bolt upright, eyes bulging. 'Why didn't he tell me? Call the police?'

'He was told not to, sir,' Batchelor said, 'by the kidnapper. Dire things would happen to Emilia unless Selwyn co-operated.'

'Dire?' Byng thundered. 'How much more dire can it be than to chop off a person's finger? At the very least she'll die of loss of blood or sepsis or whatever the medical chappies call it.'

'That's why it's important to act quickly, sir,' Batchelor said. 'I presumed your son had told you all about it.'

'My son and I haven't had a meaningful conversation since 1867, Mr Batchelor and then it was just me putting him right over his insanely liberal notions on Disraeli's extension of the vote. Now, I'm sorry I can't help you, but the timber import business is a cut-throat one and I am a very busy man. Can you see yourself out? And tell that wretched girl to stop that useless clacking outside. That contraption will never catch on.'

Since the elder Byng's mouth was now firmly shut, fringed by the silver of his whiskers, there seemed little else that Batchelor could find out. He thanked the man for his time, which was really all he had given and crossed the office threshold. He was going to take the opportunity to ask the wretched girl all about the typewriting machine and perhaps even have a go on it himself, but he saw Todmorden hovering and swept on past.

'Todmorden,' old Mr Byng growled as the retainer reached his door. 'Get my son up here now. We need to talk.'

'What do you mean, sir?' the elder Byng was sitting back in his chair, his eyes flinty hard and his Dundrearies bristling.

'About what, father?' Selwyn asked.

'That girl you married. She's been kidnapped.'

Selwyn blinked. His mouth was bricky dry. All his life he had feared and hated this man in equal measure. Often because the old man always seemed to know as much, if not more, than he did. 'I know,' was all he could think to say.

The elder Byng slammed closed a ledger on his desk and stood up, hauling down the lapels of his frock coat. 'Of course you know,' he snarled. 'But *I* didn't. I just had some scruffy street person up here, name of Batchelor. Know him?'

'Yes, Father.'

'Claims you've hired him to find Emilia. Is that right?'

'Yes, Father.'

'Why didn't you come to me?' the old man bellowed, answering his own question with every move of his body.

'I . . . I didn't want to bother you, Father. The Trust . . .'

'Yes,' the old man's sharp business brain was whirling. 'I was wondering about that. This kidnapper chappie – how does he know about the Trust?'

'He doesn't, father,' Selwyn said. 'Or at least, I don't think he does. He merely wants me to pay up or—'

'Or they'll send various bits of her to you in the post; yes, I know.'

'It's urgent now, Father,' Selwyn blurted out. 'Could you advance me the money?'

The elder Byng turned pale. He almost felt the sharp, acid pain in the area of his wallet. 'How much is it?' he asked.

'Five thousand pounds,' Selwyn said.

His father stood as though frozen to the spot. 'Impossible,' he said. 'I'm not made of money.'

'But, Father we're talking about Emilia's life.'

'That, sir, will be on your conscience, not mine.'

'The Trust, then . . .' Selwyn knew that the old man would have exactly this response; that was why he hadn't gone to him in the first place.

'You can grovel around them if you like,' the elder Byng said, 'but don't expect any help from me. You've been a disappointment to me all your life, Selwyn, a waste of space. I keep you on here so that you're not leading a life of complete dissipation. I won't have it noised abroad that my son is a layabout. But this is something you must resolve yourself – your chance to be a man, if it's not too late. Win your spurs, sir. And stop snivelling to those enquiry agents or whatever they call themselves. Damned snoopers, that's all they are. Now, get out. And, for God's sake, don't let any of this reach the newspapers.'

* * *

'Enquiry agents?' Daddy Bliss blinked. 'What's that?'

'We are,' Grand said. He didn't like this man already and he'd only been on board his ship for five minutes.

Bliss looked at the pair from his usual position across the table. The littler one was sharp, beady-eyed and didn't miss much. He was difficult to pin down, however. Clearly, he had had an above-average education, maybe even private, but his duds were nothing to write home about. The bigger one was foreign.

'And what is it you are enquiring about, exactly?' he asked.

'We have a client,' Batchelor told him, 'who came to us with a little problem. That problem led us to Dr Kempster of V Division.'

'A good man,' Bliss nodded. He was pouring himself a cup of coffee but showed no inclination to offer any to his visitors. 'But less good now I know he's passed you on to me.'

'We understand,' Grand said, 'that you're something of an expert on body parts.'

Bliss paused with the tin cup near his lips. 'I've had my moments,' he said.

'Digits?' Batchelor asked.

Bliss continued his swig, then wiped his mouth. 'Suppose you tell me *exactly* what you want,' he said.

Grand and Batchelor looked at each other. They'd known coppers who were helpfulness itself – the late Dick Tanner at the Yard had been one such. Dolly Williamson, also of A Division, more or less sang from their hymn sheet. Then there were the others – and Daddy Bliss appeared to be one of them – who wouldn't give them the time of day. But ice had to be broken somewhere or all that the Strand pair would have to show for this morning was a faint whiff of the river.

'We cannot give you our client's name,' Batchelor said, 'but we can confide that his wife is missing and he has received two ransom notes.'

'A matter for us, surely,' Bliss said, 'in my professional opinion.'

'That's just it,' Grand said. 'The notes were specific – no police.'

Bliss snorted. 'That's what they all say, isn't it? It's axiomatic among the criminal classes. I'm going to throw this brick through a plate glass window but don't go blabbing to the boys in blue. That sort of thing.'

'They sent him a finger,' Grand said.

Bliss paused in mid-swig again. 'I see,' he said. 'Hence your interest in body parts and digits.'

'Dr Kempster gave nothing away,' Batchelor lied. 'The papers are full of your river finds. What's the *Star* calling it? "The Bermondsey Horror"?'

Bliss chuckled. 'I don't know how these blokes can watch themselves shave of a morning,' he said, 'writing bollocks like that. They only do it to frighten people.'

'Perhaps people *should* be frightened.' Batchelor felt he had to defend his former colleagues. 'What with torsos floating in the Thames.'

'We've got it in hand,' Bliss assured them, 'if you'll excuse the pun.'

'The hand is why we're here,' Grand said. 'Or, to be precise, the left-hand ring finger.'

'Sent through the post?' Bliss asked.

'We believe so,' Batchelor nodded.

'Postmark?'

'Blurred to the point of invisibilty,' Grand said. 'Unreadable.'

'Hm,' Bliss nodded. 'I don't mean to denigrate the operatives of the General Post Office, but all too often those careless, lazy buggers obstruct us in the course of our enquiries. Or, in this case, yours. What about packaging?'

'Plain,' Batchelor said. 'Brown, for the use of. You can buy it in any stationers in the country.'

'String?' Bliss asked.

'Ditto,' Grand said. 'Hardware stores the length and breadth.'

'You said "ring finger".' Bliss was intrigued now. He had eleven body parts on display in Kempster's laboratory, but fingers were not among them. 'Was the ring still present?'

'It was,' Batchelor said. 'Our client confirmed it as the one he bought for his wife on their wedding day.'

'Touching,' Bliss murmured.

'There was no mention of hands in the newspaper articles,'

Batchelor said. 'Can you confirm that the parts that have turned up did not include them?'

'What did Kempster say?'

Again, the pair exchanged glances.

'He didn't believe the finger belonged to the body,' Grand said.

Bliss spread his arms. 'Well, there you are, gentlemen,' he said. 'You've already had it from the horse's mouth. I don't see what more I can add.'

Resisting the urge to continue the metaphor with Bliss as the horse's ass, Grand went on, 'There's a world of difference between a doctor's point of view and a River Policeman's,' he said.

'We were hoping to pick your brains on the body parts you've found,' Batchelor chipped in. 'Kempster has tried to reassemble the woman, but the papers were hazy as to where the various parts were found.'

'They would be,' Bliss said. 'That's partly because I want it that way. It hasn't quite started yet, but pretty soon we'll have every lunatic in London queuing up to view the remains, claiming it's his auntie, mother, daughter or the woman whose cat once ran up his alley. After that, we'll get the pillocks who claimed to have done it; anything for their fifteen minutes of fame. And of course, the other reason the papers are "hazy" as you put it, is that they're run by bloody idiots who wouldn't know a river current from their elbows.'

'So, you can't help further?' Batchelor asked.

'No, gentlemen, I'm sorry,' the inspector said.

Grand opened his mouth to say something, but Batchelor was on his feet. 'Well, thank you, Inspector.' He held out his hand. Bliss shook it.

'If your client sees reason and calls us in,' he said, 'you know where we are.'

'We sure do,' Grand said, without smiling. He tipped his hat and they left, clattering up the steps to the deck.

Constable Brandon saw them off the *Royalist* with a grin and a brisk salute.

'Might as well have asked the ship's cat,' Grand muttered as they trod the quayside stone again.

'Matthew, Matthew,' Batchelor chuckled. 'Will you never learn the skills of an old newshound?'

'What would they be?' Grand asked. 'Lounging in bars? Paying out bungs?'

'Tsk, tsk,' Batchelor chided. 'So young, so cynical. No, I mean, the ability to read upside down. Did you notice the note on Bliss's desk?'

'I saw some scribbles, yes.'

'It said "Monkey boats. Limehouse. Travellers."'

'Travellers?'

'Gypsies, Matthew. The travelling people. In this case, those who travel the canals on the barges. Now it may be that Bliss pays these blokes a visit every now and again just because he can. Or it may be because he has a link between them and the body parts.'

'Okay.'

'Did you notice something else?' Batchelor asked. 'Something Bliss jotted down with his pencil just before we left?'

'Er . . .'

Batchelor tapped the side of his nose, 'It could have been his wife's shopping list, but I don't think so. Didn't it strike you as odd that Bliss didn't ask about the size of the ransom? The money involved?'

'I assumed it was because he didn't give a damn,' Grand shrugged.

'Well, yes, that's possible. But it could be because he's got an idea who's sending notes and fingers through the post.'

'Why?' Grand asked. 'What did he write down?'

'One word,' Batchelor said, 'Knowes. K-N-O-W-E-S.'

'Can't he spell?' Grand asked.

'I've no idea,' Batchelor said, 'but I think it's a name.'

'So all we have to do is to find it,' Grand said. A cold dread filled him. He'd been here before, looking for needles in haystacks. It meant hours of his life, hours he'd never get back, poring over Kelly's Street Directories. That was if Knowes was a real name and not an alias.

'That's all,' Batchelor said cheerfully, 'and we *are* enquiry agents.'

NINE

The Street Directories were unhelpful. There were four Knowles, a couple of Knodes, even several people of Knote. But Knowes remained defiantly absent from Kelly's lists. So Batchelor took a cab (he was feeling lazy that afternoon) to Fleet Street to link up with his old cronies from the *Telegraph*. Old Gabriel Horner had long since shuffled off the mortal coil, a martyr to brandy and soda. Tom Grossmith had moved to *The Times*, as a royal correspondent, no less, wondering politely whether Her Majesty would ever make another public appearance as her devoted subjects loved her so much. That left Edwin Dyer.

Batchelor knew exactly where to find him, especially as the clock of St Dunstan's chimed four. It was tea-time and Dyer was sitting at his favourite corner table in the Cheshire Cheese, pouring gin into his afternoon Darjeeling.

'Hello, Edwin,' Batchelor slapped the man's back. 'It's been a while.'

The man nearly died then and there from juniper inhalation and croaked hoarsely, 'Jim Batchelor, you complete bastard!'

'I've missed you too, Ed,' Batchelor said. 'But it's James these days.'

'Oh, of course.' Dyer let his throat come back to normal. 'The private detective business.'

'Enquiry Agency,' Batchelor corrected him.

'Whatever.' Dyer signalled to a waiter for a second cup. 'How is that going? Beats working, I expect.'

'Well, funnily enough,' Batchelor sat himself down and leaned closer, resting his elbows on the table, 'that's more or less why I'm here.'

'Tchah!' The journalist threw back his head in mock disgust. 'And here's me thinking you just wanted to catch up with an old friend.'

'Oh, I do, Ed, I do. It's simply delightful and all that. But I need a favour.'

Dyer raised his hand and rubbed his thumb and forefinger together, as if feeling pound notes. 'That'll cost, I'm afraid,' he said.

Batchelor sighed. 'Do you remember, Ed, that little business with whatsername? You know, the Bishop of Islington's daughter? Let me see, that was back in 'sixty-five, wasn't it? You were quite smitten, I seem to remember, writing that piece on the historic churches of London. She was *hugely* helpful, I seem to remember, closeted away with you in that prebendal stall, all that time. What was her name, now? Yes.' He clicked his fingers. 'Dorothea, wasn't it? And wasn't she fifteen at the time?'

'You've always been a shit, Batchelor,' the journalist said, 'but now you're more of a shit than you used to be. What do you want to know?' He could feel the hot breath of the vengeful Bishop of Islington on the back of his neck.

'Knowes. K-N-O-W-E-S. Is that name familiar?'

Dyer twisted his face in an effort to remember. 'No, it doesn't ring any . . . wait a minute. Yes, Richard.'

'Richard?' Batchelor blinked. 'Dick Knowes? Surely not.'

'I wouldn't let him hear you call him that if I were you. He could buy both of us with his back-pocket change.'

'Really?' Batchelor frowned. 'Why haven't I heard of him?'

'I don't know,' Dyer smirked, 'you being in the enquiry business and all. He lives in Eaton Square, the shady side, naturally. Import/export.'

'Is he straight?' Batchelor asked.

'You know we don't ask that kind of question in Fleet Street, Ji . . . James. It's not seemly.'

'I mean, can we assume that his residence is the result of honest toil?'

'You can assume what you like. Let's just say the *Telegraph* was going to run a piece on him last year. Rumours of insider trading and decidedly dodgy dealings in Sumatran rubber.'

'Going to?' Batchelor picked up the key clause of the sentence.

'My editor called me into his office one day and told me to

drop it. "No story there," he said. "Move on." When I pointed out the public's right to know, he mentioned, as you did, the Bishop of Islington and his wretched daughter.'

'Tcha!' it was Batchelor's turn to say. 'And I thought I was the sole proprietor of that little gem.'

'James.' Dyer suddenly clutched at his sleeve. 'If you're going after Richard Knowes, for whatever reason, you look out for yourself. There's an ugly rumour that the man is an extortionist.'

Batchelor shrugged. An extortionist held no fears from him; apart from a few clothes and his granny's cranberry glass, he didn't have much to extort.

Dyer laughed wryly. 'Or if that doesn't scare you, then the other rumour is that he likes to hurt people. For fun and profit.' He raised an eyebrow and Batchelor looked at him more seriously. Edwin Dyer, though in many ways a rat, a weasel and several of the less fluffy rodents, knew his stuff and if he said be careful, careful he would be.

It was going to be a busy day. Grand would have his hands full, out on the Regent's Canal, checking up on all the barges. He didn't know how many there were, but he imagined a fair few. Batchelor had two tasks and he wasn't relishing either. In the morning, he was taking a very reluctant Selwyn Byng to view the dismembered body in William Kempster's basement. It seemed pointless to both enquiry agents, but it had to be done; actually, Daddy Bliss's acid note found in the letterbox by Maisie late the night before used language rather stronger than 'had' and 'done'. The threats were vague, skirting around being thrown into chokey for the rest of your natural and perverting the course of justice but they did the trick. Whoever their client was, he was to view the remains, sharpish. So Selwyn Byng received a note at his place of work, similar in general content but shorn of the police hyperbole. He was waiting anxiously on the pavement that morning; he had become rather chary of Mrs Rackstraw and so now he hung around outside until someone noticed him, rather than risk her wrath.

The door hadn't even swung shut behind Batchelor before Byng was complaining. His interview with his father and all subsequent conversations with him since Batchelor's visit to the timber warehouse had not gone well and he was a man who tended to bear a grudge. Batchelor was left in no doubt that it was all his fault; Byng stopped just short of accusing him of actually kidnapping his wife, but it was, Batchelor felt, only a matter of time. The rode in a cab – Batchelor ended up paying and made a note to add it to expenses – to Kempter's house in Battersea and rang the bell.

Nancy Kempster answered and recognized Batchelor at once. She smiled vaguely at Byng; she had a special doctor's wife expression which gave away nothing but was yet friendly and helpful.

Batchelor helped her out. 'This is Mr Byng, Mrs Kempster,' he said. 'He has been asked by the River Police to . . .'

'. . . come and view the body,' she sighed. 'I'll just put you in here, Mr Batchelor. Someone is with . . . her . . . at the moment.'

Byng was immediately aggrieved. 'If someone else has already identified—'

'No, no, Mr Byng,' Nancy Kempster said, quickly. 'Nothing as definite as that. I did start to keep count, but gave up after a couple of dozen. My husband is taking names and details, but really; it is getting a bit much. The poor woman should be given a decent burial. Apart from anything else, she isn't getting any fresher. I'll have to charge the police for the cost of the disinfectant I have had to buy.' She sniffed. 'It still comes through, though, don't you think?' She suddenly stopped, stricken. This could be the woman's nearest and dearest, after all.

Batchelor took a deep breath and almost gagged. 'Come through' was a bit of an understatement. 'Not at all,' he reassured her. 'Just a nice whiff of pine.'

'Really?' She was doubtful. 'I'll check with Felix how things are going with the current viewer and I'll let you know in a minute.'

In the mortuary, the atmosphere was rather thicker than in the sitting room above and Felix Kempster stood with his arm around the shoulders of a frail old man. He hadn't troubled him

with the torso. It was the head which would give the positive
identification, if one was to be made. He had come because he
suspected it might be his daughter, who he had last seen a few
years ago. She had been brought up nicely, as nicely as he could
manage on a Billingsgate's porter's pay. She had married young
and had a couple of children, who lived now with their father
and came to see their old granddad at Christmas and on his
birthday, which was all he could expect. Joe, his son-in-law,
had another woman now, not married, of course, because they
didn't know whether his Maggie was alive or dead, but a nice
woman, couple of children; he was lucky they still kept in touch.
But he thought about his Maggie every day, where she had
gone, why she went. He knew she had taken to drink, hung
around with sailors, lumpers; well, that's all there were around
here, didn't Dr Kempster agree? And she wore wigs, had done
since a girl. She didn't like her curly hair, wanted to look a bit
more sophisticated, she used to say, though who looks sophisticated when her wig is hanging over one eye and the gin is on
her? But . . . and the stream of words had stuttered and died
for a moment and Felix Kempster couldn't help but put a
comforting arm around the old man. But . . . his wife, Maggie's
mother, had gone to her grave crying for her girl and so he
thought he had better . . . he should come and see . . .

Kempster moved closer to the shrouded head, his arm still
round the old man. He had warned him it wasn't a pretty sight,
but he hadn't been able to talk him out of it. He had had lots
of sightseers since the posters had gone up and not a few jour-
nalists posing as bereaved husbands, sons, brothers; anything
to get them through his door. But no one who had affected him
as this man had. He didn't know whether he wanted it to be
his Maggie or not; to stem the pain and let him bury his girl,
or to leave him looking, wondering, hoping every day she might
come back.

'Ready?' he said and the old man nodded, an almost imper-
ceptible movement of an already tremulous head. He took off
the cloth with as much reverence as he could muster and he
felt the man flinch. The time since the mudlark had fished this
gruesome mask from the river had not been kind. Formaldehyde
or no, it was beginning to sag even more and the skin around

the empty eyesockets was now so thin that the grain of the oak block below showed through clearly, making a mockery of any crow's feet she may have had in life.

He felt the man gulp, forcing down the bile which rose to the throat of any normal person. Then the movement of the head.

'I shall have to ask you to answer this question,' he said. 'Is this your daughter? I need you to say yes or no, for the records.'

The old man took a deep breath and held it for what seemed like eternity. The room held its breath too; the woman on the block seemed to be asking to be found, to be allowed the peace of a name and a burial. Finally, he spoke.

'No,' he said, on a sob. 'No, that's not my Maggie.'

The door at the top of the stairs opened and Nancy Kempster took in the situation at once. Maternal instincts in full flow, she came down the stairs in a rush of compassion and swept the old man into her arms and away to the warmth of her kitchen. Kempster smiled; Nancy could mother anything, from a chick fallen out of its nest to an old man in search of peace. She would have made a better doctor than him but whoever heard of a woman doctor?

She turned at the top of the stairs. 'I'll send the next one down, Felix,' she said. 'It's nice Mr Batchelor and a Mr Byng.'

Kempster was puzzled. If this was a follow-up to the finger, they were wasting everyone's time. He had told Batchelor from the start that when the finger had been lopped off, this body had already been fished out of the Thames. But he fixed his expression to one of formal professionalism as they clattered down the stairs. He had covered up the head in the nick of time; after one near-accident, he had avoided anyone catching a glimpse while they were still descending.

'Dr Kempster,' Batchelor said, making the introductions. 'I hate to bother you, but Inspector Bliss asked that we call by.'

Kempster inwardly called Daddy a few choice epithets that only doctors used; some parts of the body lend themselves particularly well to curses. But he said, 'Thank you for offering to help, Mr Byng. I'll make this as quick as possible.' Because this was a husband, viewing the body parts was more relevant and he whipped off the cloth with little ceremony. Byng looked briefly and then shook his head. He was almost as white as the corpse and his eyelids were fluttering alarmingly.

He licked his lips and regretted it. He could taste the corpse with the tip of his tongue and thought he would never be rid of it. Kempster didn't like his colour and felt for his pulse, which was racing like an express train.

'Would you like to sit down, Mr Byng?' he said. 'I am a little concerned . . .'

'No,' Byng said. 'Let's get on with it, if you please.' He straightened his shoulders and turned to the other bench, where the shrouded head stood.

Kempster did his big reveal again – he knew that this wouldn't be a positive identification, but like his wife, he was getting tired of this woman's company.

Byng pressed his hand to his mouth and rushed over to the corner, where there was a sink. He threw up everything he had eaten in the last six hours, and then some more. Batchelor and Kempster looked anywhere but at him; after a grown man crying, the next most embarrassing thing had to be a grown man throwing up. After a while, Byng rejoined them, wiping his mouth on a handkerchief.

'I'm sorry,' he muttered. 'I wasn't really . . .' he stopped and pointed. 'Is that Emilia's *finger*?' His own finger trembled and his voice broke. Kempster had partially dissected it and it was pinned out on a board like a schoolroom project.

The doctor threw a hasty cloth over it. 'Um . . . I'm sorry about that,' he said. 'I needed to investigate . . .' he stuttered to a close. In all the difficult conversations he had had as a doctor, telling a husband that he was checking whether his wife's finger had been cut off before or after death had never been one had that cropped up.

Batchelor came to his rescue. 'If you could just put that in a report for us, Dr Kempster?' he said, briskly.

'Ah, yes,' Kempster grasped the straw as any dying man will. 'Here is it, Mr Batchelor.'

'And your invoice?' Batchelor sounded a businessman to his fingertips.

'In the envelope,' Kempster said. He had just plucked a figure out of the air; he had no idea if there was a going rate for identifying the details of a finger's disarticulation nor what it might be, should it exist. But he had remarked to Nancy that it was a shame these private cases didn't come around a little more often.

Byng was first up the steps, desperate for fresh air away from Kempster's charnel house. Batchelor turned on the first tread and raised an interrogatory eyebrow.

'Alive,' Kempster mouthed, pulling a rueful face. The conundrum of the finger didn't really have a right or wrong answer, but in the scheme of things, probably alive was better than the alternative.

Outside on the pavement on Lockington Street, Byng looked marginally better.

'I suggest you go home and have a rest,' Batchelor said. Even without the stress of the encounter, the vomiting would have made him feel wretched, he was sure.

'No,' Byng said. 'I must go in to work.'

'But . . .'

'You do *remember* my father?' Byng asked, with almost a ghost of a smile crossing his face.

Batchelor could only nod and smile back. Selwyn Byng was between the devil and the deep blue sea – the only question was whether he would burn forever in hell fire or drown.

Eaton Square could almost be called the natural habitat of Grand and Batchelor, Enquiry Agents. There was hardly a front door which didn't hide marital disharmony or a daughter who was consorting with men not deemed good enough for his little princess by a doting father. But Number Twenty-three had never sent their man round with a discreet billet-doux asking that they should attend at their earliest convenience, as long as that time came in the hours of darkness and began with a complex and secret knock at the front door.

It didn't look any different, though, from all of the many front doors already knocked on by Grand and Batchelor, either alone or in tandem. It had no brass plaque announcing that it was a business premises, it had no discreet second bell, for callers In The Know. In fact, as Batchelor knocked briskly that afternoon, it basked quietly in the warm late September sun just like its neighbours, almost purring in contentment. Batchelor and Grand had talked over their next steps that morning over breakfast – which had remained wonderfully lunatic-free – and the consensus had been that subterfuge was likely to be pointless. Dyer's advice to be careful had gone home; although annoying in many ways, he was a fearless journalist, with the missing teeth to prove it, so if he advised caution, caution it would be. A straightforward request for information would have to be the method; as a professed import/export agent, it was likely that he knew the tea and timber business inside out. An innocent enquiry about how the extortion racket was going would probably not go down quite as well.

Batchelor's first knock went unanswered and he was just about to repeat it when the door swung silently inwards. A man stood there, dressed in a perfectly cut tweed suit and a shirt so white it all but shone.

'Yes?' While waiting for a reply, the tweedy gent pulled on a large cigar. Batchelor was not an enquiry agent for nothing; this was probably not the butler. Apart from the cigar, the suit, though wonderfully tailored, could not conceal the rippling muscle beneath.

'I'm here to speak to Mr Knowes, if he is available,' he said, proffering his card.

The man leaned forward to read it, but made no attempt to take it from him. 'Enquiry agents?' he asked, an eyebrow rising sardonically. 'Enquiring into what?'

'The wife of a client of ours is currently missing,' Batchelor said, 'and we are making general enquiries.'

'And your client is . . .?'

'I'm afraid I couldn't possibly divulge,' Batchelor said, descending to cliché. 'All of our clients rely on our discretion.'

'Well, then,' the tweedy swell remarked, taking the card and stowing it neatly in a waistcoat pocket, 'how can Mr Knowes be of any help? If you can't tell him who you are asking about, I mean. If you ask in general terms whether he knows any women, the answer will obviously be yes. If you ask if he knows any missing women, I would imagine the answer will be no.'

'My questions were more to do with a couple of firms in the import/export business,' Batchelor said. 'But it would be much simpler if I could speak to Mr Knowes.'

'I'll see if he's free.' Tapping the ash from his cigar into an aspidistra pot at the foot of the stairs, the man bounded up the stairs and disappeared along a landing which doubled back to the left.

Batchelor stood where he had left him, straining his ears for the noises of a household in the grip of an unseasonably warm afternoon. There was no clashing of washing up from the kitchen, no smells of early dinner preparations. The silence was so total that he could hear the surge of blood through his own ears. So when the tweedy gent leaned over the balustrade and called down to him, he jumped visibly.

'Come on up, Mr . . . which one are you?'

'Batchelor.'

'Come on up, Mr Batchelor. Mr Knowes will see you now. And, if I can give you some friendly advice,' he said, as Batchelor joined him on the landing, 'don't be so jumpy. Mr Knowes doesn't like jumpy people. It makes *him* jumpy and . . . well, we'll just say that you wouldn't like him when he's jumpy.'

Dyer's face swam in front of Batchelor's eyes. 'Look out for yourself,' he heard faintly. 'Look out for yourself.' Taking a deep breath and squaring his shoulders, he followed the advertisement for gentlemen's outfitters, tweeds a speciality, into the room at the end of the landing.

After the mellow sunlight of the hall, the room into which he was led was stygian in its gloom. The blinds were drawn down and a small amount of light crept in along the bottom, almost taunting the inhabitants, reminding them that there was light and life outside. The room was large, but even so was dwarfed by an enormous desk in the centre of a Turkey carpet of subdued colours which stretched from the door to the fireplace to one side. The walls were lined with shelves, laden with boxes and files, for all the world like a lawyer's office; all that was missing was the twirling ends of the red ribbons tying them all closed. A lamp on the desk was turned so low that the wick was just a glowing filament of red, hardly hanging

on to life. The tweed suit glowed yellow with the memory of
summer days and it and its owner left as soon as Batchelor
was ensconced on the rug in front of the desk. He had been
an unusually well-behaved schoolboy, back in the day, but this
reminded him very much of the occasional times when he had
had to turn up in front of the headmaster, having been found
out in some minor infraction. He found himself wishing that
he had had the foresight to stuff a slim volume of Homer
down the back of his trousers, to offset the pain of the inevitable six of the best.

The best way to describe the man behind the desk was 'beige'.
His hair was virtually the same colour as his skin, which was
essentially the colour of porridge. His clothes were as impecc-
ably cut as the tweed suit, but considerably less ostentatious.
The fabric was possibly linen; Grand would know. There were
times when Batchelor wished he had listened more carefully to
Matthew's sartorial advice and this was one; clothes maketh the
man and he might be missing an important clue.

The man behind the desk was twirling Batchelor's business
card between his fingers. Two hooded eyes looked him over
from head to toe and James Batchelor suddenly felt as if his
clothes had disappeared and he stood there naked as a jay. If
Mr Knowes turned his hand to the detecting business, Batchelor
felt sure there wouldn't be room in town for both of them.

'Mr Batchelor.' His voice was as colourless as the rest of him.
'I assume that Mr Grand is . . . hmm . . . a figment of your
imagination? Something to give gravitas?'

Batchelor could hardly contain a smirk; the thought of
Matthew Grand, so alive he almost crackled, being a figment
of someone's imagination was certainly amusing. But somehow,
the thought of smiling in this room was not something he could
countenance. 'No,' he said, flatly. 'Mr Grand is real. He is
currently engaged in another matter.' He was beginning to sound
like the minutes of a really boring meeting.

'I see,' said Knowes, doubtfully. 'How can I help you, Mr
Batchelor? Hamish said something about a missing woman?'

Yes, thought Batchelor, he would be called Hamish. 'A client
of ours has had some letters which suggest that his wife has
been kidnapped,' he said. He hadn't meant to divulge this

much this soon, but there was something about the beige Mr
Knowes that seemed to drag the words out of him.

'And you think I can help because . . .?'

'I understood from a friend that you are in the import/export
business . . .'

'Did you?' Knowes allowed one eyelid to flicker. He picked
up a pen and dipped it very deliberately in the elaborate inkwell
to his right. He poised the pen above a piece of paper dead
centre in front of him. Batchelor could see, using his legendary
upside-down reading skills, that it was already neatly headed
'Batchelor?' underlined three times. 'Who is this friend, may
I ask?'

'Umm.' Batchelor looked up to the ceiling and tried to look
as if he were trying to remember. 'I can't call his name to mind
just at the moment.'

'I see.' Knowes made a cryptic note and put the pen back in
its holder. He laced his fingers together and leaned forward.
Batchelor felt that this was probably how a doctor would give
really *really* bad news. 'I don't see how I can help you, Mr
Batchelor. This lady, with no name, has perhaps been kidnapped,
by you don't know who. Do you know when?'

'Not precisely.' Batchelor shook his head.

'Where?'

'No . . . well, either Eastbourne, or London or . . .'

'All points between.'

'Yes.' Batchelor could almost hear the swish of the cane.

Knowes looked across his desk and Batchelor almost felt
him rummage in his brain. He seemed to be making up his
mind about something and Batchelor didn't like to guess about
what. Finally, he leaned back.

'Mr Batchelor,' he said at last. 'I like you. I don't know why;
your cheek, I suppose. I don't know what you have heard about
me, precisely. Or from whom. But . . . I am a man who knows
things and if I don't, I can find them out. I don't know anything
about a kidnapped woman. And you can take that as gospel.
But I can . . . ask.' He smiled; it was the slow smile of a stoat
spying a fat and oblivious rabbit. 'And when I ask, most people
answer.' He picked up the card and tapped it on the desk. 'Is
this your business address?'

Batchelor nodded.

'I'll have an answer with you by tomorrow.'

Batchelor had to ask. 'And your fee?'

'Oh, Mr Batchelor.' The chuckle was low and not without menace. 'I wouldn't ask you for money. Let's say that this one is on the house.' He touched a bell on his desk and as if by magic, Hamish was behind Batchelor and was ushering him out. In no time at all, he was on the pavement, still wondering what exactly had gone on. For some reason he didn't quite understand, he felt the need to count his fingers.

Back upstairs, Hamish awaited instructions. His boss clicked his fingers and Hamish poured the obligatory brandy.

'Grand and Batchelor,' Knowes said. 'Anything known?'

'Snoopers.' Hamish lit his boss's cigar. 'Out of the Strand.'

'Straight?'

'Snoopers? Straight? Don't make me laugh.'

'Anything for us to worry about? Business-wise, I mean?'

'I doubt it,' was Hamish's professional opinion.

Knowes held the smoke in while he ruminated. Then he let it go. 'Even so, have a word with the boys. Put 'em on their guard. Who do we know in Fleet Street?'

'Editor or hack?'

'Either.'

'Dyer – works for the *Telegraph*.'

'Yes, I remember him. Something I once scraped off my shoe. What about the Yard?'

'Palmer, Druscovitch, Meiklejohn; take your pick.'

'Oh, yes, the wise monkeys. Put Dyer on alert to spread ugly rumours about Grand and Batchelor when I give the nod. And the Detective Force can be as obstructive with them as they like.'

'You want the squeeze, boss?' Hamish asked. 'Kneecaps? Hamstrings?'

Knowes looked horrified and took a restorative swig of brandy. 'We're not barbarians, Hamish,' he said.

TEN

They had divided with the hope of conquest. While Batchelor went in search of the enigmatic Mr Knowes, Grand travelled to Limehouse, to the canals that skirted the docks. It was impossible to escape the river smell here or the clash and hurry of the wharves. The great derricks swung and swayed over Grand's head and the heavy horses clopped past him, their giant hoofs striking sparks off the cobbles. Out on the river, he could see the lightermen and the lumpers going about their business, hauling coal and cotton, spices and fabrics, in chests and bales, that had come from all over the world.

There would be little here from Grand's native America. The produce of the States came to Liverpool and Bristol, not to London and the greatest docks in the world made do with the imports from Europe and all points east; granite from the Balkans and flint from just along the coast in Kent.

They had tossed the usual coin for this and Grand was beginning to think that he had got the worst of the deal. Even if Mr Knowes was not at home, or if he was and had become defensive, the most that Batchelor could expect in terms of rudeness was an Eaton Square door slammed in his face. To be fair, Batchelor knew no more about the travellers of the monkey boats than Grand did, so it was debatable whether the London man would have made better headway than the ex-captain from the Army of the Potomac. They had all looked at him suspiciously. The women ducked their heads, averted their gaze, cuffed their naturally nosy children around the ear and shooed them away. Their clothes were gaudy with sewn edges and ribbons, their skin burned brown by the sun and the wind. The men sat sullenly on coils of rope, smoking their pipes or settling their cargo. Even the mangy dogs on the narrow boats weren't giving much away, except for the odd flea; they moved in a miasma of parasites that would have a lesser canine flat on its back in the local veterinary surgeon's office.

Grand traipsed from barge to barge, monkey boat to monkey boat until he could scarcely remember where he had been or how many he had visited. He tried to formulate a plan, moving up one side of Regent's Canal and down the other, but it wasn't that simple. Those who talked to him, in a bewildering variety of dialects, had seen nothing, heard nothing. It was nothing to do with them what happened on the canals, still less on the river. They were honest traders, going about their business. Honest.

It was dusk now as the September days shortened and chilly on the water, for all the warmth of the fading day. The lights were being lit on the decks of the barges and the lighters and a thin film of mist lent the river a ghostly appearance. The derricks hung silent after the momentum of the day, black monsters against the purple of the sky. Grand decided to try one last barge before calling it a day. The picturesquely named *Windsong* was just like all the others, a black narrow boat painted with the bright flowers that the travellers loved. The ubiquitous dog, of no breed known to man, lay curled up near the bow. It raised its head, sniffed the alien presence and gave a token growl before settling back to sleep.

'Welcome, Mr Grand.'

The voice made the enquiry agent jump. He couldn't see anybody, still less someone who knew who he was. His head spun to left and right and his hand hovered near his inside pocket, where his .32 calibre Colt lay waiting.

'Over here.'

Grand could pinpoint it now. It was a woman's voice, reedy and sharp and he made out a figure, small and hunched, sitting motionless in the stern. He edged his way past the cabin, teetering on the strip of deck. He had been doing this all day and was quite adept at it by now. He found himself looking down at an ancient crone, her silver hair strained back from a leather-brown face and stuffed under a black straw bonnet. She wore a fringed shawl embroidered with flowers over her narrow shoulders and her bony fingers clutched a clay pipe from which the smoke drifted lazily.

'You have the advantage of me, madam.' He tipped his wideawake.

The old girl chuckled, clicking her teeth. 'I know I have. I know your name, Mr Grand, but not exactly what you want.'

He eased himself down onto an upturned chest, so that their height difference was not so great. 'All right,' he said. 'I'll tell you what I want if you'll tell me your name.'

He could see her sharp grey eyes twinkling in the half-light from the *Windsong*'s lanterns. 'Have a seat, why don't you?' she said, fully aware that he already had. 'You can call me Queenie.'

'Queenie,' Grand nodded. 'And tell me, how do you know my name?'

The crone tapped the side of her not inconsiderable nose. 'That'd be telling,' she chuckled.

'Yes, it would,' Grand agreed. He could play the village idiot when he had to.

She peered closely at him. It was a kind face, all in all, open and very good-looking. 'Where are you from, sonny?' she asked him.

'I was born in Boston,' he told her, 'brought up in Washington – DC, that is.'

'I was born under a gooseberry bush,' she confided, 'but I don't feel dry land under me much. What brings you to the *Windsong*?'

'You haven't told me how you know my name,' he said.

'Look yonder.' Queenie pointed to a rope line strung the length of the *Windsong*. Tattered flags of different colours hung there, limp and hardly discernible now in the dusk. 'Every barge on the canal's got those. The first one you went on this afternoon was the *Bramble*, Ned Cattermole's boat. Then you went to the *Rhymer*, then to the *Ouzel*. You should have gone to the *Shearwater* next, but you didn't; got lost would be my guess.'

Grand sat there open mouthed.

'The flags, sonny.' Queenie took a triumphant pull at her dark shag. 'We pass it all from barge to barge. You're never alone on the canals. Bluebottles, Revenue men – you can't be too careful.'

Grand could have kicked himself. His own Army of the Potomac had done something similar in the Wilderness campaign; but he never expected it three thousand miles away in what was a very different world.

'You're looking for bodies,' Queenie said. 'The flag system's not perfect, but I gathered that much.'

'And you've been told not to talk to me,' Grand understood.

'Nobody tells Queenie who she can talk to,' the old girl said. 'But you've got to tell me why you're interested.'

'The flags'll have told you I'm an enquiry agent,' Grand said.

'It came out as "nosy bastard" in flag-talk,' she said.

Grand chuckled. 'Close enough,' he said. 'A client of mine has lost his wife.'

'Lost?'

'She's been kidnapped.'

Queenie paused, peering at the man through the pipe smoke. 'And you're wondering if this 'ere woman whose bits have turned up is her.'

'Something like that,' Grand said.

'Why come to us?' Queenie wanted to know.

Matthew Grand had no intention of recounting his associate's upside-down reading skills or the link with the River Police, so he settled for a noncommittal, 'We leave no stone unturned.'

'Good for you.' Queenie had let her pipe go out and was refilling it. 'What does Daddy Bliss say?'

'Who?' Grand had been keeping a straight face against such questions for years.

'The bastard who runs the Bluebottles,' Queenie said. 'Or at least, he'd like to think he does. If you've never met him, you're a lucky bugger. He's had it in for us travellers for years. Anybody farts on the river he's round here with his flat-feet, accusing us.'

'So you can't help,' Grand assumed.

'I didn't say that. What's the missing lady's name?'

'That's a confidence too far, Queenie,' Grand said. 'Client-Agent privilege.'

'Bollocks!' Queenie snorted, but no sooner had she opened her mouth to carry on the conversation than rattles and bells punctuated the night.

'Bluebottles!' A shout came from the prow.

Queenie was on her feet. 'Jem, you blind shithouse, you're supposed to be on watch.'

'They've come by boat,' the voice came back. 'No lights.'

Grand peered into the darkness. All he could make out was a black silhouette in the water and oars coming to the upright. There was a thud as the police boat collided with the *Windsong* and he was almost jolted off his feet, though Queenie sat on, as steady as a rock. Grand scrambled along the side, desperately trying to keep his footing and found himself facing a man with shoulders like wardrobes who he assumed must be Jem.

'Working with the Bottles, are yer?' he snarled and swung an oar which caught the already unsteady Grand below the shoulder and sent him crashing over the side into the murky waters of the canal.

At first, everything was black. There was a roaring in Matthew Grand's ears and he couldn't open his eyes. When he did open them, he still couldn't see anything. Father Thames, he knew, lay ahead of him, beyond the sluices of St Katharine's Lock. Here the canal water was slightly warmer, but it was just as wet. Grand had been swimming in the Potomac since he was knee-high to a grasshopper, but this water was full of tangled ropes and anchor chains that lay like a submerged forest all around him. His lungs were torture and he struck upwards once the shock of his fall had subsided and he crashed through the surface, gulping in the murky evening air as though it were the freshest in the world.

'Fall in the Thames,' James Batchelor had told him more than once, 'and you won't drown, you'll die of poisoning.' Grand took comfort in the fact that he wasn't technically in the river at all. His left arm ached and he couldn't use it properly, so he struck out with his right and kicked for all he was worth. There was a current here, of sorts, and it was pulling him away from the flat keel of the *Windsong* and sideways towards the Stair. He could see the police launch bobbing against the barge's hull and from the noise, a battle royal was going on on deck and in the cabins. He didn't know how Daddy Bliss's boys would fare against Jem but he was pretty sure none of them would be much of a match for Queenie.

Ahead, he could make out the black bulk of the canal embankment and worn, slippery steps leading from the water, as though the devil had made himself a slimy stairway to hell. There were ropes trailing from the quayside above and he caught one, rough and slippery under his good hand. He was just about to haul himself across onto the iron ring below the water line when he came face to face with another luckless soul who shouldn't, like Grand, have been there.

It was difficult to tell in the dim light, with the water lapping around their necks, but Grand's swimming companion had clearly once been a woman. Her dark hair was plastered to her head and weed, slimy and green, was woven into it, as if the canal had tried to make her corpse more beautiful, by the standards of the water. Her mouth hung open, unable to cope with swallowing any more and her eyes rolled white and sightless back into her head. For one startling moment as he bobbed there, almost nose to nose with the horror, Grand wanted to scream, but he checked himself. People had been finding body parts along the Thames now for days. He had merely had the misfortune to find a whole one and he was in the water with it. Well, not quite whole, as it turned out. As he steadied the bobbing body and tried to lift it to the stairs, he realized that it had no hands.

'And no feet.'

There had been a time when Dr Felix Kempster would have come running to the finding of a body. That was when he had been a young police surgeon, new to V Division and he sought, like every other medical man, to make a difference. Now, with age and experience, he doubted whether he even made a dent. The river gave up its dead when it chose to, without rhyme or reason. Kempster didn't understand tides and currents like Daddy Bliss, but he understood bodies. He could tell the careless lighterman who'd lost his footing on a slippery deck; an angler who'd slithered down the banks upstream; a suicide, pockets full of stones, who had simply had enough and had leapt from Waterloo Bridge in one last moment of despair. Or a murder, like this one.

The woman was lying on Kempster's slab the morning after Grand had found her. Rigor mortis had come and gone and it was likely that she had been in the river for about two days. There were stumps, once bloody, where her hands had been and the same at her ankles. A dark red line around her neck showed that she had been strangled with a ligature. Other than that, she had seemed in good health. His best guess was that she was about thirty, was no stranger to sex but had never given birth. The abrasions on her arms and across her back, Kempster attributed to the ropes and anchor-chains she had collided with as the river took her body, now this way, now that, upstream and down. There were no obvious signs of sexual assault, but again, the water had that annoying habit of disguising such things.

Kempster crossed his little mortuary to where the other body lay, the one that had arrived in pieces like a demented jigsaw. He was glad to have the space to check them, side by side. Most of the London mortuaries were tiny, single rooms little more than sheds annexed to police stations or workhouses. Here, an investigator into sudden death had, unlike his subjects, room to breathe.

He had been wondering for days now about the cause of death of the disarticulated woman. The only abrasions he could find were on top of the scalp, under what was left of the hair. He was fairly certain that the cause of death was a blow or blows to the top of the cranium which would have resulted in immediate concussion and insensibility. 'Grand's woman', as Kempster mentally called the other one, took longer to die. Depending on the relative strengths of victim and killer, strangulation by ligature, Kempster knew, could take up to four minutes, eternity for them both. Most telling of all, however, were the amputations. Neither corpse had feet or hands, but the disarticulated woman's had been removed with precision and speed; Grand's woman had met a butcher.

Kempster crossed the room again and dipped his pen into the inkwell. 'Death,' he wrote, 'by a different hand.'

'How you feeling now, Mr Grand?' Constable Brandon had given the man some soothing cocoa and towels when he'd first arrived, handcuffed to Gosling and Crossland. Then he'd given him a change of clothes, albeit itchy and threadbare Metropolitan cardigans and oil-cloth breeches. After all that, Brandon's question was a little pointless.

'I'll live,' the American growled. In the last twelve hours, he had been toyed with by an ancient crone, clouted by a bargee's oar, half drowned in a freezing canal and had come face to face with a corpse. Then he'd been dragged out of said canal and fitted with bracelets by two large boys in blue who must have been absent when God gave out gentleness. To cap it all, he was still in custody in the cramped hold of what the Underworld and Fleet Street called the Abode of Bliss.

'That's enough of that fraternization, Brandon.' Bliss had clattered down the steps from the halfway comfortable mess rooms upstairs and was hanging a dripping oilskin on its peg on the wall. As cells went, the *Royalist* was, to say the least, different. It had wooden walls, not stone and there were no bars on the windows. In fact, at this depth, there were no windows; just the relentless thud of the river nudging the *Royalist*'s hull, merely to remind her who was boss.

'Get up top and relieve Gosling. The others'll be back presently.'

Grand was doing his mental arithmetic. If Brandon was relieving Gosling, the chances were that there were only the two of them on the boat. Two, now that his arm had at least partly recovered and he was no longer treading water, he could probably handle. On the other hand, his first obstacle was Daddy Bliss and the man could blot out the sun with his bulk.

The inspector sat down across the table from his prisoner and pulled out a pistol from the pocket of his frock coat.

'This is nice,' he said. He spun it on his finger, cocked it and pointed the muzzle at Grand.

'It is,' Grand nodded. 'But it isn't loaded and it's mine.'

'Always carry it, do you,' Bliss asked, 'in the pursuance of your enquiries?'

'Only when I feel I might be roughed up by the law,' Grand said.

'All right,' Bliss uncocked the Colt and laid it down. 'Let's get that little matter straight from the start, shall we? What were you doing on the *Windsong*?'

'Pursuing my enquiries,' Grand shrugged as best he could with one arm still shackled to the *Royalist*'s woodwork.

'I'm sure,' Bliss said. 'But I think it's time for a little more precision, don't you?'

'As you wish,' Grand said. 'You know that Batchelor and I are investigating the disappearance of the wife of a client.'

'I do,' Bliss said.

'Seeing as how the body parts of a woman have been turning up in your neck of the woods, as it were, we naturally ask questions along the Thames.'

'Yes.' Bliss narrowed his eyes and leaned back. 'So you were just collecting tales of the riverbank when my boys and me turned up.'

'That's right. Now it's your turn to answer my question. What brought *you* to the *Windsong*?'

'Routine,' Bliss said.

'I believe the word you Limeys have for that is "bollocks",' Grand said with a smile.

'Well, well,' Bliss raised both eyebrows. 'Regular little cock sparrer, aintchya?'

'What bothers me, Inspector, is that the proprietors of the *Windsong* assumed, if I remember the brief conversation, that I was part of your routine operation, a sort of advance guard, if you will.'

'So?'

'So, that's not a reputation I want to have.'

Bliss laughed. 'I wouldn't worry what Queenie and Jem think about you, Mr Grand,' he said. 'The old girl's got a mouth on her like a gin trap and we're not likely to get much out of her. Jem however is made of less stern stuff. He's at the Wapping Headquarters now, singing like a canary.'

'What tune?' Grand asked.

Bliss laughed again. 'Come off it, Mr Grand. You know I cannot divulge.'

'Has it occurred to you, Inspector, that you and I might just be on the same side?'

'I doubt it,' Bliss said. 'But, for the record, we occasionally deal, as I am sure you do, with tip-offs, anonymous leads that usually go nowhere but we can't afford to ignore. Catch my drift?'

'I do,' Grand said.

'One such tip-off suggested that the murder of the cut-up woman might have happened on a barge. After all, pretty much every other sort of crime does.'

'So we *are* working together,' Grand chuckled.

'Not if our lives depended on it.' Bliss's smile had vanished. 'Now that you're fully rested and recovered after your unfortunate ordeal, Mr Grand, you are at liberty to leave. You'll find your clothes aired and pressed upstairs, courtesy of Constable Brandon. I'm not really at all sure about that boy – I have a strong feeling he is in the wrong profession.'

Bliss reached over and deftly unlocked Grand's shackles. Grand let his arm drop, rubbing his chafed wrist. 'And my gun?' he asked, standing up.

'I don't approve,' the inspector said, 'but as it's your property, I can hardly stand in your way.'

Grand picked up the pistol and edged round the table. As he reached the stairs, Bliss turned to face him. 'But if I find you or that snot-nosed partner of yours interfering in the work of the River Police again, I'm going to shove that up your arse. Catch my drift?'

ELEVEN

'Name?'

'Abel Beer.'

'Domicile?'

'Do what?'

This morning was not going well for Daddy Bliss. George Crossland had come down with something; Bliss could hardly expose the public to Constable Brandon. So, here he was, having to do his own paperwork. 'Where do you live?'

'Uplyne,' Beer told him.

'Where's that?'

'Dorset.'

The inspector leaned back in his chair. He'd lost count of the ghouls who had crept out of their hidey-holes since women's parts had begun turning up along the Thames. He had predicted all this, of course, but that didn't do much for his temper. 'Suppose you tell me the reason for your visit,' he said.

'My sister Mary has gone missing,' Beer said. 'I haven't seen her since early August.'

'This was in Uplyne?'

'No, here in London.'

'Where, precisely?' Bliss needed to know.

'I left her lodging with Mrs Christian in South Street, Battersea.'

'And what does your sister do for a living, Mr Beer?' Bliss was still going through the motions.

'Nothing,' Beer said. 'She's in London to settle her affairs.'

'Affairs?' That was a word that could easily be misconstrued in Daddy Bliss's world.

'To see her solicitor. She's about to come into some money.'

'And did she see said solicitor?'

'No. That's the first place I checked. He hasn't seen her.'

'So, you last saw her in early August . . .'

'And I sent her a telegram – four, in fact – and never got a reply.'

Bliss was trying to place Beer's circumstances. A man's dress, the cut of his jib, told a lot about his status. So did his manner of speaking, but Beer's West Country burr all but destroyed that. He was sharply dressed enough, but did he have the air of a man whose sister was about to inherit? He wasn't sure. 'So, you came to find her?' he checked.

'Yes. Mrs Christian hadn't seen her. But . . . and this worried me, Inspector; she told Mrs Christian that she had been assaulted by four men near Victoria Bridge one night.'

'Did she report it to the police?'

'Mrs Christian didn't know.'

'Right,' Bliss sighed. 'Well, then, we'd better have a look.' He scraped back his chair. 'I have to warn you, Mr Beer, that the corpse . . . er, the subject . . . is not a pretty sight. The doctor has tried to reconstruct the head.'

'Reconstruct?' Beer wasn't sure he had heard right.

'The skull itself hasn't turned up,' Bliss said. 'Only the skin.' The inspector was a little unnerved to see Abel Beer cross himself. That's all he needed, a bereft Papist under his feet. 'This way.'

He led the Dorset man through the labyrinthine passageways that linked Dr Kempster's laboratory to the mortuary. It was nearly eleven by this time and he hoped that Mrs Kempster wouldn't be much longer with his morning coffee, two lumps, please.

Bliss had done this so often that he had lost all sense of reverence. The disarticulated woman, turning less human every day, was beginning to annoy him now, if only because she wasn't providing any answers. He whipped away the shroud and Beer gasped. He wasn't looking at the head at all. 'It's her,' he gulped. 'It's Mary.'

Bliss frowned at him. This was not the first Eureka moment he had experienced over the last few days, but none had been as certain as this. 'May I ask how you know, sir?'

'The scald mark on her stomach,' Beer pointed. 'I was there in the kitchen when she did that. Tipped a boiling pan over herself. She'd have been eight or so at the time. I must have been ten.'

Bliss didn't like peering closely at a dead woman's stomach

with said dead woman's brother standing there, but it was all in the line of duty. He couldn't actually see anything, but the light wasn't of the best in the bowels of the mortuary and the water and time had distorted the skin. It was an acid green now, with purple edges.

'May I . . . may I take her away?' Beer asked, 'for a proper burial? Take her home?'

'Not just yet, sir,' Bliss said. 'There are formalities, I'm afraid. Paperwork. If you could call to the *Royalist*, the floating police station on the Thames, say, Thursday, we can talk further.'

'Thank you, Inspector.' Beer seemed reluctant to leave the body, but Bliss's bulk nudged him towards the door and he saw him out.

'Your coffee, Inspector.' Fanny Kempster emerged from the kitchen carrying a tray, complete with Garibaldis.

'Thank you, ma'am.' Bliss took it gratefully.

'You'll forgive me for saying this, Inspector,' she said, as she turned to go, 'and Felix will remonstrate with me, I feel sure, but you didn't tell that poor man how sorry you were for his loss.'

'That's because, m'm,' Bliss scowled at her, 'he hasn't had any loss. Catch my drift?'

They didn't need to toss a coin this time. It was Matthew Grand's call. He it was also who had struck a chord with Constable Brandon of the River Police and so the American half of the firm of Grand and Batchelor found himself sitting below decks on board the *Royalist* two days later, sipping tea from a tin cup.

'Strong enough for you, Mr Grand?' the boy asked. He prided himself on his tea-making skills.

'Delicious, Mr Brandon, thank you.'

'You can call me Lloyd,' Brandon said. After all, he *had* rinsed out and ironed his visitor's smalls. They could have been brothers under the skin.

'Fine . . . Lloyd,' Grand smiled. 'How's the case coming?'

'The case?' Nobody had ever accused the champion tea-maker of being very bright.

'The torsos in the Thames.'

'Well,' Brandon put his own cup down and became confidential. 'Oh, but no.' He clamped his lips shut, opening them a little to add, 'The inspector wouldn't like it.'

'The inspector's not going to get it, Lloyd,' Grand assured him. 'This is strictly between us.'

Brandon hesitated. He'd never met an American before and the experience had rather gone to his head. 'Oh, all right,' he said. 'The body's been identified. Not the one you found – the other one.'

'Really? Who is she?'

'A Mary Cailey, née Beer, from Dorset, apparently.'

'Apparently?'

Brandon checked to right and left, then peered up the stairs that led to the deck. 'Well, Mr Bliss has his doubts. A bloke called Abel Beer turned up and recognized the corpse as his sister, gone missing from South Street, Battersea six weeks ago.'

'Six weeks?'

'That was when she was last seen by the brother and the landlady.'

'The landlady?' Grand was losing the thread of this conversation and he sincerely hoped that Constable Brandon would never be called upon to present evidence in court.

'Oh, silly me. You don't know, do you?'

Grand smiled at the boy.

'She's a Mrs Christian, of 15 South Street.'

'Has the inspector interviewed her?'

'Said there was no point. He doesn't believe Beer's story. Says he's just a ghoul who likes looking at dead bodies. I ask you – what is the matter with people? Beer can have my job if he likes. He'd have plenty of dead bodies then.'

'Find a lot, do you?' Grand asked, 'on the river?'

'Ooh, no, not me *personally*; but the lads, you know. No, the inspector never lets me out.'

Grand laughed. 'With someone who makes tea like you do, Lloyd, I can't say I blame him.'

They didn't toss a coin for the next job, either. It wasn't like Grand or Batchelor to resort to subterfuge, let alone impersonate a police officer, but needs must when the devil drives and, all in all, James Batchelor would pass muster as a Metropolitan officer better than Matthew Grand.

'I was wondering when somebody would call.' Mary Christian was a prim lady, corseted in bombazine and quick and sure in her movements. The lodger's room at 15, South Street, Battersea, was neat without being gaudy and looked out onto the park, looking a little sorry for itself now that autumn was blowing away the tree's leaves. 'Who did you say you were, again?'

'Detective Sergeant Spinster,' Batchelor beamed. 'Thames Division.'

'I didn't know they had detectives with Thames Division.' Mary Christian frowned.

Damn. Just Batchelor's luck to find the only well-informed landlady in London. 'New directive,' he lied. 'From the Home Office only the other day. Still finding my water-feet, as it were. So, this was Mrs Cailey's room?'

'It was. Still is, for all I know. *And* she owes me four weeks' rent.'

Batchelor tutted and shook his head. 'Tell me about her,' he said.

Mary Christian had been brooding about the missing woman for a while and she felt her blood pressure rising every time. 'Well,' she said, the steam all but hissing from her ears. 'Well, she turned up on August the second, I believe it was, with a Mr Beer.'

'Mr Abel Beer?' Batchelor checked.

'I didn't ask his name. From the West Country, they were, brother and sister – though I couldn't see much of a likeness.'

'Could you describe her?' Batchelor's notebook was to the fore.

Mrs Christian looked with a beady eye at it. 'I haven't seen a notebook like that before,' she remarked. 'Not police issue, is it?' She reached out a hand to take a closer look.

'Um . . . no. No, it isn't,' Batchelor managed a chuckle. 'You are a very noticing sort of person, Mrs Christian,' he said. 'This is brand-new issue, to go with the new detectives.'

'But you're more than halfway through it,' the landlady pointed out.

Batchelor was sorry that they were not looking for staff at Grand and Batchelor, Confidential Enquiry Agents, No Job Too Big Or Too Small. This woman was a natural. 'We've been busy,' he said, shortly. 'Could you describe her?' He waited, pencil poised, for a minute description from the Walking Microscope.

'Er . . . well, she *claimed* to be thirty-three.'

'Claimed?' Batchelor queried.

'Some women,' Mrs Christian scoffed, 'lie about their age. She was forty, if she was a day.'

'And . . . *Mr* Cailey?'

'Passed away, she told me. Passed out, if you ask me. There was a smell of drink on her.'

'Indeed?'

Mary Christian spun round and slid open a bedside drawer. Alongside a Bible, lay a half bottle of gin, most of it gone. 'I don't want you to think I am in the habit of rifling my lodger's things, Sergeant,' she said, through pursed lips, 'but with Mr Christian away, I have to look out for myself.'

'Quite. Tell me, Mrs Christian, did Mrs Cailey leave anything else behind?'

The landlady opened the wardrobe. Two dresses hung there and a pair of lace-up boots stood defiantly in the corner. 'There's also a drawer of her unmentionables, but I assure you, you don't want to see them.'

The look on Mary Christian's face said it all and Batchelor thought he had better decline. 'No, indeed,' he said. 'You were describing Mrs Cailey.'

'Was I? Oh, yes. Stout. Tallish – nearly your height.'

'And when did you see her last?'

'Thursday, second of September, if memory serves. She told me she was going to get some things out of pledge and to get money from her solicitor.'

'You don't remember his name, I suppose?'

'I do,' she said, folding her arms with the air of a woman who knew something Batchelor didn't. 'A Mr Thompson, of Lincoln's Inn. No need to write it down – he doesn't exist.'

'He doesn't?'

'When she'd been gone a few days, with no word, I did a bit of snooping. After all, rent is rent, isn't it, Sergeant?'

Batchelor had to agree with that.

'I checked the directories. No such person, in Lincoln's Inn or anywhere else in the capital. She was lying. She also kept odd hours.'

'How . . . odd?' Batchelor asked.

'Very,' Mrs Christian confirmed. 'She claimed she was out all day and into the small hours visiting a friend, an old lady in Carlton Square, Chelsea.'

'No such person?'

'No such square. And there's another thing.'

Somehow, Batchelor knew there would be. 'She claimed she was assaulted by four men near Victoria Bridge.'

'Do you believe that?' Batchelor thought he had the measure of the landlady now. At least she wouldn't be able to claim that there was no such bridge, but there was a definite pattern of general mistrust.

'Well, Sergeant,' she bridled, 'in your profession, you must be perfectly aware of how beastly men are. On the other hand, in all my . . . twenty-four years . . .' She fixed Batchelor with a beady eye, challenging him to comment, but he didn't even flinch and she went on. 'I can honestly say I have never been assaulted by anyone.'

Batchelor didn't doubt that for a moment. Should the dark day dawn when they recruited women to the Metropolitan Police, he was pretty sure that Mary Christian would be the first in line to sign up for her truncheon.

'You know, madam,' he said, 'that a number of body parts of a woman have been found in the Thames?'

The woman shuddered, so perhaps Batchelor's assessment of her had been wrong. 'Yes,' she said. 'I do know. And if I must, I will visit the mortuary to make the necessary identification.'

'Very brave,' Batchelor murmured politely.

Mary Christian half-smiled at the flattery but her attention was suddenly drawn to the window. 'Oh, really, he's there again.'

'Who, madam?' Batchelor asked.

'That wretched fellow who's been hanging around here for the past week. He had the impudence to knock at my door a couple of days ago, asking if I knew the whereabouts of someone called Amelia. I told him to go away in no uncertain terms . . . I . . .'

But Detective Sergeant Spinster was already clattering down the stairs in search of a ghost.

'No, No, James.' Matthew Grand was lighting a cigar in the drawing room as dusk descended on the Strand. 'This whole Mary Cailey thing is a red herring; trust me.'

'I do, Matthew,' Batchelor said, 'and I'd go along with that. Were it not for Emilia.'

'It's not that uncommon a name,' Grand pointed out.

'Granted.' Batchelor was pouring the brandies. 'But it *is* a coincidence.'

'And you didn't get a good look at this cuss hanging around the house?'

'Vanished like a will o' the wisp. So I went back to the redoubtable Mrs Christian and asked her to tell me more about the man.'

'You suspected Selwyn Byng?'

'Of course. It's not just the name Emilia, but the whole peculiar hanging-about-the-house routine. If it wasn't for the fact she didn't call him a lunatic, it could have been Mrs Rackstraw talking.'

'But it wasn't him?'

'Mrs Christian said he was a down-and-out, scruffy, unwashed. As a charitable soul, she'd given him some money – well, it goes with the surname, I suppose. But he kept rabbiting on about Emilia.'

'*Was* there an Emilia in Mrs Christian's household?'

'Not then, not ever, as far as she could remember. Unless of course, Mrs Cailey . . .'

'. . . Is really Emilia Byng.' Grand finished the sentence for his partner. 'Nothing about this Mary Cailey having a missing finger, I suppose?'

Batchelor shook his head. 'But let's just suppose for a moment it *is* the same woman, in admittedly quite heavy disguise. She hasn't been kidnapped but is living under an assumed name in a boarding house in Battersea.'

'Why?'

'No idea.'

'But, according to Mrs Christian, she's been missing since

the second of September, a few days before the body parts began to turn up.'

'And according to Constable Brandon,' Batchelor was still trying to assemble all the pieces, 'the dead woman's brother identified her body in Kempster's mortuary.'

'Which leaves us . . .?'

Batchelor gulped down his brandy in one. 'Absolutely nowhere,' he said.

Daddy Bliss was tired of unidentified bodies. True, he currently only had the two, but for a tidy-minded man such as himself, that was two too many. The identification of the patchwork body was, in his opinion, shaky at best, but it would at least clear the mortuary of the increasingly unbearable smell to let her be buried, even if the stone she was buried under bore the wrong name. But it was the handless, footless body that was nagging at him. His head told him to blame the travellers and failing that, that damned American, with his pistol and his attitude. But his gut told him that he would waste a lot of time that way and time was something that Daddy Bliss preferred to husband, not fritter.

'Brandon,' he roared. If he tried hard enough, who knew, he might find something the lad was good at. 'Br . . . oh, that was quick.'

The echo of the constable's size elevens on the ladder had been drowned out in the reverberations of the roar in the low-ceilinged cabin and he had materialized like the genie of the lamp at his boss's elbow.

'Did you get the pictures taken of our latest visitor?'

Brandon looked interested, hopeful but, ultimately, completely at a loss.

'The floater. The unidentified . . .' Bliss closed his eyes. When would he be first in line for the good one, not behind the door when brains were being given out.

The light dawned. 'Yes, sir. All angles. Including . . .' he gulped back a little rise of bile, 'the . . . stumps.' Brandon didn't really like gore.

'Well done. How did they come out? Recognizable?'

Brandon nodded. Speech wasn't an option just now.

'Did you send to the papers?'

Again, a nod.

'And . . .?' Bliss was used to playing twenty questions with his family around the Christmas table, but at work it really was too much. His colour began to darken worryingly. Any constable but Brandon would have beaten a hasty retreat at this point, but his eyes were closed, so he missed the signs and portents.

The constable opened his eyes a crack and pointed in the general direction of the corner of the inspector's desk, where a tightly folded newspaper awaited tea-break time. Opening his lips as little as possible, he said, 'Page three,' then bolted for the ladder to fresh air and the edge of the boat.

Bliss flicked open the paper and there, sure enough, was a small, one-column piece but headed by a sketch of the dead woman, not at all a bad likeness, as these things went. The copy was fairly terse, not at all over-blown and Bliss was pleased to see that there was none of the usual English rose cut down in her prime nonsense, nor even veiled hints as to her possible occupation. In fact, to his amazement, it only had what the police had told the papers to print. He jotted a note on his blotter; this was something for his diary, that was for sure.

He went to the bottom of the ladder and called up, in rather less hectoring tones. 'Brandon?'

'Hmmm?'

It wasn't much but at least he sounded a bit brighter.

'Is this in all the papers?'

'London and South Coast.' George Crossland's face swam into view. 'Brandon's not feeling too chipper, I've sat him in the stern for a bit. Do you want me to get it out further? North? Essex?'

'No, no,' Bliss flapped a hand. At least he had one man on the strength who knew what he was doing. 'Let's see what the next few days bring. If no one gets in touch, we'll go further afield.' He stepped back into the cabin and sat behind his desk. A thought struck him. 'Crossland?'

Crossland's head appeared again in the opening to the upper deck. 'Guv?'

'Any chance of a cuppa?'

'Biscuits?'

Bliss gave a happy sigh. Yes, indeed, it was good to have at least one on the strength who knew what was important in life. 'No currants. But otherwise, whatever you've got.' He settled back with his paper, in the happy knowledge that he was not a hard man to please, not really.

Mrs Rackstraw was not an ungrateful woman, taken all in all and by and large. She lived in a nice house, in a nice street and if sometimes the men she house-kept for drove her to the brink of insanity, they were out most of the day and apart from some of the laundry, an issue on which she tried not to dwell, they were no trouble. Especially Mr James, who put her in mind of a boy she had known back before there was a Mr Rackstraw or even a thought of him. The crazy little between-maid was polishing something pointless up in the spare bedroom under the eaves, the charwoman had gone home having scrubbed every inch of the kitchen floor and sanded all the saucepans until their pips squeaked. The smell of baking wafted through the house and Mrs Rackstraw, all thoughts of lunatics tucked away in the part of her mind marked 'last week', put on her afternoon dress and settled down in her sitting room over the hall and sat back and closed her eyes. Peace at last.

In another mood, Mrs Rackstraw would have interpreted the knock on the door as just a normal person using the knocker. But as she had just dropped off to sleep and had delivered herself of her first stertorous snore, she heard it as if all the hounds of hell were yammering at the threshold. She got to the bottom of the stairs, wide-eyed and with her hair slightly awry, as Maisie, smelling faintly of paraffin and beeswax and wafting a grubby cloth, opened the door.

On the step stood, not Lucifer and his infernal crew, but a little old lady, dressed in a somewhat passé day dress under a serge cloak, attended by another woman, rather younger, a little taller but clearly, for all she was smartly dressed, a maid.

Maisie was getting better at the door opening task, but still had a way to go. 'Whaddya want?' she said, then, remembering, 'Ma'am.'

Mrs Rackstraw hung back in the shadow of the hall. There was something about these two which made her suspect that her afternoon was going to spiral down even from its current low point.

The little old lady, who looked quite sweet at first glance, tapped Maisie sharply on the chest with the handle of her umbrella. 'I am here, you rude, uncouth girl,' she turned to the maid standing behind her, who had disapproval written all over her face. 'Whatever is the next generation coming to, Enid? I despair, I really do.'

Enid pursed her lips even tighter and looked at the unfortunate Maisie through narrowed eyes.

The old lady looked confused. 'Where was I?'

'I am here,' Maisie offered, anxious to please.

'I can see that. I asked where I . . . oh, yes, I see. I am here to see either Mr . . .' she glanced at a card in her hand, 'Mr Grand or Mr Batchelor. I don't mind which, but I would very much prefer both, if that is at all possible.'

Maisie was caught on the back foot. It wasn't her place to know where the young gentlemen were, though she had been known to track Grand for miles, on her afternoon off. She glanced over her shoulder at Mrs Rackstraw. Though the woman hadn't made a sound, Maisie could tell from the pricking of her thumbs that she was standing behind her.

The housekeeper slid forward, as though on wheels. 'May I help you?' she asked. 'I am the housekeeper.'

The old lady looked her up and down with ill-disguised contempt. The woman who had trained the little guttersnipe was clearly not much of a housekeeper, but she looked more likely to know what was going on, so she decided to be polite. 'Ah, good. I wish to speak to your employers.'

Mrs Rackstraw pinned what she hoped was an ingratiating smile on her face, but having had little practice, couldn't know whether it had worked or not. 'I'm afraid neither Mr Grand nor Mr Batchelor is in,' she said.

'Then I insist that you find them at once,' the old lady snapped and as she spoke, she stepped firmly in through the open doorway. 'While you look, Enid and I will wait.'

Mrs Rackstraw didn't often lose a stand-off, but she knew this was doomed from the start. Little old ladies smelling faintly of lavender and wearing clothes almost a generation out of date always had the whip hand over a housekeeper who looked as if she could overpower a docker, on the right day. She threw open the door to the sitting room and ushered her in. 'May I have a name?' she enquired, through gritted teeth.

'Miss Moriarty,' the little old lady said. 'They'll know why I am here.'

Mrs Rackstraw closed the door with care. Slamming came more naturally to her, but there was a time and a place. Maisie was still waiting, irresolute, in the hall.

'Stop gawping, girl,' Mrs Rackstraw spat. 'Get your coat on and run round to the office. Tell whoever's there that there's a Miss Moriarty here, wants a word. And be quick about it. No mooning about.'

Maisie didn't need second bidding. Although she wouldn't be long, she would be out in the fresh air and who knew, perhaps He would be in the office by himself. She would be in the room alone with the object of her affections and it might be that when he saw her, outlined in a beam of sunlight, the golden rays touching her hair, bringing radiance to her cheek . . . She sighed as she crossed the hall, buttoning her threadbare coat. Mrs Rackstraw fetched her a firm one upside the head.

'No mooning, I said. Tell them it's urgent.'

'What's it about, Mrs Rackstraw?' Maisie felt she should have all the information.

'I have no idea,' the housekeeper snapped. 'But tell them it's urgent, all the same. Then they might come round straight away, instead of when they feel like it. Now, off you go – sooner you're gone, sooner you're back. Those knobs won't polish themselves, you know.'

And Maisie, with love to give her wings, flew down the steps to the pavement and was past the lunatic before she even noticed he was there.

TWELVE

Grand and Batchelor met Maisie just as she turned into the Strand.

Grand advanced on her kindly. He worried about the poor little soul; she didn't look fit to be out on her own and he wondered for a moment if she was running away from what she presumably thought of as home. 'Is everything okay, Maisie?' he asked, and her heart lurched.

'Oh, yes, Mr Grand, sir,' she breathed. 'Mrs Rackstraw says to come home straight away, and you, Mr Batchelor, because there's a woman.'

They both waited politely for more detail, for example, what the woman might be doing but it was clear that that was it; there was no more.

'Is the woman threatening Mrs Rackstraw?' Batchelor ventured, knowing even as he spoke how unlikely that was.

Maisie shook her head so that the loose bun at the nape of her neck swung madly back and forth.

'Is the woman . . . in trouble?' Grand had a go.

Again, Maisie shook her head. The little old lady was certainly self-possessed and well able to look after herself; Maisie knew that when she undressed tonight, she would have a bruise where the carved bill of the duck which made up the handle of the umbrella she had wielded had tapped her on the chest. Even in her own head, she dropped her voice at 'chest'. Her mother had always made that kind of thing very clear, usually with a clip round the ear.

While the enquiry agents thought of the next useful question, they turned Maisie around and headed back home. They could think as they walked, even if Maisie couldn't. Batchelor suddenly had a brainwave.

'Maisie, is the woman young? Pretty?'

Maisie didn't have to think this one through. Even the younger one wasn't what you could call pretty. She shook her head.

Grand tried a long shot. 'Did she have all her fingers?' He knew that to the young, youth and age were somewhat flexible.

Maisie was horrified. The woman had worn gloves, so it was hard to tell, but still . . . she nodded her head emphatically.

The two men decided to stop asking questions and just get home as fast as possible so they each tucked one of Maisie's arms through theirs and set off at a jog-trot. That night, checking for her bruise, Maisie would remember that half mile as the best in her life.

When they got back to the house, Maisie dived down into the area and let the men go in through the front door. Batchelor used his latchkey and as he wrestled it out of the stiff lock, Grand bent and picked up something from the mat and shoved it absent-mindedly into his pocket.

'Mrs Rackstraw?' he called. 'Mrs . . .' but before the house-keeper could appear, the door to the sitting room flew open and Miss Moriarty stood there, every outmoded ribbon a-bristle.

'Mr Grand,' she said. 'You have been an unconscionable time. You were expecting me, surely?'

'Miss Moriarty.' Grand was nonplussed. 'I'm very sorry. Did we have an appointment?'

'No,' the old lady snapped. 'But I assumed as the picture of Molly had appeared in the newspapers, you would want to see me.' She tilted her head back and looked from Grand to Batchelor and back again.

Batchelor was as confused as his partner. 'Picture?'

'Molly?' Grand chimed in.

Miss Moriarty was annoyed. Beyond annoyed, in fact, but she didn't have the vocabulary to let them know it. 'I am very annoyed, gentlemen,' she said. 'Enid and I have travelled up from Eastbourne, at no little discomfort and, if I may be so bold as to discuss finances, at no small expense. And now, I find you are not expecting me.' She gave a snort and gathered herself together for a huge shrug which used her entire body from her toes to the top of her head. 'I must ask myself what kind of business you purport to run.'

Grand opened his mouth, but she hadn't finished.

'I don't expect you are even looking for my niece Emilia any more, are you? No. I thought not.'

Batchelor had spotted a flaw in her conversation. 'I thought you mentioned someone named Molly.'

'Of course I did, you stupid man,' Miss Moriarty said, raising the umbrella ready to strike. 'Molly Edwards. Emilia's maid.'

Things were beginning to fall into place. 'You're here about the maid,' Batchelor said.

The old woman's eyes opened wide and she was lost for words but only for a moment. 'Did I not just say so?' She turned to Enid, waiting patiently at her shoulder as always. 'Enid. Did I not just say so?' Her cheeks were beginning to look a little purple.

'Miss Moriarty did mention Molly,' Enid said, in calming tones. 'And I think, if I may be so bold, gentlemen, that a sit down and a cup of tea . . .' she caught her mistress's eye, '. . . with a spot of something warming in it, perhaps, just for the cold, you know . . .'

Grand jumped to attention and switched on the old down-home charm. 'Miss Moriarty,' he said, his accent thick enough to spread on toast, 'I'll call for some tea of course. There is something to go in it right there, on the sideboard. Something to eat, ladies? Scones? Cake?'

The two Eastbourne ladies looked at each other and twittered. A little cake never went amiss. Enid nodded. 'Cake, yes. Cake would be nice.'

Grand stepped into the hall to call down for Mrs Rackstraw but, as ever, she scared the bejabbers out of him by stepping out of the shadows at his elbow. 'I'll bring some up, sir,' she said, all the venom of a ruined afternoon in the last syllable. Grand returned to the sitting room, wondering again whether it was worth keeping her, even for her pig's feet pie or whatever it was that sent Batchelor into a happy stupor.

'It's on its way,' he said, ushering the women to seats by the fire. 'Now, let's start again, shall we? You're here to tell us about Molly's picture in the paper . . .'

The Gothic monstrosity that was Holloway Gaol stood in Parkhurst Road. Poplars and rhododendrons screened its gates but the red-brick towers beyond held inmates who had little interest in botany. Increasingly, because of the way society was going and they now allowed women to vote in municipal elections, female prisoners were taking over the prison world.

That, in a way, was why Daddy Bliss was there that day; not in search of an inmate who had blotted her escutcheon, but of one of the staff, who had not.

She hadn't changed a scrap. And scrapping was what Bridie O'Hara did for a living. She was actually the Chief Wardress at Holloway, but it amounted to the same thing. Bliss had not seen the woman for years and yet he recognized the set of her shoulders and the width of her back even in silhouette on the first landing. Her voice hadn't changed either. Someone was singing in her cell, 'Villikins and His Dinah' but it ended in a falsetto shriek that a eunuch would have been proud of. Bridie O'Hara didn't approve of singing. Not on her watch.

He saluted as she swept past him and he waited until they were alone in the wardresses' office. 'Bridie, my little vixen.' He let his arm creep around the solidity of her waist.

Her response was short and sharp and definitely not in the *Women Wardens' Handbook*. It was accompanied by a slap round the side of the head. 'Don't you "vixen" me, Daddy Bliss; I'm not in the mood.'

'But, Bridie . . .'

She placed her hands on her ample hips and scowled at him, like a bulldog chewing a wasp. 'Bridie, my arse,' she growled. 'That's Wardress O'Hara to you, Inspector. Or are Mrs Bliss and all the little Blisses a figment of my imagination?'

'Now, B . . . Wardress O'Hara,' he got as close to her as he dared. 'I had hoped we could let bygones be bygones.'

'Would that be the bygone when you failed to turn up at St Bartholomew's-the-Less on Wednesday 13 June 1862? The very same day that I was there in my best dress with a bridesmaid in tow and a nice old boy of a vicar? You're lucky I didn't do you for breach of promise.'

'I am,' Bliss agreed. 'Very lucky indeed. But there's been much water under Waterloo Bridge since then.'

'Ah.' She let her hands fall. 'So this is not a social call, then? Mrs Bliss, inexplicably, hasn't left you. And you haven't come to rekindle the flame.'

'Bridie,' he said softly, 'when I hear your Irish lilt . . .'

'Bliss!' she snapped. 'Come to the point.'

'Escapees.' The inspector knew when it was time to obey an order. 'Or the recently released.'

She pursed her lips. 'You're trying to place that corpse in the Thames, aren't you?' she asked.

Bliss smiled and shook his head. 'As smart as you are beautiful,' he said. She ignored him and flipped open a ledger on her desk. The writing was copperplate, the photographs unflattering.

'Take your pick,' she said. 'These five are the latest releases. But the last two have got out since your body turned up, so you're looking at these three.'

Bliss was. Carmen Valladolid was black as his patrol jacket, so he could discount her. Annie Parminter was six foot two with a hare lip. He had to look twice at Veronica Cartwright. The short-cropped hair was certainly a possibility, but the details recorded a withered left arm, so Bliss had to let her go too.

'They're all ticket-of-leave women, of course,' Bridie went on, 'so we have addresses on them all. If you've got access to some real policemen, they could check for you.'

Bliss ignored the slur. 'And the escapees?'

Bridie paused for a moment until the blood stopped pounding in her ears. 'Escapees?' she muttered. 'Escapees? This isn't Broadmoor, you know.'

Daddy Bliss was aware of that, but he found the comparison odd anyway. 'Broadmoor?' he repeated.

'Lunatic asylum,' the wardress explained, as though to an idiot.

'Yes,' Bliss said. 'I know. I wondered . . .'

'Well, they *do* let people escape. I'm thinking of the murderer Bisgrove. Scarpered over the roof and just vanished. He's been on the run for weeks now, months, even.'

'We haven't seen him on the river,' Bliss assured her.

'Nobody's seen him,' Bridie said. 'That's not the point. What I'm saying is, at Holloway, *nobody* gets out. Nobody at all.'

And she cracked her knuckles, by way of confirmation.

Miss Moriarty had, in the end, been quite succinct in telling her tale. A slug of brandy to within an inch of the top of the teacup had made her rather less bellicose and – for the moment at least – rather more forthcoming and less judgemental. Enid would have to reap the whirlwind of the aftermath as they went back to Eastbourne, but she was used to that and knew that it would bring the advantage of an evening of peace with her employer spark out on the sofa.

The old lady could tell them little about the maid, save that she had been with Emilia for some while without a blot on her character. Being found in the river without certain essential body parts Miss Moriarty was prepared to overlook – it was thoughtless, true, to bring such unwonted attention to the name of Westmoreland. She had broken off at this point to smack her lips and look enquiringly at Grand.

'Is this a Westmoreland special blend?' she asked, sucking it through her teeth and looking wistful.

'It is,' said Grand, impressed. 'In fact, Mr Teddy Westmoreland blended it just for me and it is called, in fact, Grand Blend.'

Miss Moriarty's eyes opened wide. 'What an *honour*,' she breathed and then blushed. 'I have a blend named after me as well, you know; well, not *after* me, but in my honour.'

Batchelor, who had rather tired of Grand flashing his special blend status about, smiled thinly. 'What is it called?' he asked. Surely not Annoying Old Bat – that just wouldn't sell well at all.

'*Amore*,' the old lady said, lowering her eyes. Then, she looked up at them defiantly. 'It didn't work out.'

'Ah.' Grand looked at Batchelor, eyebrows raised. Would someone please change the subject? After what seemed like an age, his help came in the shape of someone at the door.

Batchelor beat him to it by leaping up and, with a cry of, 'I'll get that,' left the room at a trot.

Miss Moriarty, recovered from her sentimental moment, began to gather up her umbrella, bag and other sundries. 'I hope I have been of help, Mr Grand,' she said. 'I appreciate that this may have brought us little further in your search for poor, dear Emilia. I fear that the finding of Molly's body must only make us think the worst. But hope springs eternal, does it not?'

'Indeed it does, Miss Moriarty,' Grand said, extending a hand. 'Can I call you a cab to take you to the station?'

Miss Moriarty inclined her head. Colonials were *so* polite. 'Thank you, Mr Grand,' she said. 'I had thought to visit my nephew-in-law, but I think that your tea may have been a little strong.' She put an age-crazed hand to her brow. 'I feel a little giddy.'

Grand caught Enid's eye but the maid gave nothing away. Stone-faced was an understatement. 'Perhaps you should go straight home. We could visit Mr Byng for you, to give him your—'

'Regards,' Miss Moriarty broke in. 'My regards. Not kind regards. Just . . . regards.' She pressed a lace handkerchief to her lips. 'I blame him, Mr Grand,' she said, in a strangled mutter.

Grand's eyes almost popped out of his head. 'Blame him for . . . murder?'

'Good grief, no,' she said, fetching him one with her umbrella. 'I mean for causing poor Emilia to go missing. If it wasn't for his . . .' she closed her eyes tight and raised her chin resolutely, '. . . carnal, animal lusts, she wouldn't have come to visit me, would not have been on that train where clearly a maniac was lurking. Poor Molly would still be with us.' She glared at Grand. 'In short, if he had been at all able to control himself, we wouldn't be here having this conversation.' She looked towards the door. 'What has happened to Mr Batchelor? Did you not have someone at the door?'

Grand frowned. She was quite right. 'I'll go and check . . .'

As he spoke, the door opened and Batchelor sidled in. 'My apologies, Miss Moriarty,' he said. 'I just need a short chat with my colleague. Would you?' He tossed his head in the direction of the door, his smile a rictus grin.

Grand, nodding his apology, followed him into the hall. 'What?' he snapped.

'We have visitors,' Batchelor announced.

'I know.'

'Not *them*. Two other visitors. The Westmoreland brothers.'

'Well, why didn't you show them . . .' Memory dawned. 'Ah, I see. It didn't work out.'

Batchelor cast his eyes up. It always dawned eventually. 'Yes. I thought perhaps it still rankled.'

Grand was surprised. 'Still? Surely, it must be . . . I was going to say centuries, but decades, at least?'

'Even so.' Batchelor looked towards the closed door. 'Still delicate, perhaps?'

'You're right. I'll show the ladies out. You keep the gents busy. Did they say why they were here?'

'Mmm . . .' Batchelor had heard the door opening and was stuck for anything intelligent to say.

'Why who was here?' Miss Moriarty might be old and a touch raddled, but she had the hearing of a twelve-year-old.

'Umm . . . clients,' Batchelor said. 'Confidential, you know the sort of thing . . . umm . . .'

Miss Moriarty looked at him with gimlet eyes. 'You look very guilty, young man,' she observed. 'And in my experience, young men of your stamp don't look guilty for no reason.' She tapped him smartly around the ankles with her umbrella and crossed the hall to fling open the study door. The two men thus revealed froze; they looked like a *tableau vivant*, just not very *vivant*.

'Teddy. Micah.' Her tones were cut glass and froze the blood.

'Miss Moriarty.' The brothers spoke in unison, lifting their hats politely.

She shut the door and looked with clamped lips at the enquiry agents. 'I believe I *will* go straight to the station. I believe my nephew-in-law lives at Milner Street, number eight. Do you know it?'

Grand looked at Batchelor. He knew London like the back of his hand and Grand had never really bothered with the minutiae. After all, one didn't keep a Londoner born and bred and bark oneself.

'Joins Cadogan Square and Lennox Gardens, doesn't it?' he checked.

She nodded. 'It is just on the corner, where Clabon Mews crosses the street,' she said. 'I have no idea how he affords such an establishment. I would imagine that his father helps him out, though that old skinflint would see his own mother starve before he gave her a penny. Or at least, that has always been my impression. I don't gossip, so I can tell you no more.' She flung an acid glance at the closed door behind which Mr Teddy and Mr Micah cowered. 'I will wish you good-day, gentleman,' she said. 'I hope your . . . visitors . . . help you.'

And with that, with Enid in her wake like an enormous liner propelling a tiny tug, she swept out.

Teddy and Micah Westmoreland sat on either side of the study fire, as if they had been there all their lives. The glow from the flames lit their soft white hair and their pink cheeks; they looked like two men without a care in the world until they looked up and then it showed in their eyes.

'I am so sorry about that,' Batchelor said, crossing the room to take a chair next to Micah. 'She just . . .'

'Oh, yes, she would,' Teddy said softly. 'Jane was always very headstrong. And beautiful, in her day.'

Micah leaned forward. 'Don't dwell, Teddy,' he advised. 'It didn't work out and that's that. Cousins marrying. Not a good idea. It might have been all right for the Egyptian pharaohs but that was *so* then. Surprised the prayer book doesn't have something to say on the matter. Anyway,' he cleared his throat and didn't look as his brother used a discreet handkerchief to dab a corner of his eye, 'we're here on rather more germane matters, gentlemen. We have received this.' He rummaged in a pocket and came up empty. 'Do you have it, Teddy?'

The other brother looked perplexed and then also rummaged. 'Sorry, Micah,' he said. 'I do have it, yes.' He pulled out a piece of paper which he smoothed out on his knee before passing it to Grand, who had pulled up a chair from behind the desk. 'We got this this morning. We thought . . . well, we thought you should see it.'

Grand leaned over with the paper so that Batchelor could see it. In crude, pencilled letters, the message was clear. 'If You wunt to see yur nice agen, Yu'd better let that money go. No Trust is Wurth a Lif. Believe me. If Yu dont do it, she's ded.'

Batchelor took it and folded it neatly. 'May we keep this?' he asked and both men nodded.

'I never want to touch it again,' Teddy said with a shiver. 'It has made me feel quite unwell.'

'Was there an address?' Grand asked. 'A postmark, even?'

'No. There wasn't even an envelope. Someone gave it to the old watchman on the main road outside the warehouse and he brought it round.'

Grand, who had met the man, held out little hope but asked anyway. 'Could he describe the man who gave it to him?'

Teddy snorted. 'He couldn't describe his own reflection,' he said. 'We should move him on, really, but he does no harm. But for once even he had to notice who he was talking to. It was a woman.'

'A *woman*?' Grand and Batchelor spoke in perfect unison.

'Yes. She was dressed in black from head to toe, he said. But a fine figure of a woman, apparently. Tall, with . . . what was that word he used, Micah?'

'Kettledrums, Teddy.' Micah turned to Grand. As a foreigner, he might need translation. 'That means she had a fine pair of . . .'

'Yes.' Grand smiled. 'I do know. So, she was a good looker, was she, this woman?'

'He didn't see her face. She was wearing a veil. But if you ask me, he was too taken up with her—'

'Yes, Micah, thank you.' Teddy took back the initiative. 'Of course, with that old fool, who knows how long he had had the note? He *said* she had just given it to him, but it could have been days. He's as mad as a March hare and drunk most of the time.'

Batchelor asked the question which was hanging in the air. 'And have you released the money?'

'Alas,' Micah said. 'We can't. I know that sounds as though we don't want to, but believe me, we do. We want to have Emilia back as much as Selwyn . . .'

'More, probably,' muttered Teddy.

'Tush,' said his brother, flapping a hand at him. 'You don't know that.'

'Never liked him.'

'No, perhaps not. But she did, and that's the main thing. Where was I?'

'Wanting to have Emilia back,' Grand supplied.

'Yes. But we can't release the money. It is tied up tight. The trust matures on her thirty-fifth birthday or on her death. And that's it. It is an endowment, you see. It doesn't exist as such, by which I mean there is no pot of money, as the writer of this seems to think. We don't have it in a sock under the mattress. The money left by our cousin was used to buy an insurance policy which will mature on the thirty-first of August 1888 and not a moment sooner. Except, as we have said, on the occasion of her death.'

'The letter-writer certainly has a very simplistic way of looking at things,' Grand pointed out. Money, making it and moving it about was what his family had done for generations and to him, the endowment was the obvious way of leaving money to a loved one. But he could see that people who were not in that world could quite literally believe in the sock under the mattress.

'He seems to be a very simple soul all around,' Teddy said. 'Look at the writing. The spelling.'

'We have,' Batchelor said. 'In the other notes we have seen, it is the same; the letters are cut out of the *Telegraph* but even so, the misspellings are there. But look here . . . and here . . .' He picked up the note and pointed to a couple of words, 'This "simple soul" can spell "believe" and also gets the punctuation right in "she's". We think the writer of these notes is as educated as we are, gentlemen, he's just trying to look simple.'

Grand pressed his lips together in thought. The next thing he said would cause offence, he just knew it. 'It could be a she, of course,' he said, quietly.

Teddy and Micah took offence. 'Do you mean,' Micah said in a voice made high and clipped by tension, 'that you believe it to be from Emilia?'

'I didn't say that,' Grand said. 'But it should be something to consider, don't you think?'

'No,' Teddy said. 'No, I don't think it is worthy of even a second's thought.'

'We have some upsetting news,' Batchelor said, gently. 'We have just heard from Miss Moriarty that a dead woman fished out of the Thames is Emilia's maid, Molly Edwards.'

The two tea-blenders were struck dumb, then Micah recovered. 'Are you suggesting,' he said, and his tone left the enquiry agents in no doubt that he was furiously angry, 'are you suggesting that *Emilia* could be responsible for all this?'

'It has to be considered . . .' Grand began.

'No, no it does not,' Micah thundered. 'Emilia is an angel,

the loveliest girl you could wish to meet. She doesn't have a dishonest or cruel bone in her body.'

'That's what we've heard, but—'

'But nothing.' Teddy got up and slapped his hat onto his head. 'Look elsewhere, sirs. It is nothing to do with Emilia. Some evil person has her in captivity, or worse. That's where you should be looking, Mr Grand, Mr Batchelor. Among the worst that London has to offer.'

Micah took up the tale. 'Scour the rookeries, Mr Grand. Look among the lowest in the land. That's where you will find our Emilia.'

'Alive or dead,' Teddy said, with a catch in his voice.

With tears in their eyes, the old men stumbled from the room and, pausing only to tussle briefly with Mrs Rackstraw who was polishing the door knob in the pursuance of her duties, left the house silent and wondering.

Batchelor took up the ransom note again and looked at it closely. Grand poked the fire in a desultory way. They had a lot to consider.

'If you ask me,' Mrs Rackstraw said, poking her head around the door, 'those two would take another look. A bit too anxious to put somebody else in the frame, in my opinion.'

When neither man replied, she gave one of her enormous sniffs, which, though wordless, said so much and went back to her polishing – there was no way now to reclaim her very interrupted afternoon.

After a while, Batchelor spoke. 'Could she be right?' he asked.

'I'm seldom wrong,' the housekeeper told him, through the door.

'Is he in?' Batchelor asked with one foot on the gangplank of the *Royalist*. 'Is he out? Is he shaking it all about?'

Constable Brandon looked down from the deck rail.

'It's all right, Lloyd,' Grand said. 'Remember my colleague, Mr Batchelor? He doesn't get out much himself. We were hoping to see the inspector.'

There was a muffled roar from the hull and a flock of seagulls heard it and took off, screaming, preferring to find a nice quiet storm somewhere out to sea.

'Yes,' Brandon grimaced. 'He's in.'

Grand and Batchelor clattered onto the planking and disappeared into the hatch. The daylight barely reached here on the waterline and a lantern flickered, swaying gently to and fro as the Abode of Bliss groaned and swung at its moorings. The great man himself looked up at them over a pair of rimless spectacles, the ones he wore in court to make him look more intellectual.

'Gentlemen,' he swept the glasses off and threw them down on his table. 'To what do I owe the pleasure?'

'We know who the dead woman was.' Grand got straight to the point. 'Mine, I mean; not yours.'

'Really?' Bliss raised an eyebrow. 'And how do you know that?'

Batchelor produced a newspaper from his pocket. 'The *Eastbourne Intelligencer*,' he said, throwing it down on Bliss's table, 'if that isn't a contradiction in terms.'

Bliss put his glasses back on and picked it up. 'The Wessex Truss Company?' He felt he had to ask.

'Next page,' Batchelor explained.

'Ah.' Bliss found it and ferreted among the papers on the Canterbury. 'Snap,' he said, passing a newspaper of his own across the desk.

'What's that?' Grand asked.

'That,' Batchelor sighed, 'is the *Illustrated Police News*. The last I looked it was not written by policemen nor did it carry much in the way of news. All we can agree on is that it is illustrated.'

'Never mind about all that,' Bliss said. 'I had that likeness placed in a number of newspapers in the hope that someone would recognize the deceased.' He frowned at Grand. 'Odd that it should be the self-same person who found her in the first place.'

'Not guilty, Inspector,' the American said, rearranging a discarded oilskin in order to find a seat. 'The woman you want is Miss Moriarty.'

'Moriarty?' Bliss repeated. 'What a ludicrous name. Should I know her?'

'I doubt it.' Batchelor perched on the corner of the table. 'Eastbourne born and bred, apparently.'

'Good for her,' Bliss nodded. 'What's the link?'

Grand took a deep breath then let it go with a hiss. 'How much do you want to know?'

Bliss narrowed his eyes at him and leaned forward. 'Mr Grand,' he said, heavily. 'I am a rather senior policeman in the service of the Queen, God bless her. If that still leaves you in doubt, the answer to your question is; everything.'

Grand took a breath again and started, enumerating points on his fingers and keeping an eye on Batchelor, in case he left anything out. 'We were approached by one Selwyn Byng, a timber importer, whose wife had been kidnapped . . .'

'And he didn't come to the police because . . .?' Bliss was not going to make this easy.

'Because the people who had kidnapped his wife said he wasn't to; if he did, his wife would be killed.'

Bliss thought for a moment, then nodded. 'Go on.'

'We weren't at all convinced, to be absolutely honest, that any such crime had taken place. In fact, we were almost certain that his wife had left of her own free will.'

Batchelor held up a finger and interrupted. 'She had been staying with her aunt in Eastbourne . . .'

'Miss Moriarty?' Bliss hazarded and the two enquiry agents nodded their approval of his detective skills.

'. . . because,' Grand resumed, 'she didn't want to be tempted into . . . what's that word you use here when you want to be polite?'

'Congress,' Batchelor supplied.

'That's the one. I don't think of it that way, as you might expect. Tempted into congress with her husband, because she was in mourning for her father, who had been squashed by a load of tea.'

Bliss leaned back. He had told less unlikely tales to any one of the numerous little Blisses many a time. He was enjoying himself, in a strange sort of way. These two were good company, you had to give them that.

'At least,' Batchelor continued, 'that was the husband's story. But there were holes in it and Miss Moriarty, the aunt, told us about the maid.'

'Any maid in particular?' Bliss asked, wryly.

'Mrs Byng's maid. She had travelled with her up to London but Mr Byng hadn't mentioned her at all. So we more or less told him to go away and stop bothering us.'

'That was very . . . altruistic of you,' Bliss remarked. 'Most gentlemen in your line of work will take on any job for the per diem and expenses.'

Batchelor pulled a face and gestured with his thumb at Grand. 'Private means,' he mouthed.

Bliss glanced across but Grand didn't seem to have taken offence. 'That must be nice,' he acknowledged. 'But if it makes you more honest, then I'm all for it. So . . . you told him to go away and . . .?'

'He came back a day or so later with a finger.'

Bliss leaned forward again. 'It's all beginning to take shape,' he said. 'This would be the finger you brought to Dr Kempster.'

'It would,' Grand agreed. 'We wondered if it might go with your own bits and bobs, but it was too fresh.'

Brandon, who had been eavesdropping on the deck, moved away and leaned over the side for a while.

'Then I found the other body, of course,' Grand said. 'And as she had no hands, we can't tell if the finger was hers.'

'So, that's easy then,' Bliss said, standing up and reaching for his cap. 'It's the wife. Why didn't you say so?'

'Because it isn't,' Batchelor said. 'It's the maid. Miss Moriarty and *her* maid, Enid, recognized her at once. Unfortunately, they don't know much about her, except that her name is Molly Edwards and she had been Mrs Byng's maid since before she got married. Enid seemed quite upset by it all; I understand they had got quite friendly while Mrs Byng was visiting.'

'Was it the wife's finger, though?' Bliss was trying not to get confused.

'Byng was adamant it was. It had her ring on and he seemed very sure. But I'm not certain whether anyone could tell from such a small part, unless there is some handy scarring, or something.' Grand was really thinking aloud.

'This Byng is a timber importer, you say. I think I should go round and have a word.'

Batchelor hopped down from the table and dislodged a

teetering pile of files. 'Sorry,' he muttered, trying to catch them. 'Were they in any particular order?'

Bliss shrugged. Brandon was in charge of that kind of thing, insofar as Brandon could be in charge of anything. 'Possibly. Now, which timber importers?'

'Could we go first?' Grand asked. 'He's a rather nervy gentleman and if you suddenly confront him, I can't really predict how he will react.'

Bliss looked thunderous. He didn't really believe in nerves, having never been aware of having any himself. A nervy suspect was a collared suspect, in his book. 'Well, I . . .'

'Just give us an hour,' Batchelor said.

Bliss looked at the clock. 'I'll give you until tomorrow,' he said. 'First thing.'

'That's very generous,' Grand acknowledged. 'If we find anything else out, shall we . . .?'

'Keep it to yourselves until tomorrow? Yes, that would be marvellous,' Bliss agreed. Even policemen had the right to some time off and he had had his conscience pricked by his meeting with Bridie O'Hara. Mrs Bliss and all the little Blisses didn't see half enough of him.

'We'll do that thing,' Grand said and he and Batchelor made their way back into the open air, bidding a farewell to Brandon's heaving back.

THIRTEEN

The doorkeeper at Sillitoe, Byng and Son was clear when he eventually slid open the little hatch in the wicket gate. Neither Byng, senior or junior, was available at the moment.

'Do you mean not *available*, or not here?' Batchelor wanted to be sure.

'Mr Byng is at home,' the doorkeeper said. 'Mr Selwyn is also at home.'

Grand blinked. That sounded a very subtle distinction. 'Same place?' he ventured.

'No.' The doorkeeper was a man of few words. 'Mr Byng and Mr Selwyn don't live in the same establishment. I don't rightly know where Mr Selwyn lives. Somewhere posh, I expect.' That was the only hint that perhaps Mr Selwyn was not the man's favourite of his employers.

'Where does Mr Byng live?'

'Ooh, more than my job's worth to tell you that,' the door-keeper said.

'Let me be sure of this,' Grand said. 'You don't know where Mr Selwyn lives. You *do* know where Mr Byng lives, but you won't tell us.'

The doorkeeper looked upwards, thinking for a moment, then nodded. 'On the button,' he said and slammed the hatch. 'Bloody foreigners,' he muttered, spitting into a sawdust-strewn corner. Coming over here, asking personal questions. He'd have to make sure Mr Byng and Mr Selwyn knew that he had sent them packing; not that there would be a tip, not from those two. Tight as a gnat's arse, the both of them. He settled down in his chair again and slowly, the dust of the timber works settled too, coating him in a fine layer as soft as sin.

'Oh, I almost forgot.' It was late and the lamps of Alsatia flick-ered out one by one. Matthew Grand was rummaging in his inside jacket pocket. He tore open the envelope and read the contents.

'What's that?' James Batchelor was scanning the evening papers for news of more body parts.

'Well,' Grand leaned back in his chair, the letter in one hand. 'I thought it was the half past two post. Some tight cuss too mean to pay for a stamp . . .'

'Whereas?' Batchelor looked up.

'Whereas it's a letter from our friend Richard Knowes.'

'Really?' Batchelor stopped reading. To be honest, he hadn't expected to hear anything more from that quarter. 'Don't tell me, it's composed of letters cut out from the *Telegraph*.'

'So young, so cynical,' Grand chuckled. 'No, it's in a fair round hand.'

'Knowes himself, then.' Batchelor craned his neck to see it. 'Not Board School handwriting, that's for sure. What does it say?'

'Says he's drawn a blank,' Grand told him. 'He's talked to people who in their turn have talked to people. Nobody in his line of work is much interested in the Byngs – too far down wealth's ladder, apparently. Now, if we're interested in a little scam involving Lionel de Rothschild or one of the Barings, he can shed a little light; for the usual consideration, of course.'

'Which is?' Batchelor asked; it would be an education to know what information at that level went for these days. When he was working in Fleet Street he could find out most of what he needed to know by passing over a couple of shillings. Somehow, he didn't think that Richard Knowes dealt in small change.

Grand turned the page over. 'He doesn't say, but I guess, bearing in mind his calling, it will involve a large percentage and somebody's kneecaps.'

Batchelor sighed. 'Matthew,' he said after a while, 'we're getting nowhere fast. Time for a recap.' The correct word, as James Batchelor knew perfectly well, was recapitulation, but the man's journalistic training died hard and as far as Matthew Grand was concerned, 'correct' was only a serving suggestion when it came to the Queen's English. They adjusted their chairs and faced the wall. Mr and Mrs Gladstone stared back at them from their sepia photographs, jaws of granite and eyes of steel. Since *he* was the famous politician and she was merely loaded and fond of ice-cold baths, *he* sat in the chair and *she* stood at his shoulder, restraining him, if the rumours were true, from hurtling out of Number Ten in search of fallen women. Across the fireplace, in which the embers were glowing towards an ashy end, Mr Disraeli stood by himself, reptilian, oily. *Mrs* Disraeli was notable by her absence. The two greatest politicians of their age loathed each other with a passion and their ideologies were poles apart. The only thing they had in common were the enormous ink moustaches that Grand and Batchelor had added to their portraits, Mrs Gladstone looking particularly fetching in hers. Whatever the provocation, clients were *never* shown into this room.

'You first.' Grand lit a cigar and threw another one to his colleague.

'Selwyn Byng,' Batchelor said, holding the brandy decanter up to the gas light, 'comes to us distraught at the disappearance of his wife.'

'Emilia,' Grand chimed in, 'who has no money in her own right but who will inherit a tidy sum on her thirty-fifth birthday.'

'Said money,' Grand poured for them both, 'being tied up in the tea business . . .'

'. . . the trustees of which can't release the money, even to get her released from captivity, always assuming she is held captive.'

'The person or persons unknown have sent ransom notes to her husband, but no one has seen them arrive. And now, one to said trustees, possibly delivered by a woman.'

'Emilia was last seen,' Grand said, taking his glass from Batchelor, 'as she left Eastbourne, where she had been visiting an aunt in the company of her maid.'

'Miss Moriarty being the aunt, Molly the maid,' Batchelor added. 'But there's a problem with that.'

'Tell me about it,' Grand murmured.

'Well, we don't know for certain whether she actually got on the train at all, do we? I mean, we know from Byng that she never arrived in London, at least not on the train he met. And people can't just disappear from a moving train, can they? Unless . . .'

'Unless she got off at any of the stations in between,' Grand nodded. 'How many is that? You're the local.'

Batchelor shrugged; he wondered when Grand would acclimatize to the size of England as opposed to the great outdoors that was America. In Grand's head, local was anything within about five hundred miles. In Batchelor's experience, in London local was only within the borough or, in certain cases, the tenement. 'I'd have to check Bradshaw,' he said. 'There are a lot of variables, such as whether she caught a stopping train, a fast, semi-fast.'

'Semi-fast?' Grand wasn't sure he would ever completely understand this country.

'That's a—'

Grand held up his hand; he didn't really want to know. 'However many it is,' he said, sipping his brandy, 'we don't have the resources to check them all out. Nor to go house to house in Eastbourne, for that matter. And there's the little matter of the maid,' he continued. 'We know *she* got to London, because I had the pleasure of bumping into her in the canal basin one very dark night. I'm still trying to forget.'

'Sans hands and feet,' Batchelor nodded. 'Now, why would anyone do that? I mean, the other woman was well and truly disarticulated. Virtually nothing about her is recognizable. Yet Molly's face, surely the most recognizable thing about a person, was intact.'

'The finger,' Grand said. 'Emilia Byng's finger, complete with wedding ring. What if the finger isn't Emilia's at all, but Molly's?'

'So the ring is the real thing, but the finger is somebody else's. That would square with Kempster's opinion, that the ring hadn't been worn by the finger for very long. But why?'

Grand leaned back again, his eyes flicking from Gladstone to Disraeli, but there was no hint of help from either of them. 'What if our kidnapper's getting cold feet?' he asked.

Batchelor looked at him sidelong. 'Is that a joke, Matthew? If so, it is in remarkably poor taste.'

'Dick Knowes has no information and if rumours are true, he knows every confidence trick and piece of skulduggery going on across the country at any one moment.'

'So?' Batchelor wasn't following.

'So, what if it's an amateur? Somebody who's never done this before? All right, Emilia Byng is in line for a fortune, but it's not a fortune by Knowes's standards – it's penny-ante. Also, Knowes will know that she hasn't got it yet, not by a long chalk – he's bound to be in with every banker in London, and I use the word advisedly. If he had done this, he wouldn't have done it, if you follow. He's far too professional.'

Batchelor clicked his fingers. 'So, the kidnapper's rattled. He's out of his depth – and that's not a joke either. Perhaps he saw it as some sort of game, get a few thousand from Byng and then go on his way. He may even be a friend, acquaintance, neighbour – someone who would know there was money, but not how tightly it was tied up. But now, it's serious.'

'Perhaps it got serious at Eastbourne Station, when he realized, late in the day, that Emilia had a maid in tow.'

'Or at Waterloo – we still don't know where he snatched them from.'

'If it was a snatch – he might have just persuaded Emilia he was there to pick her up . . .' Grand was putting his ducks in a row and could almost see the light at the end of the tunnel, mixing his metaphors as only a West-Pointer can. 'But he has two women on his hands, not one.'

'Not a problem if it's a gang,' Batchelor pointed out.

'True, but if he is a loner. If he's green, unsure of himself . . .'

'. . . Emilia may have worked on him.' Batchelor was refreshing their drinks. 'Come all doe-eyed and sobbed about her loving husband, her dear old mum, her fluffy little kitten . . .'

'So he relents,' Grand sipped his brandy. 'Not to the extent of letting her go, of course, but by cutting off the maid's finger, not hers.'

'And putting Emilia's ring on it, just to show he means business.'

'But why kill the maid?' Grand mused. 'I can't imagine that Emilia would be in agreement with that. They've been together a long while, according to Auntie Moriarty; everyone says she is a kind woman. The Westmoreland brothers seemed very fond of her, for example.'

'Perhaps he had to,' Batchelor said. 'Or perhaps she died.'

Grand waved a hand across his throat. 'Strangled,' he said.

'Hmm, yes . . . perhaps she was screaming. I know I would scream the place down if someone chopped my finger off.'

Grand, who had seen far more than fingers chopped off without the soldier in question making a sound, forbore to comment, but Batchelor did have a point. 'And there'd be blood, as well.'

'Yes. True. So he kills her and dumps her in the river, to shut her up or for whatever reason. Perhaps she tried to escape . . .'

'You're being a bit too much of a journalist now, James. Let's just go with the facts. He sees the news of the dismembered bits in the river and thinks why not add one more.' Grand's cigar had gone out through neglect and he relit it. 'I wonder what Bliss is going to do?'

'About what, in particular?'

'Well, thanks to us, he now knows who Molly was. He's identified one of his floating bodies.'

'We had to tell him, Matthew. We've always said . . .'

'. . . that if a serious crime has been committed, we must inform the police.' Grand finished the sentence for him. 'Yes, I know. But we must try our best to stop him pestering Selwyn Byng. Because once he gets involved in that, we can say goodbye to *ever* finding Emilia alive. If we're right about our amateur kidnapper, he'll panic. Emilia will become a third body in the Thames.'

'We owe it to Byng to tell him,' Batchelor said. 'And now we have an address from Miss Moriarty, we should go round. It's not fair to anyone to let them get bad news from Bliss. There is one thing we can be sure of, though,' Batchelor stubbed out the remains of his cigar. 'Daddy Bliss won't be sharing this information with any of his Metropolitan colleagues. He'll want this collar for himself. And that'll slow him down. He's given us till the morning, but I reckon it'll be at least tomorrow afternoon before he gets round to it. After all, he's only got six blokes and one of them just makes the tea and does the ironing . . .'

'Now, James,' Grand wagged a disapproving finger at him. 'I won't have you taking the rise out of Lloyd Brandon.'

'. . . and six miles of river to police. I'm prepared to bet the machinery of Daddy Bliss grinds slow.'

Every fibre of Inspector Bliss's body told him not to do it. All his years of experience, of rubbing shoulders with coppers great and small, of going head-to-head with the riff-raff of London, told him, 'Don't sent Lloyd Brandon out.'

But the boy had turned his doe eyes on him and had looked so pitiful and Gosling and Crossland had argued his case so persuasively, that the inspector had relented and given him the red port-lantern.

'Watch the tide, Brandon,' Bliss had said, his face grim, his eyes hard.

'Yes, sir.' The young man's excitement was bubbling over. At last he'd be in a skiff of his own, the only Bluebottle on his stretch of the river. His old mum would be *so* proud. And he couldn't wait to tell her.

'And watch the wind,' Bliss called as the constable reached the bottom stair. 'Keep away from the sluice at Woolwich – there's things in the water there'll kill you.'

'Yes, sir.'

Brandon was up on deck now, looking upstream where the Tower stood, dark and brooding under its turrets. And downstream, where the tall spars of the clippers kissed the sky. The river had never looked – or smelled – so lovely as on this October morning. And he didn't see the green, grey rolling fog at all. All he saw then was the skiff roped to the *Royalist*'s hull, bobbing on the dark waters below him. He clattered down the steps and swung out onto the ropes, lowering himself too fast as it turned out and burning his hands. He winced in pain and blew on them before casting off and hauling on his left oar. For a while, he went around in a complete circle, then remembered to use his right and pulled away from the stern of the Abode of Bliss.

Up on the deck, the inspector watched him go, shaking his head. 'Above all,' he said softly to himself, 'don't talk to any strange men.'

The morning had gone quite well as Brandon rowed between the colliers. He heard the shouts of the lightermen and the scream of the gulls high overhead. He saw the tiny people, like ants, on both river banks, going about their lives with bustle and purpose. A sensitive soul was Lloyd Brandon and he knew that every one of those ants had a tale to tell, sorrows to bear, reasons to be cheerful. He was that rare kind of copper who sees a glass half full, not half empty; but perhaps that was because he was still only twenty-one years old and usually made the tea.

He didn't hear it at first. Something floated past the skiff and he prodded it with an oar. 'Never let an object pass you by,' he heard Daddy Bliss in his ear as he had for months now, even though the man himself was over a mile away on board the *Royalist* and the *Royalist* had disappeared around the bend. The thing in the water twisted at the sudden intrusion of his oar. It was a hessian sack, empty and stamped with a brand name he didn't recognize and it seemed to be tied to something at one end. He was so busy trying to see what it was that he didn't hear the shout from the south bank. When he did, he tried to pinpoint it. The river's sounds played funny tricks at the best of times and along this stretch they were the oddest of all. He steadied the skiff, trying to make his limited horizon come into focus.

There was a man waving to him from the bank, shouting, 'Over here! Over here!' over and over again. Daddy Bliss had dinned it into him – 'They'll come running to you, lad, because you're wearing the blue; because you've got the metal letters on your jacket. Some of 'em will've lost their cat; some of 'em want to know the time. But some of 'em . . .' and Daddy Bliss's face had darkened and his voice dropped an octave, 'will have been assaulted and raped. And it's your job to listen to 'em all. Catch my drift?'

Brandon turned the skiff, feeling the craft lurch under him as he hauled on the left oar and lifted the right clear. The figure on the shore, bobbing with the ebb-tide, was still shouting at him, 'This way! Come on! Hurry!' He looked like a lighterman by his clothing and he'd been joined by another. By the time Brandon's skiff had crunched its blunt nose into the struts below Hope Wharf there was quite a crowd, all jostling each other.

Brandon waited until someone had caught the prow and helped him onto the foreshore. He sank up to his ankles immediately and climbed out of the sucking mud with as much dignity as he could muster.

'Now then,' he said, remembering to keep his voice low and level. 'What seems to be the trouble?'

'What are you?' a docker asked him. 'A bleedin' doctor?'

Brandon decided to take a leaf out of Daddy Bliss's book.

Nobody spoke to a Bluebottle like that. 'No,' he said, looking the oaf squarely in the face. 'I am an officer of the Metropolitan Police. I'm going to have to ask you all to move along, gentlemen.'

'With pleasure,' said the docker. 'When you've done something about this.' He pointed to the ground as the little crowd backed away to give the nice constable room. Brandon followed the man's finger and found himself looking at the body of a woman. It didn't matter to Brandon that this one was at least in one piece and didn't appear to be shy of any major part of her anatomy. Seconds after he had first clapped eyes on her, he was looking at nothing; he was just lying neatly alongside her on the foreshore below St Mary, Rotherhithe.

'What did you say his name was?' George Crossland was running his finger over the latest Met reports.

'Who?' Gosling asked.

'The mad bloke, got out of Broadmoor.'

'Bisgrove, Daddy said.' Tom Gosling was making the tea, what with Lloyd Brandon lying in St Thomas's with unspecified complications due to mud inhalation.

'Killed a bloke somewhere in the West Country. Fight over a woman, apparently. Daddy was vague about it.'

'What, the murder?'

'No.' Gosling passed the steaming mug to him as the *Royalist* swung in the morning tide. 'How he came upon the case. Know what I think, George?' The man settled himself down, elbows on the table.

'In most matters, Tom, yes, but perhaps not on this occasion.'

'Well, Daddy mentioned the name shortly after his return from Holloway. And you know what that means, don't you?'

A silence, punctuated by a sudden creak of the *Royalist*'s ropes. 'I'm waiting to be enlightened, Tom,' Crossland said.

'Bridie O'Hara,' Gosling leaned back, arms folded, as if he had solved a murder all by himself.

'What?' Crossland's eyes widened. 'The ex-Mummy Bliss? Before the current one, I mean.'

'Well, technically, she was never *actually* Mrs Bliss. He jilted her.'

'The beast!'

Gosling nodded sagely and sipped his tea. He looked remi-
niscently back into the past, when Bridie O'Hara had been a
red-headed heartbreaker who had caught the eye of Daddy Bliss
and many another copper. 'She was . . . well, let's just say I
wouldn't have kicked her out of bed. Any more than Daddy
did, or so they say.'

Crossland looked suitably impressed. He hadn't seen Daddy
as a Lothario. He must look more closely next time he was on
board.

'So, we're supposed to be on the look-out for this wandering
lunatic, are we? Like we haven't got enough on the river as it is.'

Matthew Grand trusted James Batchelor to find even an obscure
street in London, but he trusted a cabbie more. Despite
Batchelor's insistence that a nice walk through Green Park and
up Constitution Hill would be splendid on this crisp autumn
morning, the American had his hand in the air before the
Englishman had finished speaking. The cabbie passing on
the other side of the road pulled in his hack and they were soon
bowling along west towards Milner Street. Batchelor was right;
a brisk canter through Green Park was indeed bracing, but Grand
preferred it that legs other than his own were doing the work.

'I always thought you army men were keen on walking,
hiking, that kind of thing,' Batchelor observed.

'Yes, I would say we are.' Grand sank back against the leather
worn thin over the years by the backsides of various fares. 'I
like a walk as well as the next man, I would say.'

'And yet, here we are.' Batchelor spread an expressive arm.

Grand was puzzled. 'A week-long hike in the Adirondacks,
yes,' he said. 'A summer spent walking through the Appalachians,
I have no problem with that. But a forty-five-minute stroll on
sidewalks; that, I can do without. And anyway, as you say,' he
said, his timing perfect, 'here we are.' He gave the cabbie
the fare and a lavish tip, as always. Batchelor had learned
over the years not to bother asking for a receipt; petty cash
reconciliation was something that happened to other people as
far as Matthew Grand was concerned. He knew about money,
true; but only when it had a fair few zeros.

Eight Milner Street was a very pleasant house indeed, separated from the pavement by a basement area, reached by narrow winding steps; the main door was set a half a storey above street level. The steps to reach this door were wide and white, scrubbed daily by a tweenie and then rubbed over with a stone to keep them in the peak of gleam. The door itself was painted a deep, cherry red and the knocker and other door furniture almost hurt the eyes, they were so burnished and bright. Crisp curtains framed the windows on either side of the door and high above their heads, a maid was working hard, if the feather duster being shaken out of the window was any guide.

Grand and Batchelor stood on the pavement and looked up. This was not what they had expected. They had begun to form the opinion that the Byngs lived a fairly humdrum life, not exactly in a suburban villa, perhaps, but in some mews, with no room to swing a cat but with pretensions to gentility. Byng senior in a house like this, yes; they could picture that. But the Byngs junior – it stretched credibility. Perhaps Miss Moriarty had got it wrong.

'No point in just staring at the place,' Grand said. 'Let's see if he's in.'

They bounded up the steps and instinctively looked behind them to make sure they hadn't left footmarks – it would have been a travesty. But no, the steps still gleamed. Batchelor rapped smartly on the knocker and they both stepped back to wait for the answer.

'What do you reckon?' Batchelor asked. 'Maid?'

Grand looked along the façade. 'No. I reckon a butler.'

Batchelor nodded. 'Could be,' he mused. 'Could be a butler.'

The word was still on his lips when the door swung open on perfectly balanced hinges and the man himself stood there, tall and stately, perfect from his Macassared hair to his patent shoes, by way of a striped waistcoat and cutaway tails.

'Yes?' he intoned, his voice a mellifluous hum. 'May I help you, gentlemen?'

Batchelor felt awkward. He knew his shoes needed a proper clean, not just the Maisieing they received when she remembered. His trousers, likewise, were crumpled and in definite concertinas behind his knees. His waistcoat lacked a button and his collar had seen better days. He shuffled slightly and felt himself blush.

Grand was more secure sartorially, but even so was caught on the back foot. This was altogether too grand, even for him. He cleared his throat.

'We are here to see Mr Byng. Mr *Selwyn* Byng.' He still wasn't convinced he was at the right address.

'Mr Byng is currently at his toilet, sir,' the butler said, his voice coming from the depths of a honey-filled well. 'If you would like to follow me and wait in the withdrawing room, I will see if he can attend you.' He leaned forward and seemed to inspect the two as if they were something on a microscope slide. 'Who should I tell him is calling?'

Grand handed him a card, which he took between a supercilious finger and thumb.

'Please,' he swung open a door, 'if you would wait in here, I will ascertain whether the master will see you.' There was something in his tone which made it clear that they should have used the tradesmen's entrance or, for preference, not have come at all.

The room into which the butler ushered them was in the very height of fashion. There was hardly a flat surface which was not smothered with knick-knacks and the fringing and furbelowing made the two enquiry agents feel almost breathless. The whole space was stifled and airless and neither of them dared move for fear of toppling some artefact from its perch. There wasn't a fingermark or smudge to be seen; it was a little like being buried alive.

There was something about the setting that made casual conversation all but impossible and they stood there like a couple of shop mannequins. After a while, Grand eased out his pocket watch, being careful to keep his elbows tucked well in. 'Ten minutes,' he muttered out of the corner of his mouth. 'Five more, and we go and look for the cuss. I can hardly get my breath in here.'

'It's very . . . fashionable.' Batchelor ventured. 'Like a room set up in Debenham's. It must have cost a packet.'

Grand carefully leaned sideways and peered at a whatnot. 'It did. This one still has a price tag on it.'

Batchelor turned gingerly.

'Don't look, James. It will only upset you.' Grand had winced at the price, which seemed a little steep to say the least. It begged the question why Selwyn Byng didn't just dip into his back pocket and pay the money the kidnappers were demanding. 'By the way, I've been thinking. Did that butler look familiar to you?'

'No. I've never seen him before. He just looks like . . .' Batchelor scoured his memory, 'well, every other butler I've ever seen. You keep rather more aristocratic company than I do, Matthew. That's probably why he looks familiar.'

Grand thought for a moment and then shrugged, carefully. That might be it. But he was still puzzling over it when the door opened and Selwyn Byng entered.

'Sorry to keep you waiting, gentlemen,' he said. For someone who had been at his toilet for at least twenty minutes, he looked as much like an unmade bed as ever. There are people who don't really suit clothes and Selwyn Byng was definitely in that category. 'Symes didn't want to disturb me. I was at my toilet.'

'Yes,' Grand said. 'He said. I don't want to beat about the bush, Mr Byng, but an Inspector Bliss of the River Police will be visiting you later, at your place of business, I would imagine. We wanted to warn you.'

Byng went pale. 'Police? What does he want?'

'Well, he has some rather upsetting news,' Batchelor said. 'They have found a body . . .'

Byng went even paler and clutched at the back of an over-stuffed button-back chair, his fingers digging into the pile of the velvet. 'A . . . body . . .?' he croaked and slid gracefully to the floor.

Batchelor looked at Grand. 'Sorry,' he said. 'I was trying to break it to him gently.'

Grand was kneeling beside the prostrate man, loosening his collar and slapping his face, none too gently. Byng groaned and tried to sit up. 'Stay lying down for a moment,' Grand said. 'You've had a shock.'

'A body?' Byng said as though unconsciousness had not intervened. 'Is it . . . is it Emilia?'

'No. But it is her maid, Molly.'

'Molly?' Byng struggled to his feet. 'Molly? Are you sure?' Grand nodded.

'But . . . how did you find out? That it's Molly, I mean. How did she get in the river?'

'Did I say she was in the river?' Batchelor wasn't an enquiry agent for nothing.

'No,' Byng said, smoothing out the velvet pile where his fingers had dragged it. 'But since you said River Police, I put two and two together.'

Batchelor had to concede the man had a point. 'We don't know how she got there. Mr Grand here actually found her.' That seemed a better way of putting it than the actual description of him bumping into her handless corpse in the filthy water off Limehouse.

Byng stared at Grand. '*You* did? How did you know she was there?'

Grand was a little nonplussed. 'It was accidental,' he said. 'I wasn't looking for her. I . . . fell in.'

Batchelor let him get away with that small inaccuracy.

'But that's not all,' he continued. 'Emilia's uncles have had an anonymous note. In writing this time, not cut out letters. We assume it is from the kidnappers, even so. It demands that they release the funds, or the worst will happen.'

'The worst?' Byng clutched his arm. 'Surely not!'

Grand frowned and then the penny dropped. 'No, Mr Byng, I don't mean that. I mean that Emilia will be killed.'

'Oh.' Byng didn't look exactly relieved, but his fingers released Grand's arm and his hand swung down to his side. All of the life seemed to have gone out of him. 'Oh. I see. Are there funds? Can they be released?'

'It's an endowment,' Grand told him. 'Until it matures, there are no funds.'

'That's what I was led to understand,' Byng said, his voice flat.

Batchelor caught Grand's eye and leaned forward. 'Mr Byng. I can't help noticing that you keep a very expensive establishment here. The furniture in this room alone would more than pay the ransom that is being asked. Could you not . . . well, could you not simply pay what they want?'

Byng's eyes flashed. 'Do you not think I would if I could, Mr Batchelor? I have approached any number of dealers in furniture and fine things and they wouldn't give me even half of what I need for everything I own. Sadly, as soon as fashionable items such as these leave the shop, they are almost worthless.' He slapped his palm to his forehead. 'If only we had known. But Emilia loves nice things and . . . we weren't to know. We were just building our little nest. Making it nice for when . . .' he stifled a sob, 'when little feet came pattering.'

Neither Grand nor Batchelor was exactly an expert on children, but it struck them both that this was scarcely a room conducive to the pattering of little feet. But what did they know?

'And your father . . .?'

'Still adamant, I fear.'

Grand and Batchelor came from very different homes, with money a talking point in both, though from opposite ends of the spectrum. But they both knew that had they needed something, even the skin from a parent's back, that something would have been delivered, no matter what the cost. Byng senior must have a heart of stone.

'My father is not an affectionate man. He doesn't really . . . understand.'

Nods were the only answer. Nods and averted eyes.

'What about Westmoreland Tea?' Grand said. 'I have to say that I didn't used to be a tea drinker, but your Uncle Teddy has converted me. Surely, they do well?'

'I don't think so,' Byng said. 'Appearances are deceptive. There are so many tea importers, so many shops that sell it but somehow Westmoreland don't get the big orders. Fortnum's, now, or one of the big grocers, an order from them would transform the business, but too slowly to help my poor Emilia.' He trumpeted into his handkerchief. 'I need money now. This *instant.*' He stamped his foot like a child. 'Or I fear I will never see her again. Alive or . . .' he choked. 'Alive or dead.' He turned his back and blew his nose again, then put his handkerchief resolutely away. 'But for now, gentlemen . . .'

Before he could continue, there was a genteel tap on the door and the butler's head appeared round it. 'If I may make so bold, sir,' he said to Byng, 'there is an important appointment imminent.' He nodded politely to the enquiry agents. 'If you recall, you asked me quite specific to remind you.'

Batchelor gave him an old-fashioned look. Specific? Perhaps

the man was foreign, brought over with a load of lumber and trained up. But Byng had jumped to attention.

'Symes,' he said. 'You are quite right. I will have to ask you to leave now, gentlemen. I do have a very important appointment which won't wait.' He glanced up at the butler. 'Are the gentlemen here, Symes?'

'It wants half an hour as yet, sir. But you asked me to remind—'

'Yes. Well done, Symes.'

The man's head withdrew and the door began to close.

'Oh, and Symes?'

'Yes, sir?' He reappeared.

'That's "specifically", not "specific".'

'Thank you, sir. I will make a note.'

When he had gone, Byng smiled at the others. 'Foreign,' he said.

Batchelor metaphorically patted himself on the back.

'Welsh. But we do what we can. Let me show you out.'

'No need, really . . .'

'No, no, I'm going that way anyway. Big old place like this, it's easy to miss your way.' He opened the door and ushered them through. Symes was waiting just by the front door and pulled it towards him, stepping back with a flourish. 'Thank you for letting me know about poor Molly,' Byng said. 'And about Inspector Bliss. Please excuse the rush, but I must keep this appointment. A special delivery from Peru – very tricky, Peruvians, you know. They drink special tea and all sorts. Poor Symes is kept on his toes catering for them, are you not, Symes?'

'Indeed to goodness, look you,' the butler said, impassively.

Byng clicked his tongue. 'Welsh!' he said. 'You can take the butler out of Haverfordwest, but you can't take the Haverfordwest out of the butler, eh, gentlemen? Goodbye.'

In a blink of an eye, the two men were on the other side of the front door. 'That was odd,' Grand said, thoughtfully.

'He's an odd bloke,' Batchelor said. 'Look at how he behaved when he came to us first. Like some wandering loony. You can't expect normal from anyone in the Byng family, I'm beginning to think. Look at his father, skinflint that he is. Won't even help out with money to save his daughter-in-law.'

'Unless he's in on it,' mused Grand. 'With her, I mean. Helping her to teach her husband a lesson.'

'Do you think he'd do that?' Batchelor was incredulous.

'You used to be a journalist. Surely you have seen odder things than that.'

Batchelor riffled through the filing cabinet of his brain and mentally ticked off the stories stored under 'damned peculiar' and 'almost incredible' and nodded. 'You're right. Compared to many people in London, they come under the heading of "perfectly normal".'

'Quite. Anyway, let's get back to the office. Those lost dogs won't find themselves, you know. Oh, God – watch out!' Grand pulled his friend out of the road where he was standing ready to cross. A dray-horse pulling an open cart missed Batchelor by a whisker; he felt the animal's hames scrape past his chest. There was a clash of steel-shod hoofs on the cobbles and the snort and whinny of a horse.

'He nearly got me,' he said, his throat dry with shock. 'Where the hell did he come from?' He shook his fist at the driver who sat impassive on his perch. 'Imbecile!' he shouted. He took a deep breath. 'Before we go and find those dogs, a drink, I think, don't you?'

Grand patted his arm. 'Definitely. Home or away?'

'There's a pub just near here, isn't there?'

Grand looked puzzled. Of course there was; this was London, after all. 'I expect so,' he said. Shock could do odd things to a man.

'Away, then. I just need a sit down.' He sniffed his sleeve and held it up to Grand's nose. 'Saddle soap. *That's* how close he came.'

'There, there,' Grand said. 'He missed you and that's the main thing. Come on. I'm buying.'

Batchelor shrugged. He had never even thought it might be otherwise.

Eyes watched them go. Some were hot with love, some swivelling with madness, others keen and calculating. But ignorance, for the agents that morning, was very heaven.

FOURTEEN

The lamplight was reflected in the raindrops that spattered the windows. Felix Kempster was looking at them, tiny pinpricks of light that now and then ran in long tears to the bottom of the pane.

Fanny Kempster knew the signs. She had married a brilliant man eight years ago, but, more than that, she had married a good one. And here he was, wrestling with a death he could only explain in strictly medical terms, remembering a face he couldn't identify.

'Difficult one, dear?' she asked, looking up from her crewel work, one of those mundane but beautiful things that reminded them both that there was more to life than sudden, violent death.

'More difficult for Daddy Bliss, I'll wager.' The doctor was finishing the notes he had begun in the mortuary, preferring the warmth of the drawing room to the cold antiseptic slabs.

'Tell me about this one.' Fanny knew it helped her husband to talk at moments like these.

'She was in her mid-twenties, I'd say, younger possibly but no older than twenty-six.' He didn't have to check the ledger he was writing in. 'Well-nourished, good-looking before the river got at her.'

'Children?' Fanny could almost picture the tiny faces, tear-stained as they waited for a mother who would never return.

'No,' her husband said. 'But she was . . .' even with his wife, he kept his language circumspect, although he knew she was all but unshockable, '. . . no stranger to a man's attentions, shall we say? In fact, quite the opposite, although there was no coercion involved, I would say.'

'So not rape, then?' Fanny believed in calling a spade a spade.

'Er . . . no.' Even after eight years, she could still pull him up short. 'I would classify the signs as showing enthusiasm but no force.' He felt himself blush and blushed some more at the realization.

'Were there any mutilations?' Fanny Kempster was a doctor's daughter as well as a doctor's wife. Not for her the smelling salts, the avoidance of all things nasty and the usual euphemisms of her class. And not a blush mantled her pretty cheek.

'None.' He shook his head, glad to be in more manageable conversational waters.

'Cause of death?'

'Strangulation,' he told her. 'Ligature. Usual bruising under the jaw line. There was some bruising to the face, probably a fist, but it could have been post mortem.'

'Where did they find her?'

'On the foreshore at Rotherhithe. Some lightermen, yesterday morning.'

'Do we know who she was?'

Kempster sighed. 'Not a clue. She was fully clothed. I made an inventory. All good quality stuff, so we can assume middle class. There were no laundry marks on her underwear but her bodice was made by Jesmer and Jay's.'

'Oxford Street,' Fanny said promptly. She was a lovely woman, but she *did* have a tiny shopping habit.

He smiled at her. 'I thought you'd know it,' he said. 'The police will follow that up, though if it wasn't tailormade, that'll probably lead nowhere. She was married, or at least engaged for a long while – there was the groove left by a ring on the appropriate finger. I am assuming married, though, because of . . .' He cocked his head at her. That conversation didn't need to be revisited.

She reached across and patted his arm. 'You are such a darling,' she muttered. He had seen so much and yet he could still be embarrassed talking to his wife. It made him the man he was and she never failed to appreciate it. 'How long had she been in the water?' she asked, to change the subject slightly.

'That's tricky,' Kempster admitted. 'Not long, I'd say. And that's what gave Daddy Bliss his first headache.'

'Why?'

'Well, apparently, the first copper on the scene was a rookie, one of Daddy's Waterbabies with the accent on the baby. He took one look at the deceased and promptly passed out.'

'Ah, London's finest,' Fanny beamed.

'Precisely. Anyway, another Police boat saw the commotion and came to the lad's aid.'

'So where does Daddy's headache come in?'

'By the time the second skiff got there, yet another copper had arrived, from dry land, I mean. He took charge and there was an unseemly contretemps over jurisdiction – the River Police or M Division.'

'Oh, really! They're like squabbling children!' Fanny had no patience with red tape, especially when it got tangled around Felix.

'Daddy arrived with his usual suave charm and persuaded M Division that it would be better for their collective knee-caps if they gave the body to him.'

'What a foul man he is.' Fanny shook her head.

'Agreed,' Kempster said. 'But he's *our* foul man. His second headache is caused by the fact that *this* woman doesn't fit the pattern of the others. No mutilations.'

'Which means . . .?'

He looked at her. 'Either our murderous friend was interrupted on this one and didn't have time to remove various body parts . . .'

'. . . or?' Fanny Kempster was there already, but she knew it helped her husband to spell it out.

'Or there is not one killer on the river, but two.'

It was days later that William Bisgrove came face to face with fate. He was shambling along South Street again, the trees of the park rustling as the evening breeze tried to part them with their autumn leaves. There it was, a piece of paper fluttering on the lamp post as he passed it. 'Metropolitan Police,' it read. 'Have you seen this man?' William Bisgrove had. Not once, but many times. Every time, in fact, that he had looked in the mirror. He read the print below the engraving, just to make sure. 'William Bisgrove. Aged 32. Height, 5ft 9in. Brown hair. No distinguishing features. Wanted for murder.'

That wasn't right and Bisgrove became indignant. He hadn't killed anybody. It had all been a misunderstanding. And if only he could find Millie, she would speak for him. He looked across the street, to the warm lights twinkling in the windows

of Number 15. That's where she had been when he saw her
last. But she hadn't seen him and that old cow who was
her landlady said she'd gone. And she'd chased him off too,
with a broom the last time. She was lying, of course. That
was why he'd come back. And now, this.

He was about to tear the poster down when he saw the
very same old cow coming out of the house; Millie's house.
He turned his back, pulling up his collar and ducked into the
shadows. The old cow pulled her bonnet strings tighter and
shuddered at the weather. She hated going out at night but she
had places to be and needs must. As she passed the lamp post,
a flutter caught her eye. Under the pale green glow of the gas,
she read the words, 'Metropolitan Police' and the other word,
'Murder'. Then she saw the face.

The old cow gasped, clutching at her throat and looking
wildly about her. She tore the poster down and hurried back to
the safety of her house. It was *him*; the lunatic she had seen
loitering about several times, looking for some woman called
Millie. She'd been kind at first, but kindness had turned to
irritation and then downright annoyance and she'd taken a broom
to him. She knew now that she'd been right to do it. The man
was a stone killer. She'd known that all along. And as she
slammed the door behind her and slid the bolts, she knew what
she had to do. Go to the River Police, to that nice Detective
Sergeant Spinster and make the streets of London safe again
for women and children.

'Who?' Daddy Bliss looked over his rimless spectacles.

'That's what I said, Inspector.'

'Yes, thank you, Gosling. I'll take this from here. Haven't you
got any skins need oiling?' He waited until the constable had
clattered up the stairs. 'Now, then, Mrs . . .?'

'Christian,' she said. She had no intention of sharing her
given name with this oaf. 'I wanted to see Sergeant Spinster.'

'Well, as I suspect Constable Gosling will have told you,' Bliss
said, 'we have no one of that name here.'

'Of course you do,' she snapped, tired already of the rudeness
of the river's finest. 'Shortish gentleman, quite good-looking in
a detective sort of way.'

'Well, that's just the problem, madam, we don't have detectives in the River Police. We uniformed boys have to do it all.'

'But not since the new directive, surely? Haven't they told you?'

'Who, madam?' This conversation had a curiously circular motion about it.

'The Home Office, of course. Do try and keep up . . . Inspector, is it?'

'It is, madam, and I can assure you there are no new directives covering detectives, not from the Home Office or anywhere else. Now, if I can't help you, I assure you no one can. What's the problem?'

'This.' She rummaged in her handbag and fished out the tatty poster, thrusting it at Bliss. 'This madman has been lingering about outside my house.'

'Has he indeed?' Bliss's eyebrows rose. He had long ago stopped seeing the need to impress Bridie O'Hara, but it would be a feather in his cap to be able to say that he had caught the only lunatic ever to have escaped from Broadmoor. 'Where was this?' he asked.

'South Street, Battersea.'

Bliss sat bolt upright. 'You're Mrs Christian,' he told her.

She was unimpressed. 'First you deny any knowledge of Home Office procedure and then you tell me something I already know; something I told you not two moments ago.'

'No, I mean you are Mary Cailey's landlady.'

'I am,' Mrs Christian said. 'But that's not why I'm here. I am being pursued by this raving madman Bisgrove.'

'Pursued?' Bliss checked.

'Well, perhaps pursued is too strong a word, but bothered, certainly. He seems to think I know someone called Millie.'

'And do you?'

'No. Well, yes. There was an Millie Dysart who ran a dame school when I was a little girl, but she's long dead so it's clearly not the same woman.'

Bliss looked at her, his eyebrow cocked.

'Don't look at me like that,' she said. 'I like to be accurate.'

Getting back to the subject, Bliss asked, 'Why did Bisgrove want her?'

Mrs Christian sighed. 'Look,' she said, as though to the ship's cat. 'I appreciate you feel you have to ask questions, but I can't answer any of them.'

'Very well,' Bliss said. 'Just let me ask you one more, however. Why does this Bisgrove think that Millie has anything to do with you?'

'Again, Inspector,' Mrs Christian was patience itself, 'I have no idea. Does the name mean anything to you?'

'Do you have stout locks on all your doors?' Bliss asked.

'Indeed I do,' she assured him. 'And a maid with shoulders like tallboys. Mr Christian is away at the moment, but I expect him back soon. You suspect this maniac will return?'

'It's possible,' Bliss admitted. 'That's the thing with maniacs. You're never sure what they're going to do next. Perhaps I had better tell you about Millie.'

'I wish you would,' she said.

'I don't want to alarm you unnecessarily.'

'Get to the point, Inspector.'

'Very well.' Bliss reached down a ledger from the groaning shelves that formed just part of the *Royalist*'s filing system. He flicked through the pages until he found what he was looking for. 'Millie Paget is a milkmaid living in Wookey Hole, Somerset. Two years ago last August, she was . . .' he glanced up to meet Mrs Christian's basilisk stare, '. . . entertaining a gentleman in a field, just off Pelting Drove.'

'Disgusting!' Mrs Christian shuddered.

'Quite. The entertainment was just about to reach its climax, so to speak, when William Bisgrove came along. The local police believe he had been watching the couple for some time and that, for reasons best known to himself, he emerged from his hiding place and brained the wholly unaware gentleman with a rock, shattering his skull.'

Mrs Christian shuddered again, but this time words failed her.

'He was apprehended and Millie Paget was, of course, the principal witness for the prosecution.'

'He was found guilty, I assume?'

'As Judas Iscariot,' Bliss confirmed. 'But some do-gooder intervened and claimed that the said Bisgrove was as mad as a tree. So they put him in Broadmoor.'

'From where he escaped.'

'Regrettably, yes. But with this new sighting of yours, I think we can say that our net is closing in on him. In other news, I assume you've heard nothing of Mrs Cailey?'

'Not a word. She was neither of the women I saw in Dr Kempster's mortuary, so we're no further forward, are we?'

'Yes and no, Mrs Christian,' Bliss said. 'Tell me; this detective you're looking for, the shortish, good-looking one – his name couldn't have been Batchelor, could it?'

'Don't be ridiculous, Inspector,' the landlady said, gathering up her cape, umbrella, gloves and other impedimenta before clambering up the ladder to the deck. 'Do you take me for a complete fool?'

'Well, well; if it isn't Sergeant Spinster.' Daddy Bliss was not smiling. He wasn't even tapping the peak of his cap as he might have done in greeting a member of the public or a junior colleague. His hard grey eyes were boring into James Batchelor's.

'To what do we owe the pleasure?' Matthew Grand wore his poker face, sensing his friend's discomfort.

'I doubt it'll be a pleasure for long,' Bliss said. 'Impersonating a police officer is a serious offence.'

'And yet you do it all the time.' Grand gave him a smile as wide as the Hudson.

'I'm sure Mr Batchelor can speak for himself,' Bliss said, 'in connection with his recent misrepresentational visit to Mrs Christian.'

Batchelor screwed up his face and sighed. 'It's a fair cop,' he said.

'James . . .' Grand felt the ground shifting under him. An enquiry agent with a record was scarcely unusual, but it didn't exactly bring the clients in either.

Batchelor held up his hand. 'No, Matthew,' he said. 'If you can't beat 'em, join 'em, eh, Inspector?'

Bliss's piggy eyes narrowed still further. 'If you're suggesting some sort of collusion . . .' he began.

'That's exactly what I'm suggesting,' Batchelor said and offered the man a cigar from the box on the desk.

'First you impersonate a policeman, then you bribe one. Not your day, is it?'

'We *are* all on the same side,' Grand reminded him. 'Justice. Law and Order. No stone unturned etcetera, etcetera.'

'But sometimes,' Batchelor offered Bliss a chair, 'just sometimes, in the interests of those things, we have to bend the rules a little. We don't carry one of those little Metropolitan tipstaffs to give us powers of arrest, so we have to be a little creative.'

'You could always enlist,' Bliss suggested.

'And earn what you do?' Grand was aghast. 'That wouldn't cover the cost of the paper clips. And Mrs Rackstraw would resign for sure; she feels demeaned enough that we are enquiry agents; policemen would place us beyond the pale.'

Bliss took his time, then sank into the more-than-comfortable armchair positioned just the right distance from a roaring log fire. He looked around him, at the sparkling glass, the gleaming mahogany, the bookcase full of files, standing to attention speaking of successful cases completed and a well-filled client list. 'Yes,' he said. 'Looks like you two are doing all right.' The offices of Grand and Batchelor made the bowels of the *Royalist* look like the Black Hole of Calcutta. The cigar was still on offer and Bliss took it, savouring the moment as Batchelor struck a lucifer for him. 'And was Mrs Christian of any help?' he asked.

'No.' Batchelor blew out the match. 'Although there was a man acting suspiciously outside her house.'

'Oh?'

'She told me he had been hanging around for days in search of someone called Emilia.'

'So?'

Grand was beginning to wonder just how much the inspector was bringing to the table as part of this new alliance.

'Our client, Mr Byng,' Batchelor went on, 'the one we told you about; his missing wife is Emilia.'

'So . . .?'

'So, isn't it rather a coincidence that *two* men are looking for someone called Emilia?'

'You're assuming the bloke hanging around outside Mrs Christian's wasn't your Mr Byng.'

'It didn't sound like him from that good lady's description.'

'Tell us, Inspector.' Grand changed tack. 'Have you been to see Mr Byng yet?'

'Not yet,' Bliss admitted. 'Pressure of work; you must know how it is.' He waved to the bookcase. 'Of course, now, with this latest body . . .'

'Latest body?' Grand and Batchelor chorused.

'Well, keeping that out of the papers is one of the minor miracles we achieve daily in the River Police. One butchered corpse in the river caused bedlam. The second was even worse. When the great British public hears there's a third, we can all forget about leave until the bloody river freezes over.'

'Have you identified her?' Grand asked.

'No,' Bliss said. 'On account of how I want to keep it quiet.'

'Was she . . . intact?' Batchelor enquired.

'Had all her parts, yes. If you mean was she *virgo intacta*, as the medical men have it, Dr Kempster says no. At it like a weasel, to coin a phrase. But not an unfortunate; at least, not by her clothes.'

'Where was she found?' Grand asked.

'On the south bank,' Bliss told him. 'Near Rotherhithe. Could it be the elusive Mrs Byng?'

Grand and Batchelor looked at each other. 'Anything's possible,' Batchelor nodded.

'How did she die?' Grand asked.

'Strangulation by ligature,' the inspector was blowing smoke rings to the ceiling.

'Like the one I bumped into in the water that night.'

'That's right,' Bliss said. 'Byng's wife's maid. It could be that our Mr Byng is in for another shock. I'll get him. Where's he live, again?'

'Milner Street,' Grand said. 'But could we do that, Inspector?'

'Yes,' Batchelor said. 'We owe him that at least.'

'And,' Grand continued, 'despite our new-found collaboration, he is technically *our* Mr Byng, not yours.'

'If he can tell us who this third woman is,' Bliss sighed, 'I don't care whose he is.'

*   *   *

Grand and Batchelor stood on the kerb outside the office and watched Bliss as he walked down the Strand with a sailor's rolling gait.

'Do you think he does that on purpose?' mused Batchelor. 'That Jolly Jack Tar thing? Surely, he was never in the navy?'

'I have heard that he gets seasick on windy days,' Grand said, 'but if it pleases him and keeps him somewhere this side of bearable, I say we leave him to it. Now then,' he looked left and right along the street, 'a cab.' Without looking at Batchelor, he carried on, 'I know it's only a hop and a skip to Milner Street, but I suspect that we'll find *our* Mr Byng at the warehouse. I don't get the impression that Byng senior will be giving him time off to grieve for his wife's maid.' He clicked his fingers at a passing hackney and the driver pulled up in a skitter of hoofs and a jingle of bits. 'Limehouse,' Grand told him as he climbed aboard. 'Soon as you like.'

The two were tossed back in their seats as the cab took off at a brisk trot. The horse, for once, wasn't a spavined old nag but a new one just off the farm and it hadn't learned yet that there would be no sugar lump or sweet apple for work done above and beyond the call of duty. It bowled east along Thames Street and swung round the Tower as it headed for the quays, the titupping horse making good time. The cabbie leaned back and turned to his fares.

'You'll never guess who I had in the back just yesterday night,' he told them.

'Wouldn't we?' Grand said. Batchelor leaned on his elbow and watched the warehouses rock past; he had heard every cabbie story going but Grand still found them interesting. 'Who?'

The cabbie laughed. 'Only that Alfred Lord Bleedin' Tennyson, that's all.'

'Tennyson, goodness.'

'Yes.' The cabbie sucked his teeth reflectively. 'Miserable old bugger.'

The enquiry agents waited for more pearls but there seemed to have been nothing. The cabbie swivelled round on his perch and flicked the horse lightly with his whip. 'Here we are, gents,' he said, drawing up his cab. 'Do you mind getting out here, only, the horses don't like to go too near this warehouse. It's the whine of the saws, I reckon. Or the smell of the glue they use for laminatin'. Never been too sure, but this un's a skittish un and I wouldn't want to take the chance.'

'That's all right, cabbie,' Batchelor said, getting down and stepping back so that Grand could pay.

The driver touched his cap and nodded his thanks for his tip.

'Receipt?' Batchelor asked Grand as the hack disappeared around the corner. 'For the petty cash?'

'Sorry,' Grand said, shouldering open the big gates which led to the timber yard. 'Forgot. What with the excitement about Tennyson and all. Poet or somesuch, isn't he?'

Batchelor glared at his back but with the usual lack of effect. And to be fair, it did seem churlish to be maundering on about petty cash reconciliation when they might be giving a man the worst news he could have; that his wife was dead, brutally murdered and thrown into the river like so much garbage. He trotted for a pace or two to catch up with Grand and all too soon they were outside the respective offices of Byng and Byng.

'Mr Selwyn is in with his father,' the factotum told them. 'Would you like me to . . .?'

'No, no,' Grand said. He knew that if he were to be receiving bad news, he would rather have his father by his side than no one, but his father was not Byng senior. On the other hand, Selwyn did have a bit of a habit of keeling over when things got stressful, so another pair of hands might come in handy. 'We can speak to Mr Byng in front of his father.'

'Oh, dear,' the factotum said. 'I'm afraid Mr Byng's father is dead.'

'Dead?' Grand's eyes nearly started out of his head. 'When?'

The factotum rolled up his eyes and counted on his fingers. 'Eighteen forty-two,' he said. 'A sad day, yes indeed.'

Grand raised a finger to ask a question, but Batchelor had seen where the confusion had arisen.

'We mean,' he said, 'that we can speak to Mr Selwyn in front of his father.' He turned to Grand. 'Mr Selwyn and Mr Byng are—'

'Yes, yes,' Grand was testy. What was the matter with this godforsaken country, where common sense always took second place to fancy speaking. 'I know.' He tapped on the door.

'In!' The imperious voice could only belong to Byng senior.

The factotum rushed to open the door. The proprieties had to be followed as far as possible, even with colonials involved. 'Messrs Grand and Batchelor, sirs,' he said hurriedly and stepped aside.

'Again?' Byng hardly looked up. 'Selwyn, are these men here to see you?'

'Yes,' Grand said and Selwyn Byng looked surprised to hear the answer coming out of someone else's mouth. 'We need Mr Byng to come with us to the mortuary in Lockington Street. There is no good way of telling you this, Mr Byng, but a body has been found and we need you to see if you can identify it.'

Selwyn Byng looked up and anxiously licked his lips. The combination of potentially annoying his father and the threat of another dead body to look at was really almost more than he could take. He felt his head going a bit swimmy and he held on to the edge of the desk. 'I know about that, don't I?' he asked, his voice a distant, dry croak. 'It's Molly, isn't it? You already know that. Didn't Miss Moriarty . . .?'

Selwyn's father rose from behind his desk like a tsunami. 'Selwyn,' he snapped, banging his fist on the desk. 'Had I not known your mother to be the most chaste and loyal of women, I would doubt that you were in fact my son. That and the Byng nose, of course, which you bear with little grace, I must say. Take it like a man, man. If you need to look at this wretched maid, then do so.' He turned to Grand and Batchelor. 'If you would be good enough to be as quick as possible, gentlemen; my son has lost a great deal of time in the office of late, due to this silly misunderstanding with his wife.' He stood, knees bent and backside poised to regain his chair. He looked at them from under beetling brows, eyes sharp and hostile on either side of the Byng nose. 'Well? Don't let me keep you.'

'I'm afraid it isn't that simple,' Grand said. He really, *really* didn't like this man and he could feel the anger bubbling up just under his diaphragm. 'The body in question is not that of the maid, Molly, but possibly of Mrs Emilia Byng. It will be a distressing and upsetting experience for your son even if it isn't – I doubt he will be in any position to return to the office and I for one do not intend to escort him back here. In fact, I think it would be best if you had him home with you for a day or so. He doesn't look at all well. In fact . . .'

But he was too late. Selwyn Byng, pausing only to vomit copiously over his father's desk, had crumpled up and lay on the floor, his knees drawn up, whimpering quietly to himself.

Byng senior looked with distaste at his only child lying at his feet. 'Take as long as you need,' he muttered, pushing back his chair. 'And do, by all means bring him back to my house afterwards, that is if you think that is a better choice than a bed in some asylum. He certainly can't go back to that poky place of his – he'll need a few creature comforts I suppose, if the news is bad.' He looked up at them and for a moment a concerned parent looked out through those sharp, cruel eyes. There was a question in his voice.

Batchelor answered it. 'We can't be sure, sir, but . . .' he shrugged.

Byng touched a bell on his desk and the factotum returned. 'Help these gentlemen with Mr Selwyn, would you?' he said curtly. 'And bring a mop.' He stood up and reached his hat down from a peg on the wall behind him. 'I'll be at my club.' He strode to the door. 'And open a window. I could never stand the smell of despair.'

The door slammed behind him and Grand and Batchelor, supporting the almost catatonic Byng between them, watched him go in horror.

'Nice man,' Grand muttered.

'The death of his wife changed him,' the factotum said, sternly. 'He loved her too much, I suppose. It left no room for Mr Selwyn and now he can't accept he's all he has. This business of Mrs Selwyn has made him rather worse . . . is it true? Are you really taking Mr Selwyn to see if . . .' he glanced at his junior boss, '. . . if she's . . .?'

'Dead,' wailed Selwyn Byng. 'Dead, dead, dead.'

Normal condolences were both premature and inappropriate, so the enquiry agents settled for patting him randomly on the shoulder, arm, hand, whatever came near as he threshed and twitched his way out of the office. They were both thinking the same thing; it was going to be a long, long afternoon.

FIFTEEN

Byng recovered himself a little in the cab on the way to the mortuary but he was still in shock. Grand, who had seen more unpleasant sights as a young man than Byng would see in a lifetime, was trying to be generous, but he had been taught to not meet trouble halfway and so had little patience with Byng's constant pessimism. Batchelor had led a more sheltered life than his partner but on the other side of the coin had spent a harrowing few months as a cub reporter taking down the details at inquests and so had, at second hand, more experience of bereavement than he had. But both, in their various ways, tried to buck Byng up by talking over his head about the many people they had known who had been missing for weeks, months, years even and had yet popped up, alive and kicking, in the end. But before the journey was over, his silent tears and hand-wringing had almost worn them out and it was a sombre trio which alighted from the cab in Lockington Street. It was a measure of Batchelor's depression that he didn't even mention receipts.

The mortuary was not a welcoming place. The powers that be had never really seen the need for fripperies; after all, almost everyone who went in through the door went in feet first (when present) so they were in no state to care and the living who tended the uncaring dead had long since ceased to notice the algae-streaked tiling, the flaking paint and the windows obscured by spiders' webs as thick as bombazine. Fanny Kempster worried about her husband working there, day in and day out, and had at one time tried to add a feminine touch. Here and there, on windowsills and shelves, were the remains of her efforts: jam jars with a few withered wild flowers; a china figurine, only slightly chipped; two Staffordshire dogs, though not a pair as they both faced the same way, resolutely looking out through the door, to the world of light and life.

It was really no place to bring a husband already almost insane with grief and worry but it was where the body was and so needs must when the devil drives. At least the woman was shrouded in a fairly clean sheet, her clothes decently hidden in a hamper rather than strewn about as was often the case. Selwyn Byng had struck lucky; the deceased who might be his wife had been tended by Felix Kempster's own caring hands and not by the usual casual ones of the mortuary attendant. Fanny had insisted – although the woman's private life seemed to leave something to be desired, she dressed like a lady and so she needed a little extra care for when her nearest and dearest came to see her.

Even so, most of that extra care was lost on Selwyn Byng. He stood, leaning heavily on both Grand and Batchelor, as Felix Kempster respectfully lowered the sheet which was shielding the dead woman's face. He had done his best with her hair, he had closed her eyes, he had made sure that the river's depredations were minimized with a touch here and there of his wife's rice powder and pale pink rouge, happily lent for the occasion. There was a bunch of chrysanthemums in her folded hands. She didn't look peaceful as such, but she certainly didn't look like a woman tossed and rolled for a day or two in a tidal river and then washed up on a shingly strand.

The two men edged Byng nearer. He didn't speak and after a moment or two, Grand peered into his face. 'You'll have to open your eyes, Selwyn,' he said, gently. 'There's nothing nasty to see, honestly there isn't. She just looks as though she's sleeping.' He might have been speaking to a child. From the small studio portrait he had seen he was sure enough that it was Emilia Byng but only her husband could say for sure. '*Please* open your eyes, Selwyn, just for a moment.'

He watched as the man's eyelids fluttered and first one and then another eye opened then almost instantaneously closed again, squeezing together as though glued. Byng nodded his head and kept on nodding, tears oozing out from under his lashes and washing down his cheeks. He opened his mouth to howl but nothing came. He sagged and would have fallen had it not been for his supporters, as firm and trusty as any on a shield on a tomb. Kempster lowered his eyes and his lips moved in a short prayer. He was not a religious man over and above the common, but he always said a few words over the dead; so many had no one else but he and even when they had, he said them, all the same. 'Into your hands, Lord, we commend her spirit,' Batchelor heard, as he and Grand half dragged Byng out into the hall, away from the smell of formaldehyde and river mud, away from the green-streaked tiles and dead daisies.

Kempster joined them in the waiting area, where Byng was now stretched out on a bench, his breathing stertorous, his face like grey wax.

'He's taking it hard,' the doctor said. He had watched many men identify their wives, their children, their mothers, fathers and friends before now but few had reacted like this.

'It's been a while coming,' Grand said, keeping his voice low. 'I think from the moment he got the first letter, he has been expecting something like this.'

'Letter?' Kempster was confused. 'She's been writing to him, has she? I hope you haven't misunderstood, gentlemen; this isn't a case of suicide, you know. It is definitely murder. Strangulation by ligature.'

Grand had seen the mark, inadequately covered by one of Fanny Kemspter's last year's scarves and nodded. 'Anonymous letters.' He tried to speak without moving his lips too much. 'She had been kidnapped.' The final word defeated his ventri-loquial attempt and he gave up, using a whisper instead.

'Kidnapped? Of course.' Kempster was putting things together. 'The finger.'

Batchelor hushed him. Byng was beginning to come round.

'Sorry.' The doctor dropped his voice. 'I see now. Yes, I can see that he would be under a lot of strain. But even so, I don't like his colour. Would you like me to give him something? A sedative?' He glanced down with professional detachment. 'A pick-me-up, perhaps. He certainly needs help of some kind.'

Byng suddenly spoke, his eyes still closed. 'I don't need drugs, doctor. I need to know who killed my wife. Who killed my little Emilia, who never did anyone an ounce of harm in all her life.'

The three men stood looking down at him. It was what everyone wanted; but how could they find out what had happened when the information was so scrappy, when Byng was so highly strung that you could practically play a jig on him? Grand turned to Kempster.

'Yes. Give him something. Whatever it takes to bring him round.' He only just stopped himself from suggesting a corpse-reviver, but Kempster got the message.

'You know where my house is?' he asked and the enquiry agents nodded. 'Walk him round there and I'll meet you in a minute. Fanny will make you comfortable and meanwhile, I'll send to Daddy Bliss that the body has been identified. He'll want to interview Mr Byng, I would imagine . . .'

'No,' screamed Byng, fluttering his hands in front of his face as though warding off moths, 'no, no, no police. They said no police. It's police that have brought Emilia to this place. No police, no, no . . .'

Kempster took a deep breath and raised his eyebrows then continued with barely a pause. 'Though I know that he often makes an exception, so what I will say is that Mrs Byng has been identified and that Mr Byng is currently having a well-earned rest.' His eyebrows continued their semaphore and Grand played along.

'That would be a good plan, Dr Kempster, thank you so much. Meanwhile, we'll see you at your house shortly, shall we?'

And nodding and smiling, they all went their separate ways, Byng's feet trailing behind him and his head lolling, Kempster hurrying off to the dispensary to make up something to bring round a dead man.

Fanny Kempster was, of course, more than equal to the occasion and she soon had Selwyn Byng ensconced in her husband's favourite chair by the fire, with a rug around his knees, a hot bottle at his feet and a cat on his knee. In her experience, there was nothing like a purring cat to calm a person down and although Grand and Batchelor had smiled condescendingly, they had to admit it seemed to be working. The grieving widower's fingers smoothed the thick coat of the calico cat and his breathing had slowed. His colour was coming back and the tense cords in his neck had all but disappeared. The cat, used to alarums and excursions, slept on through the racking sobs, but apart from them, the man in the chair could have passed for almost normal.

The sound of a key in the door made all but Byng turn and Fanny bustled off to bring her husband up to date on his patient's

condition. The low voices in the hall added their hum to the
general homely quiet of the Kempsters' sitting room and seemed
to lull Byng even further into a better place. But both Grand
and Batchelor knew that he would have to come out of it
soon; was it better to leave him there for a while longer, or get
the whole thing done and dusted and get on with finding who
had killed Emilia Byng?

Felix Kempster, followed by his hovering wife, came quietly
into the room but couldn't resist a chuckle when he saw the
cat, which simply cocked an eyebrow at him and carried on
purring. Sitting opposite the sobbing man, the doctor leaned
forward and slid expert fingers under his wrist. After a moment,
he let go and patted the man's hand. 'Feeling a little better,
Mr Byng?' he asked gently.

'A little,' the man sobbed. 'A little calmer, yes.'

'Well, my wife has gone to rustle up a warm drink for you,'
Kempster said. 'I have given her a powder to add to it which
will help you feel calmer still. No, no, don't worry.' He hastened
to explain. 'It isn't a drug, just a herbal remedy which my
patients find useful when they are overwrought. Ah, here she
is. You'll find it very palatable. Just drink up and we'll be back
to have a chat in a moment.'

With a final pat on Byng's hand, he relinquished the seat to
his wife and went over to where Grand and Batchelor patiently
waited. Batchelor sniffed the air. 'Surely, that's . . .'

Kempster shushed him. 'Laudanum,' he mouthed. 'Yes, that's
right. All herbal.'

Grand shrugged. A poppy was a herb, taken in the widest
sense, so Kempster hadn't exactly lied. 'How long do we have,
before he goes out like a light?' he asked.

'Well,' Kempster said, 'it isn't a precise science. And I did put
a small amount of accelerant in there to counteract the . . . er . . .
herbs, because I was worried about his colour. But I should think
in the region of ten, fifteen minutes. But surely, he can't help you,
can he? He never met the kidnappers, I assume, so . . .'

'Well,' Grand said, speaking low, 'the kidnappers knew
enough to get in touch with her uncles, they knew about the
trust.' He saw Kempster's eyes glaze with incomprehension.
'You'll have to just try and keep up, doctor, I'm sorry, we don't

have time to explain. So we think it must have been someone she knew, or at least who knew the family.'

Kempster's expression took on a man-of-the-world cast. 'Knew her very well, I think, gentlemen. There were signs of . . . well, I don't have to draw you a picture.'

'Really?' Batchelor's eyebrows rose and he moved in closer. 'Rape, you mean?'

'Not unless the man was a real gent,' Kempster whispered. 'There were no signs of coercion. No rope marks on ankles or wrists. No . . .' his natural diffidence took over and he stopped.

'I think we get the picture.' Grand was thoughtful. 'We had wondered if she had gone off with someone, right from the get-go.'

'That would fit the pattern,' Kempster said. 'She was well-nourished and though the food in the stomach was almost digested to nothing, there was nothing to suggest it was anything other than a well-balanced meal. My experience of people kept captive is small, as you may imagine, but in cases of post mortems of, say, workhouse inmates, a basic diet shows very differently compared to something you or I might eat. So someone she knew would be a good guess.'

'Or someone she came to know,' Batchelor said, thoughtfully.

'Sorry?' Grand was lost.

'Someone who snatched her and was a stranger at first but who she came to like. To love and trust, even.'

'Is that likely?' Kempster asked. 'Surely, she would hate her kidnapper?'

'Not necessarily,' Grand said. 'Now James has mentioned it, I have heard of girls in the West being taken by Indians and living happily with them, having children. Forgetting English, even.'

'Cynthia Parker,' Batchelor said.

'Fancy you knowing that.' Grand wasn't often impressed by his colleague, but he was now. He précised the story for Kempster. 'She was taken hostage by the Comanches, was it, or the Sioux . . .? Anyway, that isn't important. The important bit is that she assimilated into the tribe and it wasn't until she was rescued that she had all sorts of problems. I grant you it took years, but who knows – Emilia had been parted from her husband for a while, so she may have been hungry for affection and simply bonded with her kidnappers.'

While they talked, Fanny Kempster was tempting her patient to drink up his potion. She had sweetened it with honey and sprinkled some cinnamon on it and although to an educated nose it smelled of the poppy, to anyone else, it was simply a creamy milk drink. Byng, after his initial lassitude, drank it happily and drained the cup. Checking the dregs to make sure he had taken everything, she scrambled to her feet and went over to touch Grand on the elbow. 'He's drunk it all,' she whispered. 'You don't have long. I'll leave you to it, gentlemen.' With a smile she slid silently from the room.

Grand and Batchelor watched her go. 'You're a lucky man, Dr Kempster,' Grand told him and the doctor smiled and dipped his head. There wasn't a day that he didn't give thanks for his wife, but it was nice when someone else noticed as well.

The three men took seats alongside Byng around the cosy fire. 'Are you feeling a little stronger now, Mr Byng?' Kempster asked, again slipping his fingers around his wrist to check his pulse.

Byng looked at him, just slightly cross-eyed. 'Yes. I feel . . . I feel more relaxed now. I know Emilia is dead . . . and she's never coming back . . . but somehow, I can stand it. Whatever was in that drink, doctor?' His pupils stood wide. 'It tasted very good, I'll say that for it.'

'Good.' Kempster patted his hand. 'That's good. Now, Mr Grand and Mr Batchelor have a few questions for you, if you feel up to it.'

Byng nodded, slowly and deliberately. 'Umm-hmm. I can manage a few,' he said, good-naturedly. Neither of the agents had ever seen him so pleasant and they could now see what Emilia had married him for. With a smile on his face, no matter that it was a little vacant, he was quite handsome, in a ferrety sort of way.

'We'll keep it brief, Selwyn,' Grand said softly. 'Can you think of anyone who might want to hurt you?'

'Hurt me?' Byng was confused. 'It's Emilia who's been hurt.'

'Yes, but everyone knew how much you loved her. Taking her would be a way of getting back at you, of hurting you. Is there anyone who would do that, do you think? Do you have any enemies?'

Byng shook his head but soon stopped. He smiled up at Kempster. 'Giddy,' he said.

'Be quick,' Kempster said quietly to Grand. 'He's starting to go.'

'So, now you've had a think, is there anyone?' Batchelor prompted.

'There was Murphy Minor at school. He hated me. He kept making me apple pie beds.' He gave a reminiscent little chuckle. 'But I put woodlice in his tuck box so that showed him.' He looked down at the firelight reflected in the brass of the fender and turned his head this way and that, watching the light change.

'Quick,' urged Kempster.

'Since then,' Grand said. 'Who has hated you since then?'

Byng looked hurt. 'No one hates me, I don't think,' he said. He held out his hand to the fire. 'Look,' he said to the doctor, 'pink.' He smiled again, then frowned. 'Except my father of course. He hates me.' A tear ran down his cheek. 'Always has. Always will. He didn't hate Emilia, though. He loved Emilia. Everyone loved Emilia . . .' And with that, his head dropped forward onto his chest and he was asleep, drifting on clouds of poppy.

Fanny Kempster was, as always, keen to join in the discussion of the case, but the three men could see an embarrassing conversation in the offing and persuaded her to sit this one out. Incest was a tricky enough subject without it becoming a family issue.

They sat around the desk in the doctor's surgery for a long time, busying themselves with cigars and a small snifter of brandy each before finally, Batchelor cracked.

'Would Mr Byng senior really . . .?'

'I don't know the man,' Kempster said, 'but it certainly isn't unknown. I've had cases . . . mostly with blood relations. Of course, it isn't strictly incest without a blood link, but I think most people would frown . . . oh, dear, this is most difficult . . .'

'She was a very pretty girl,' Batchelor said, 'but not one to make a man mad, I wouldn't have thought.' He didn't think that counted as speaking ill of the dead, more a damning with faint praise.

'Look at the state her husband's in,' Grand said. 'She certainly has incited a grand passion in him.'

'Yes, but . . .' Batchelor had nothing more to add.

They sat there, intent on their cigars, until the gloom in the room was such that only the glowing tips revealed their presence. Mr Byng senior, they were all thinking. There's a turn-up for the books.

Daddy Bliss was up to his rowlocks in the dealers of horror, those ghouls who crept from the rat-infested wainscoting at moments like these, determined to see for themselves the ghastly spectres thrown up by the river. So it came as no surprise to Inspector Bliss that yet another ghoul turned up on the gangplank of the *Royalist* late that September Thursday, one that Constable Gosling had allowed on board. She was a well-set-up woman, perhaps thirty, with blonde hair swept up under a fashionable bonnet. Her boots were spring-sided and the train of her skirt was looped up to show just an inch or so of lace to keep the hem out of the river mud. Bliss sat at his table under the swaying oil lamp, blinking and trying to take it all in.

'Who did you say you were again?' he asked.

'Cailey,' she said. 'Mary Cailey. Mrs.'

Bliss never liked to appear taken aback, especially not by a woman. 'So . . . reports of your demise were exaggerated, then?'

'Who said I'd demised?' Mrs Cailey wanted to know.

'Well, your landlady thought it might be a possibility,' he told her.

'Christian?' Mary Cailey almost spat the word. 'Interfering old trout. I never liked her, not from the first day.'

'Then there was . . .' Bliss checked his ledger, open on the table in front of him, '. . . a Mr Abel Beer, who positively identified a corpse found in the river as you. He *is* your brother?'

'Sadly, yes,' she sighed. 'But Abel's a few trapeze artistes short of a circus. He loves all that sort of thing. Cried for days when Granddad died and he couldn't stand Granddad. Bloody drama queen.'

'Then there's your *other* brother, Mr Ambrose Beer. He *thought* it was you.'

'Until recently,' Mary Cailey scowled, 'Ambrose thought babies came from gooseberry bushes. Not quite the ticket.'

'And of course, your sister . . .'

'Millicent would say anything Abel told her to. Look, Inspector, I'm not too proud to admit that the Beers of Wookey aren't made of the sterner stuff. Well, there's still a lot of in-breeding, if you know what I mean, in the West Country. That's partly why we moved to Uplyne.'

'But you . . .'

'I was lucky enough to escape all that. Every generation produces a normal one and I'm it.'

'So where have you been, Mrs Cailey?' Bliss asked, 'if you haven't been bobbing about in the river or lying on a mortuary slab?'

'If you must know,' she said, 'I have been to Scotland with a gentleman.'

'His name?' Bliss, like Grand and Batchelor, liked to leave no stone unturned.

'Is none of your business,' she told him flatly.

'And your solicitor, Mr Thompson of Lincoln's Inn?'

'Don't know what you're talking about,' she shrugged.

'And the dear old lady you spent time with, at an address in a London square that doesn't exist?'

'I don't know what they're putting in your tea,' she remarked with a laugh, pointing to the tin cup on the table.

Bliss, of course, wasn't laughing. 'I could charge you with wasting police time,' he said.

'Look,' she snapped. 'I only come here out of the goodness of my heart. I read in the papers about the missing Mrs Cailey. Well, I'm not missing. I never was.'

'Indeed not. Constable Gosling,' the inspector bellowed up the stairs.

'Sir?' The constable appeared in the hatch doorway.

'Take Mrs Cailey to 15, South Street, Battersea Fields, will you? The landlady there is Mrs Christian and Mrs Cailey owes her several weeks' rent. See to it that she pays, will you?'

''Ere,' Mary Cailey shrieked as she felt the constable's iron grip on her elbow. 'You can't do that!'

'Yes, he can,' Bliss assured her. 'He's the River Police.'

And Mary Cailey was still shouting the odds as Constable Gosling hailed a cab on the moonlit dockside and bundled them both into it.

'What was all that, Inspector?' Constable Brandon was up on deck with his boss, a steaming mug of tea in his hand.

'That, lad,' Bliss said, 'was the unusual sight of a member of the public helping the police with their enquiries.'

'Did I overhear right,' the constable asked, 'that all her family identified her as the second . . . you know . . . body?'

'They did,' Bliss took the cup that cheered, 'and I'm still, after all these years, amazed by the stupidity of folk. It's my guess that our Mrs Cailey earns her money on her back – or any other position her gentlemen friends require of her. Her brother Abel may or may not act as her pimp and they thought they'd try a new manor here in London. I don't know much about this Wookey place, or Uplyne, but I'm prepared to bet they're quite small, Metropolis-wise. More money to be made where the streets are paved with gold, eh?'

'But, all her family . . .'

'Identified her, yes. Perhaps I should have paid more attention to the one eye in the middle of their foreheads. More likely, they sniffed some sort of reward and thought they could cash in.'

'Whereas . . .?'

'Whereas it's my guess that said Mrs Cailey had met a client who whisked her away – maybe even to Scotland, who knows? She invented the business deal, the solicitor, the old lady, just to keep Mrs Christian quiet. As for the four men on Victoria Bridge, that sort of thing says it all, doesn't it? What class of woman is most likely to be set upon by roughs, Brandon?'

'Er . . . the underclass, sir.' Even in the moonlight and the *Royalist*'s swaying lanterns, Bliss could see the constable blush.

'Exactly. Nobody's knocked Her Royal Highness the Princess of Wales about much recently, have they?'

'No, indeed, sir.' Lloyd Brandon was sure of that. 'The only question is – who knocked the women in the river about?'

Bliss paused in mid-slurp. 'That's right, boy,' he said, patting the lad's shoulder. 'And that's why I keep you on. Somewhere underneath that lily-livered exterior, there are the faint stirrings of a policeman.' He pulled a face. 'And talking of faint stirrings,' he said, 'any sugar in this tea?'

SIXTEEN

By the time the cab had rattled through Southwark, Mary Cailey had calmed down. She had been this close to policemen before, but not from this constabulary and she didn't quite know what Inspector Bliss had in mind for her. Wasting police time, he had said, but that could be the least of it. And there was the matter of the unpaid rent to that miserable old cow who had briefly been her landlady. All in all, the decision made by Abel and herself to move to the pastures new that were London had not worked out too well.

'It's nice of you to see me home,' she smiled at Tom Gosling sitting alongside her in the cab. 'Not that I've actually got a home, of course, not anymore.'

'All in a day's work, madam,' the constable said. He'd been up and down the river a few times, had Tom Gosling and he knew every ploy in the book. In a minute, this woman would not only be asking him to let her go but suggest he pay her back rent too.

'No, I feel really bad about those stories I told that nice Mrs Christian. And your inspector, too, come to think of it. He must be a really great bloke to work with.' She grinned up at him.

'Oh, the best,' Gosling assured her.

'I think it's time I told you the truth.' She bowed her head.

Here we go, thought Gosling.

'Your inspector, brilliant man that he is, was absolutely right. There is no solicitor in Lincoln's Inn. Nor is there a sweet old lady in Chelsea – well, there are probably loads of 'em, but I don't know any. That was all Abel's idea.'

'Abel Beer,' Gosling checked. 'Your brother.'

'And my . . . what do you call them here? My bully.'

'Oh, you mean pimp,' Gosling realized. 'I believe the term "bully" went out with the late Mr Dickens.'

'He made me do it.' Mary Cailey was sobbing demurely. 'Ever since we were kids. He'd hire me out to his mates, in the barn, down the orchard. You show me yours and I'll show you mine.'

Gosling started and then realized that this was simply part of the narrative and sat back again.

'They'd pay sweets at first. Then it gravitated – is that the word?'

Gosling shrugged. It might have been.

'Gravitated to money. And there was no stopping him. For every quid he made, I got five bob.'

'Hardly seems fair,' Gosling commented.

'You're right, Constable . . . er . . .?'

'Gosling, miss.'

'Constable Gosling.' She laughed through her tears. 'That's funny.'

Tom Gosling had lived with his surname for so long now, he'd ceased to see the funny side. 'Is it really?' he asked.

'No, I mean, when I was a *little* girl, back in Wookey, I used to look after the geese. I used to love feeding the goslings. All warm and fluffy.'

Was that a gloved hand fondling the constable's knee or had he imagined it?

'Of course, as we got older and Abel began to charge more for my services, those services got ever more . . . shall we say . . . adventurous?'

'Did they now?' Gosling was trying not to look at her.

'Oh, I don't suppose any of it would turn a hair here in London, but back home . . . Well, I mean . . .' She reached over, cupping her hand as she whispered in his ear. He missed some of it due to the noise of creaking harness and clopping hoofs, but he got the general gist. '. . . with two choirboys . . . in the squire's parlour . . . well, I'm not sure how he got there . . . I'm not sure who he was, but he was wearing – briefly – the get-up of a bishop.'

'Fascinating,' said Gosling, beginning to feel a little hot under the collar in spite of himself. 'Well, here we are.'

They were. The cab rocked to a halt outside Number 15 and the constable was only too pleased to leap out onto the pavement. He paid the cabbie, well aware of Daddy Bliss's constant warnings about bribe-taking and turned to face his ex-fellow traveller.

Gosling stood rooted to the spot. Mary Cailey was in the grip of an assailant, as the constable would have put it in court. In short, a mad bastard in threadbare clothes had her held fast from behind, one arm across the woman's breasts, the other holding a knife at her throat. Mary Cailey's eyes were wide with terror and her mouth was open in a silent scream. As though her attacker realized the danger, he clapped his hand over her mouth and pulled her backwards towards the shrubbery.

'Now, then,' Gosling held up his hand, about to take a step forward. 'We don't want any trouble, do we?'

Gosling had talked down lunatics before, those dribbling, wild-eyed men who haunted both banks of the Thames. He knew the drill – keep the movements slow, the voice soft and gentle.

'Who are you?' the attacker asked him.

Mary Cailey recognized the West Country burr at once, but the subtlety was lost on Gosling.

'I am Constable Thomas Gosling of the River Police,' he said. That was another part of the drill – honesty.

'The river, eh? You're as lost as I am, copper.'

'You know my name, sir,' the constable said. 'Might I know yours?'

'You might,' he said, 'if you kept your eyes open and read your own posters. I am William Bisgrove if you want to know. And I didn't kill nobody. Did I, Millie? You'll tell 'em, won't you?'

There was a muffled scream from Mary Cailey.

'I don't think the lady can tell us anything, Mr Bisgrove,' Gosling said, 'with your hand over her mouth. Why don't you let her go . . .?'

'No!' Bisgrove pulled the terrified woman further towards the park. 'It's taken me months to find her. I'm not letting her go now.'

'No, no,' Gosling was understanding itself. 'No, of course not. I didn't mean let her go completely, just let her breathe. She's turning a funny colour.'

In the street lamp's green glow, Gosling couldn't see what colour Mary Cailey had turned, but he was playing for time. If he could just reach the truncheon at his belt . . .

'And you're not going to scream, are you, Millie?' Gosling was nodding furiously, urging the woman to play along. It all fell into place now, the reports that he had read in the files and the *Police News*. Bisgrove had escaped from Broadmoor and a woman called Millie was involved in his case. Mistaken identity? Probably, but mistaken identities got people killed.

Mary shook her head frantically.

'I'm sorry, Millie,' Bisgrove hissed in her ear. 'I didn't want it to come to . . .' He stopped, frowning. 'Wait a minute,' and he let his hand fall. All Tom Gosling's urgings of a moment ago had achieved nothing. As soon as her mouth was free and the blade tip had left her neck, she screamed with a noise that could shatter glass.

Gosling saw his moment and lunged. His truncheon was in his hand and he threw himself at Bisgrove. The man turned, but too slowly and both men landed in the leaves blown by autumn into damp piles. The constable found his feet first, but he swung too high with the truncheon and the hardwood merely whistled over Bisgrove's head. The West Countryman hurled himself forward, driving his shoulder into the pit of Gosling's stomach and the policeman went down.

Mary had run to the steps of Number 15, hammering on the door for all she was worth. She saw a net curtain shiver to one side and heard the rattle and scrape of bolts. The door swung inwards and Mary Christian stood there, already in her night attire but brandishing a poker in her hand. Both women stared at the scene below them. Tom Gosling was kneeling upright, his own truncheon held horizontally under his chin by William Bisgrove, who was deciding whether to break the man's neck or not.

'Don't!' both women screamed and Bisgrove stopped. For a moment, he blinked, glancing around him, unsure of exactly where he was. Then he relaxed and brought the truncheon down on the policeman's cranium. Gosling slumped onto the leaves like a child suddenly overtaken by sleep and lay there, curled and looking almost comfortable.

To the horror of the ladies, Bisgrove was making his way towards them. This was Battersea. Nobody else was going to come running at the sound of a woman's scream and the thudding on a door. Life was all too precious for that. Bisgrove, with the truncheon in one hand and the knife in the other, took the first step, then the second. He ignored Mary Christian completely. The last time he'd seen her she'd chased him with a broom; now she was shaking a poker at him. Unpleasant, these London landladies, and no mistake.

He followed their gaze, to the fallen policeman. 'He'll be all right,' he said. 'Just a bit of a headache, that's all.' He threw the truncheon down on the leaves beside him.

Then he fixed his hypnotic gaze on Mary Cailey. He slipped the knife back into his coat pocket. 'I'm sorry, ma'am,' he muttered. 'I thought you were somebody else. You look *so* like my Millie, but now I see you up close, I can see I was wrong.' He turned to go, then stopped. 'But I *will* find her,' he said, 'my Millie. She's out there somewhere. And I'll clear my name. You see if I don't.'

And he was gone, another shadow in the shadows.

James Batchelor looked in the mirror in his bedroom and couldn't decide whether his tie was wonky or whether there was a serious flaw in the glass. As he twisted this way and that, it did seem to fluctuate, so he decided to go and ask Matthew Grand, who was more adept at such sartorial detail. He tapped on his bedroom door and was invited in.

'Matthew, does this tie look right to you?'

Grand looked at it with his head on one side and grimaced. 'It depends,' he said, enigmatically, and went back to primping his own appearance in the mirror above the washstand. Maisie stood ready with hot water and a soft, warm towel. Batchelor gave her a sidelong glance and made a mental note to discuss engaging a valet; this household was definitely too female and the hot look in Maisie's eye was more than a little unsettling.

'On what?' He stepped over to the mirror and examined himself over Grand's shoulder.

'On whether you want to look as if you tied that tie this year or about five years ago. It is a little passé, James. Look at mine. Lady Caroline says it is up to the minute; up to the second, actually. Ow!' He jumped back. 'No more hot water, Maisie, please. You nearly scalded me, there.'

'Sorry,' the girl muttered and looked down mulishly. Grand might be up to the second, he might even be a good enquiry agent, but when it came to spotting doglike devotion under his very nose, he left a lot to be desired.

'As for your tie, it will do as well as any other. I've been to this theatre before; you will see all sorts there, so you won't stand out.'

'Are you sure?' Batchelor gave the errant tie another tug. 'I wouldn't want to let you down.'

'No, really. I have met Lady Hester before as well; a lovely woman. Not at all . . .'

'Not at all what? Picky? Good-looking? Normal? What?'

'I was going to say not at all one to bother if her escort's tie isn't in the first flight of fashion. She is something of a blue stocking, so you two can talk poetry or whatnot all night if you want to. That's all. She is perfectly pretty, perfectly normal.' Grand turned from the mirror and grabbed Batchelor firmly by the shoulders and gave him a shake. 'You look very much the man about town. Handsome, wouldn't you say, Maisie?'

Her eyes widened and she took a deep breath. 'That depends,' she blurted out, and fled.

'Sometimes I wonder if that girl is quite the ticket, James, I really do.'

Batchelor rolled his eyes, but it would get neither of them anywhere to get involved in long explanations now. 'As long as you're sure the tie will pass muster, we should be going. Don't want to keep the ladies waiting.'

Grand laughed and shrugged into his jacket. 'You can tell it's a while since you accompanied a lady anywhere, James; the last lady I kept waiting was my mother when I was born two weeks later than expected. Since then, I have done nothing but wait for them. But you're right, we should be gone. We don't want to miss the first turn. As memory serves, it is quite funny. Some kind of comic juggler, but I won't spoil it for you.'

And, putting aside the cares of Selwyn Byng and the rest of the world, they went down the stairs, chattering like schoolgirls.

Mrs Rackstraw watched them go from the shadow under the stairs. She was glad they were having a night off; they were spending too much time with lunatics, and that rarely ended well, as she knew only too well. To stop herself from dwelling too much on painful memories, she made her way to the kitchen, to find fault with some of Maisie's handiwork; that always made her feel rather better.

Despite – or it may be because of, Batchelor didn't like to overthink it – his unfortunate tie, the evening was going well. Caroline and Grand didn't seem to notice anything or anyone around them, having eyes only for each other. Batchelor and Hester were in the middle of a complex argument on the subject of the symbolism of Morris's *The Earthly Paradise*. Were Batchelor to have been questioned and he decided to tell the truth, he had hardly any idea what the woman was talking about, but her eyes were soft and blue, her lips pink and sensuous and her cheek smooth and rosy, so he didn't really care. He had not fallen into the obvious trap of saying how much he admired the man's fabric designs and so the evening was going well. The bell for the second half sounded and the ladies suddenly realized that a call of nature was essential and went off, twittering together as Grand and Batchelor made their way back to their box.

'What do you think of Hester?' Grand said.

'She's very pretty,' Batchelor said. 'And intelligent, of course. Lovely, in fact.'

'You don't mind, then?' Grand was enigmatic.

'Mind?'

'About the wooden leg.'

'The *what*?' Batchelor was aghast. He now had only one choice; he either made his excuses and left or made the best of it. 'She doesn't limp or anything . . .' His eyes were wide and stricken.

Grand nudged him. 'Just joshing,' he said. 'She has as many legs as you require and from what I hear, they are stunners. Play your cards right, James my boy, and you'll find out tonight.'

'I wouldn't be so crass.' No man had a higher horse to mount than James Batchelor.

'Crass won't come into it,' Grand assured him. 'She's been having an affair with some old geezer in the city or something for years, so she's no prude, I can assure you. But if you'd rather take your time, well, some women like that too.'

Batchelor was still aghast but not in quite the same way. The non-Puritan half of him was rather looking forward to the rest of the evening. The lights began to dim and the women rejoined them in the box, Hester snuggling up close to Batchelor and stroking a thigh with a practised hand. Yes, this evening could end very nicely, thank you very much!

The second half of the show was announced by the master of ceremonies as a drama set in an old haunted house, fit to chill the blood. The curtain rose and slowly the limelight picked out the detail of the set which seemed to be mostly made up of cobweb-hung furniture of antique style. The silence was split by a scream followed by a scraping violin from the orchestra pit and a girl dressed in very little ran into the middle of the stage and stood there, eyes wide and arms outstretched to the audience.

'Help me,' she cried to every man in the theatre. 'My wicked uncle Septimus is trying to kill me. Hark!'

Every ear strained to hear it and yes, there it was, the dragging step of a deranged guardian in search of young flesh to strangle and destroy.

'He comes!'

On a drum roll and a clash of cymbals, a misshapen creature lurched on from the prompt side, causing all the women in the audience to gasp and clutch their companions. Because of the position of her hand, Hester's clutch also caused Batchelor to gasp, but he turned it into a cough and it went unnoticed.

The evil creature on the stage had wild white hair and an outdated suit of clothes. His feet were encased in oversize shoes which gave him a lop-sided gait. One arm seemed longer than the other, but that was probably caused by the enormous hump on his back. He drooled. His eyes swivelled madly in his head. All in all, when the director had chosen him for a homicidal maniac, he had done his job well. With a background of screams from his ward who hid behind furniture, always making sure to leave a pert bottom or heaving bosom on show, he capered to and fro, brandishing a blood-dripping knife which had appeared from nowhere.

Grand leaned across to Batchelor and whispered, 'Not very realistic. Whose is that blood, for instance?'

Batchelor laughed and whispered back, 'I expect the comic policeman will soon solve that.'

Nodding and smiling, Grand straightened up and turned back to the stage, then stiffened. He looked at Batchelor to see if he had seen it too.

'Matthew?'

Yes, he had.

'Is that . . . can it be?'

'It certainly seems that way. It's Selwyn Byng's butler.' Grand disentangled Lady Caroline's arm from around his neck. 'Do you think we ought to follow this up?'

Batchelor looked down at his lap. Lady Hester's fingers certainly seemed quite firmly enmeshed in his unmentionables and it might be rude to intervene. 'No, we can catch him back-stage after the performance.'

Grand's eyebrows rose to unprecedented height. 'If you're sure . . .'

'I'm quite sure,' Batchelor smiled. 'After all, he isn't going to lose all that makeup in five minutes, is he?'

'True.' Grand settled back. 'Later, then. We'll catch him later.'

There had been no discernible 'later' that night. Before the enquiry agents knew what was afoot, they were being bundled out of the carriage at their doorstep, with a delicate sheen of lip rouge on their cheek and some rather tumbled underclothing. The ladies were already in a giggling huddle before the carriage had turned the corner; what a night *that* was.

'So, the mad old uncle, then?' Batchelor said over his shoulder as he tried to fit his key into the lock.

'I said I'd seen him somewhere, didn't I?' Grand was just a little smug.

'Yes, I don't really understand that,' Batchelor said. 'Had you seen that performance before?'

Grand shrugged. 'Bits of it.' He only ever saw bits of anything when out on the town with Lady Caroline. 'They change the sketches from time to time. I seem to remember him being the evil squire last time.'

'Well spotted, anyway,' Batchelor said. 'I'm not quite sure whether we're any further forward, though. I grant, it's unusual to have a butler moonlighting as an actor, but perhaps he doesn't get top wages.'

'Or an actor moonlighting as a butler,' Grand pointed out.

'True. What do they call it? Resting? Selwyn keeps a rather splendid house for someone who clearly gets a pittance from his father. Perhaps he can't afford a full-time butler.'

'True. And he didn't have any other staff as far as I could see. Did you notice anyone else?'

'No. It could be he just runs on a minimum, so he looks the part of the city gent. His father obviously lives high off the hog.' Batchelor finally succeeded in working the key and they tiptoed across the hall. 'He called the house in Milner Street poky. He must live in a palace to call it that.'

'Or he could just not want to give Selwyn the benefit of being a person in his own right. I've known people like him – hates his children but doesn't want them to leave home and live separately. Wants to control everyone.'

Batchelor nodded. 'You might be right at that. Byng senior is too tight to let anyone go.' He giggled, the champagne again asserting its ascendancy. 'I've heard he doesn't fart. Too mean to part with it.'

Grand guffawed. Batchelor wasn't often funny, but that struck him as very funny indeed. As did the gas light on low to show them their way along the landing. As did his wardrobe and his bed, turned down lovingly by Maisie. He might not have seen the funny side of the girl standing motionless in the shadow cast by the drawn curtains, but that didn't matter; he was already asleep.

Breakfast was a solemn meal. Mrs Rackstraw tried her best to raise the mood with a few well-chosen sallies on the state of the nation but they fell on deaf ears. And whatever Mrs Rackstraw knew about the University Tests Act could be written on the head of a pin, when all was said and done. Maisie lay the toast extra quietly on the plates and picked out the more challenging bits of peel from the marmalade before placing the bowl in front of the object of her affections, but all to no avail.

Eventually, Batchelor raised his head from where it had been resting in his hands. 'I suppose,' he ventured, in a low voice and taking care not to move his mouth too much, 'we should go and see Mr Byng, senior.'

'Why?' Grand asked. 'Remind me again.'

'We wondered,' Batchelor said, trying to be heard over the drummer sitting just behind his eyes, 'you, me and Inspector Bliss, whether he might have been rather more friendly than is expected with his daughter-in-law.'

'Oh, yes. I remember now. I suppose we should go and ask him. But . . . he doesn't need money, does he?'

'Who knows who needs money?' Batchelor asked, rhetorically. 'But it might not have been about the money, it might have been to destroy his son.'

'And Emilia was in on it, you think?' Grand's brain cells were beginning to line up again and he risked a piece of toast, giving up when the knife scraping against its surface hurt his ears.

'Yes. Don't you?'

'Hmm. I don't know what to think.' Grand shut his eyes. 'I can't think, not really.' He carefully put down his knife and rose to his feet. 'Look, James, I'll tell you what I am going to do. I'm going to have a lie down. Send word to Daddy Bliss that we are going to see Byng senior and does he want to come. But later. Much later. How about after dark?' And very slowly and carefully, he made his way to the stairs. Batchelor could hardly bear to watch him; it was not a nice thought that, if anything, he himself looked a lot worse than that. He closed his eyes and tugged the bell pull; Maisie could go. She should be out and about in the fresh air, girl her age. She was looking a bit peaky. He felt the air change as someone self-effacing came into the room and slowly, with lots of false starts, he finally gave her her instructions then, as she almost danced out of the room, let his head loll forward onto his chest. His last thought as he passed out was that he never, never *ever* wanted to spend another evening with Ladies Caroline and Hester. In fact, if he set eyes on them ever again, it would be too soon.

SEVENTEEN

L ater that day, as dusk was falling over London and hiding all her little imperfections and gilding her glory with pure gold, Grand, Batchelor and Bliss met on the pavement outside the Byng residence in Holland Park. Its perfect white façade gleamed in the sunset of the autumn evening and every window showed a glow of candles and lamps. Someone was definitely at home. The enquiry agents were feeling more their usual selves; a diet throughout the day of dry toast, tea and sips of seltzer had finally done its work and they could hardly wait to lock horns with Byng. Bliss was, as always, less enthusiastic. He felt ill at ease more than a street or two away from the River and this place was positively landlocked. He had read what notes he had on the Byng case and although the father had seemed a good collar at the time, now he wasn't half so sure. But he was always up for a bit of overtime; Mrs Byng hadn't had a new hat in a while, or so she told him every hour on the hour, so he would go along with this insanity, see where it led them. He was a man down while Gosling recovered from his brush with the lunatic, but things had quietened down on the river now the body count stood at zero. In any event, this evening should be good for a cigar or two, not to say a decent brandy. He mounted the steps and smartly knocked on the door.

It was opened by a shadowy figure who ushered them in. When Batchelor, bringing up the rear, got through the door, the butler or whatever factotum it had been, had disappeared. The last hangover fragment in his brain made him think of *Beauty and the Beast* and invisible servants. Shaking his head to rid himself of the fantasy, he caught up with the others as they went through an open door into an opulent study.

If Mr Byng was tight-fisted at his place of business, he stinted on nothing in his home. The room was elegant, tasteful and the very antithesis of his son's home, but welcoming and warm. The fire crackled and the smell of apple wood overlaid the scents coming from bowls of potpourri placed strategically around on the gleaming mahogany furniture. Byng had clearly been seated by the fire but now stood up and came towards them, hand outstretched.

'How may I help you, gentlemen?' he said, pleasantly.

The three looked at each other. They hadn't expected this but in some respects, it made his role as kidnapper and seducer seem more realistic. If he could be so different here from when he was at the timber warehouse, how many other personas did he have tucked away somewhere?

'Now that we have identified the body of your daughter-in-law, sir,' Bliss said, 'we must interview everyone who could possibly shed light on the subject. And you, as her father-in-law, are naturally our first port of call.' He couldn't help the odd nautical phrase; it had started as an affectation and now it was part of who he was.

'I am confused, Inspector. Your card here tells me you are from Thames Division – the River Police.'

'That is correct, sir.'

'And these gentlemen are *private* detectives.'

'Enquiry agents,' Batchelor corrected him.

'Is it usual, Inspector, for an officer of the police, whom I must assume to be a professional, to carry out his enquiries with amateurs in tow? You'll be bringing some dotty knitting spinster with you next.'

'Funny you should say that, sir,' Bliss said, looking meaningfully at Batchelor, but he wasn't laughing.

'I do see that you need to pursue enquiries,' Byng said, turning back to his seat by the fire, 'but I don't see how I can help. I didn't . . . socialize . . . with my son and his wife. I disapproved of their marriage, of their domicile, of their . . . frankly bizarre way of living. I see Selwyn every day in the office. I had no need of his companionship in the evenings too.'

'But Emilia?' Grand asked. 'Surely, you were fond of Emilia?'

Byng waved his hand inviting the men to sit. 'She was a nice enough little thing. Far too young to marry, in my opinion. I believe that young people should see the world, experience things before they marry. She had become a little housewife,

far before her time. And now what? She is dead on a slab and
had no idea of what she could have been.' He picked up his
cigar and puffed it vigorously. 'Sad, I suppose.'

Batchelor was relieved to see him revert to his previous
self; the Nice Byng was a little frightening. 'Of course it's sad,'
he burst out. 'Your son is prostrated.'

'Yes, he is.' Byng didn't argue with that. 'He is always prostrated. It's a shame you never saw him when he stubbed his toe.
Same thing.' Another puff and a swig of brandy. 'He is just
rather dramatic. He'll get over it.'

This didn't strike any of them as the demeanour of a man
whose mistress was dead in horrible circumstances, but he was
a difficult man to measure. While Grand and Batchelor cast
around for the next subtle question, Bliss went in for the kill.

'It is our belief, Mr Byng, that you collaborated with your
daughter-in-law to make your son think she had been kidnapped.
You then demanded money with menaces. We also believe that
you and your daughter-in-law were indulging in unnatural
practices which eventually led to her death.'

Batchelor leaned across and whispered in the policeman's ear.

'Yes, and the death of her maid, Molly.'

Byng was in the middle of a glug of brandy and almost
choked. After going a very alarming purple, he recovered himself
and looked at the men with bulging eyes. 'Are you all *mad*?'
he said at last. 'Whyever . . . well, I hardly want to give credibility to such an insane idea. Me and Emilia? Never in a million
years. I like women, not chits like her. And as for . . . what
was that other thing?'

'Demanding money with menaces,' Bliss repeated.

'What do I want with money got in such a way? Can you
not see the way I live?'

'Living like this doesn't necessarily mean you can afford it,'
Grand pointed out. His family had grown rich in the early days
from defaulted mortgages.

'True,' Byng conceded. 'But I can. And what's that about a
maid? I didn't even know she *had* a maid. No, gentlemen,' he
said, 'I could call my legal representatives, I suppose, or send
around a note to Edmund Henderson – presumably you know
he is Commissioner of Police – who happens to be a member

of my club. I could send for a footman or two to give you all
a sound drubbing and throw you out into the street. But I think
what I will do, and this will cause less trouble all around, is to
tell you that you are wrong on every count and leave it at that.
My word as a gentleman should suffice.'

'It certainly should,' Grand said, 'but you can surely see we
need more proof than that. Someone to swear to your every
movement since Emilia disappeared would be helpful. And I
don't expect you can produce *that*.' He sounded confident
enough, but actually could feel the ground shifting under their
feet. What had seemed so certain was now far from that.

'I can't supply just one person, of course I can't. Could you?'

The others shook their heads.

'But two or three people . . . I think I can do that. For my
day at the office, of course you have any number of people
to choose from, including Selwyn, if I am allowed to use
someone so inextricably linked with this whole sorry business.
For my journey to and fro – well, I have a groom of course,
who drives me and brings me home. For my evenings and
nights,' he got up and went to a door they hadn't noticed,
concealed by book shelves, 'you'll have to excuse me a
moment.' He put his head around the door and they heard him
say softly, 'Could you just step this way, my dear? Some
gentlemen need to see you for a moment.'

In a slither of silk and a flash of diamonds at her throat, a
woman entered the room and stood at Byng's side, holding onto
his arm and looking up into his face. 'Of course, dearest,' she
said. 'How can I assist?' She turned her beaming face to the
three men, all now on their feet. 'Whatever I can . . . oh!' Her
face lit up. 'James! Matthew! How lovely to see you again! Are
you feeling better?' She looked up at Byng again and said, 'Mr
Batchelor and Mr Grand felt rather unwell at the theatre last
night, my darling. Caroline and I had to take them home.'

Byng bent and kissed the top of her head. 'So kind,' he
murmured. 'So, gentlemen, will that be all?'

Bliss looked at Grand and Batchelor and if looks could kill
he would have had two more bodies on his hands.

Grand spoke for them all. 'Yes, that will be all,' he murmured.
'Good night, Lady Hester.'

She sketched him a small curtsy.

'Goodnight, Matthew,' she said. 'Goodnight, James. Sleep tight.'

The last the men saw of them was Byng standing like a conqueror, his arm around his prize, lit from behind by the firelight.

'Well,' Bliss began.

'Don't,' Batchelor said. 'Just . . . don't. I'll walk home, thank you.'

'But it's miles,' Bliss pointed out, but he was already gone.

Mr Micah and Mr Teddy both liked a bit of Doric. Both had a niggling respect for Ionic as well. Kensal Green cemetery offered both those architectural styles and more, so they approved Selwyn Byng's choice for the laying to rest of Emilia even before they had sorrowfully accepted the black-edged invitation to her funeral.

They were less happy about the catacombs but as the rain drove down in torrents that sad Friday, it was probably just as well. Messrs Jay had pulled out all the stops, the grim black stallions under their nodding plumes shaking rainwater all over the devout few who had lined the road, taking off their caps as the cortege passed. Inside the hearse with its black struts and ostrich-rich canopy, the curved glass revealed the coffin of Emilia Byng, resplendent in the finest black tupelo straight from the warehouse of Sillitoe, Byng and Son at wholesale rates; Byng senior was, after all, not completely without finer feelings. The dark wood was finished off with brass fittings and festooned with flowers, the lilies of death.

Alongside, the mutes walked silently, their tall wands black against the grey of the sky, their faces a tragic white thanks to generous application of greasepaint, the real tears of the rain mixing with the glycerine ones they had painted on.

In the first carriage behind the hearse, Selwyn Byng rode alone, his face an immobile mask, his shining black topper cradled in his lap. Behind him came Micah and Teddy Westmoreland in their carriage, dabbing their eyes at the sorrow of the day. Next came Mr Byng senior, again alone, his eyes hollow, his mouth set into a tight, disapproving line. The others

Grand and Batchelor didn't know, until they recognized Miss Moriarty's coach. The old girl looked terrifying behind her veil, like death itself sunk deep into the plush velveteen. As befitted someone of her age and so that she didn't miss a word that might be said, either to her or about her, she carried a Vulcanite ear-trumpet swathed in black silk. Enid carried the necessary medicaments in her clutch bag. They probably had a holiday in the Yorkshire town of Whitby for all the jet jewellery that the ladies wore that day and the monogram of Sillitoe, Byng and Son shone everywhere from each mourning coach and the harness of the horses.

As non-family members, Grand and Batchelor were not given the honour or the luxury of a coach of their own. A cab had brought them to the great mausoleum gate of Kensal Green and they waited there to watch the sad procession pass. It came to rest outside the Anglican chapel that Messrs Griffith and Chadwick had designed forty years before. It was beginning to show its age, with green water-marks dripping down the corners of the once immaculate stone portico but most people drawing up in front of it were not in the mood to notice its shortcomings. A lawn-sleeved vicar with an umbrella waited to welcome them. Selwyn Byng had put his hat on now and had to be supported by various people as the coffin was lowered gently out of the hearse and onto the broad shoulders of the pall-bearers. The horses shifted as the weight lessened on their hames and Grand and Batchelor followed the dripping procession inside.

Like the pied piper, the vicar led them down a tight spiral staircase that curved away to the left. The pall-bearers were past masters at this but all of them secretly cursed Selwyn Byng for his instructions. Most people held the service on the ground floor and their nearest and dearest were lowered to the catacombs by the clever hydraulic gadget installed for just that purpose. Neither Grand nor Batchelor had been here before but the place looked like something from *Varney the Vampire* or *The Castle of Otranto*. The stanchions were brick clad, turning to stone at the ceiling as copies of a Medieval vault. In rows on each side lay coffins, the wood draped in greenish, once black and purple, velvet, the brass studs glowing eerily in the light of the lanterns and candles carried by the vicar's people and the mutes. It had been chilly enough in the rainswept entrance, but here below ground-level the cold was augmented by a different kind of damp, one that seeped through the bones of the living from the bones of the dead.

Here and there stood monuments, granite columns snapped off as cruel death snaps a life. Angels sat weeping, their heads in their hands and little cherubs stood solemnly over the graves of children. The bell that clanged above tolled for them all.

The enquiry agents watched everyone from their positions at the back. The mourners were few in number but all seemed heartfelt and as one in their loss. Selwyn Byng sat alone in the front pew, his back straight but it was clear that he stood there at all only by a superhuman effort of the will. Teddy and Micah, as always, were towers of strength to each other, leaning one to the other and wielding identical black-bordered hand-kerchiefs when it all got too much. Miss Moriarty had chosen a seat where she couldn't see Teddy; some things still couldn't be borne, especially at a funeral. Enid passed her a discreet flask from time to time, spirits to keep her spirits up.

The coffin, carefully manoeuvred down the treacherous stairs, was installed on trestles in front of the altar and the vicar cleared his throat. He was pretty sure he was getting a cold and joined the pall-bearers in silently cursing Selwyn Byng for dragging him down to this inhospitable place. 'Dearly beloved,' he began and Emilia Byng began her journey to a better place.

The vicar moved to the lectern for the last reading – he did so wish these people wouldn't leave all the talking to him, his throat really was quite sore now – and, flicking over the damp pages of the Bible, began the familiar words, 'For everything, there is a season and a time for every purpose under heaven . . .'

While he spoke, a man still wearing his top hat, moved among the congregation. As he passed Grand, he whispered in his ear, 'The corpse's brother would take wine with you.' Grand looked startled. He hadn't known that Emilia Byng had a brother.

'It's just an old custom, Matthew,' Batchelor murmured in Grand's other ear. 'We're invited to the baked meats afterwards, that's all.'

'Oh, I see. That's a surprise. Selwyn hasn't caught my eye once today.'

'He's probably trying to put all this behind him,' Batchelor said, trying to be generous, though how he could just forget the past weeks and their terrible denouement, he couldn't imagine. Most people would wake up screaming every night for the rest of their lives.

The small company tackled the stairs as the strains of the final hymn still hung in the air. Already, the carping was beginning, now that the serious work of grieving could be put aside. The mourning clothes might be worn for a year, but the mood didn't have to be sombre. Miss Moriarty poked Enid in the ribs and hissed, 'Do you always *have* to sing an octave above everyone else? It was like standing next to a canary.'

As always, the patient Enid took no offence. 'That hymn is a tricky one,' she said. 'I wish they didn't always have it at funerals. "Love Divine, All Loves Excelling" – clearly the choice of someone who never goes to church. Such a peculiar key, it's in.'

'Musical, are we, now?' Miss Moriarty grumbled. 'Is there any medicine left?'

Teddy and Micah seemed to have aged a decade. It crossed Grand's mind that perhaps they were the only two to honestly mourn Emilia. They toiled up the steps as if going to the gallows. Selwyn Byng was waiting for them at the top and bent his head immediately in earnest conversation, from which Teddy recoiled in horror. Micah, slightly deafer, took longer to realize the subject but also reacted with distress, pushing the widower away with a frantic flapping of his hand. He and his brother veered away before they reached the small anteroom where the funeral feast waited.

With a glance at each other, Grand and Batchelor followed them and caught them up just as they were getting into their carriage.

'Mr Westmoreland, Mr Westmoreland,' Grand said, nodding to each twin. 'Are you quite well? We noticed . . .'

Micah blinked away his tears. 'Oh, Mr Grand,' he said. 'It's you. Thank you so much for coming to say goodbye to our dear Emilia. It is such a pity you never knew her, such a lovely girl.' He looked under damp lashes at Teddy, who had slumped back on his seat. 'We've taken it hard, as you see.'

'We couldn't help but see Mr Selwyn Byng speak to you just now,' Grand said, gently. 'It seemed to upset you even more.'

'We wouldn't ask, if it weren't important,' Batchelor chimed in, 'but everything anyone has to say must be followed up if we are to find who killed Emilia and Molly. Even things that people say without thinking, literally anything could lead us to the killer.'

Micah was stricken. 'Poor Molly!' he cried. 'We haven't given her a thought!'

'I understand that Dr Kempster has arranged a decent burial for her,' Grand reassured them. 'He is a kind man, if sometimes made a little brusque by his calling. And his wife would have made sure it was all done with respect. Molly had no family to speak of, so I guess she's just another orphan of the storm.'

'That's something off my mind at least.' Teddy had opened his eyes and was looking rather less like a corpse. 'But I will never forgive Selwyn, never.'

Micah nodded. 'It was the grief talking, I am sure, but he asked us, at the top of the steps just now, with his wife lying cold and alone below us, whether . . .' He pressed his lips together and dabbed his eyes.

'He asked us,' Teddy said, leaning forward, 'he asked us when he would get the trust money. Apparently,' the word came out like a bark, 'apparently, it's expensive, burying a wife.'

There seemed little more to add and it was only decent to let the old men go back to the security of their tea-scented rooms, where they could mourn their Emilia and the dead, dusty days in peace. The enquiry agents stepped back from the carriage and, with a click of the tongue and a flick of the whip, the driver took them away.

'The four o'clock post, boss.'

Hamish handed over the letters on a silver salver, etched with the arms of Buccleugh. Richard Knowes took the first, sniffed the envelope and ignored the rest; until, that is, his eyes alighted on a letter with a WC postmark. He tore it open.

'Well, well, well,' he chuckled. 'Here's a turn-up for the books. It'll cost, of course, but . . . we've had a request for help, Hamish.'

'What, a begging letter?' Hamish was horrified. Charity never moved further than home in his world.

'Of a sort.' Knowes sat back in his captain's chair and gave the orders. 'Got a pair of scissors?'

Hamish had. Not the ones he kept down his trousers to threaten people with, but a rather genteel pair Mrs Knowes also used for her crewel work.

'Is there a newspaper to hand? Or, failing that, the *Telegraph*?'

There was. Hamish had a sure thing going at Newmarket tomorrow and the runners were all listed there.

'I want you to find the words and letters that make up this short piece of prose, Hamish.' Knowes handed him the enclosure from his letter. 'Then I want you to cut them out and glue them onto a backing sheet. Plain stationery, of course, and pop it in the post for me.'

'Right, guv. You don't want it hand delivered?' Hamish fingered the knuckleduster in his pocket – he did so love a spot of hand delivery.

'No, in the post. Follow the spelling to the letter, but the gist is that we know all about a certain someone from what his wife told us before we strangled her and tossed her in the river. There's mention of a certain amount of cash . . .'

Hamish looked at his bit of paper and shrugged.

'. . . but that hardly seems worth our while. Make it ten, don't you think? Anyway, it's all written down there. Want me to read it out, make it simpler?'

Hamish grinned. 'Don't you worry about this bit of prose, guv,' he said. 'That sounds like poetry to me.'

'It's that lunatic.' Mrs Rackstraw had thought she had seen the last of him, what with his wife having turned up dead and all. The papers had been full of it and there wasn't a soul in London didn't know about the grisly end of young bride Emilia Byng and the plight of her grieving husband. She had adjusted her corsets meaningfully at the breakfast table in the kitchen and said darkly that grieving he might be, but he was still a lunatic; and here he was again.

Grand and Batchelor looked up. 'Mr Byng,' Grand said,

pleasantly. 'To what do we owe the pleasure? You could have paid our bill by post, you know. You didn't have to call round.'

'Bill?' Byng looked blank. 'Bill? Why should I pay your bill? Emilia is dead. However, that's not why I'm here. I got this this morning, in the first post. Look!' He held out a crumpled piece of paper and shook it under Batchelor's nose.

Backing away slightly, he took the paper and spread it smooth on the cloth. '*Telegraph* again, I see. Let's see what it says . . . hmm. It appears to be from our friend the kidnapper.' He pushed it across so Grand could read it too. It certainly did seem depressingly familiar.

'"While we had yur wif wiv us she spild a lot of beens about you bring ten fousand in cash to Durand's Wharf Thursday midnight com alone or we nark to the esclops."'

Byng was bouncing from foot to foot in his frustration. 'What can it mean?' he said.

'Esclops is underworld slang for the police,' Batchelor said, but the widower was clearly in no mood for a literal translation.

'Sit down, Selwyn, do,' Grand suggested, pulling out a chair. 'Well, this all depends on you, really, doesn't it? *Does* this man, or men, perhaps I should say as he says "us", have anything he can use against you? What might Emilia have told him?'

'Nothing,' Byng snapped, dropping into the chair. 'My life is an open book. I have never even been spoken to by a policeman before all this. I've never even scrumped an apple.'

Grand could believe that. Scrumping apples called for a certain amount of personality and spunk and Byng didn't appear too well off for either.

'So, in that case,' Batchelor said, 'don't go. Why pay money – ten thousand, Matthew, that sounds a lot, doesn't it? – why pay someone to keep quiet about nothing at all?'

'On the other hand,' Grand said, 'if you are ready to go into danger, Selwyn, we could apprehend Emilia's murderers. That would be something, surely?'

'But . . .' Byng looked unsure. 'How do we know it *is* her murderer who has written this?'

'The spelling, for one thing,' Batchelor said. 'It is fake.'

'It just looks like an uneducated person to me,' Byng said. 'Someone who just . . . well, who can't spell.'

'I have a way of proving it,' Grand said, and leaned over to pull the bell which summoned Maisie like the Demon King. Sure enough, the echoes were still ringing when she appeared in the doorway. 'Maisie,' Grand said, 'did you go to school?'

'A bit, sir. I had to help Ma with the little uns most of the time, though.'

'Well, sit yourself down a minute. No, don't worry, Mrs Rackstraw won't mind.'

Maisie amused herself for a moment with the thought that you didn't have to be stupid to be seriously unintelligent. But she sat down as requested.

'Now,' Grand fished for a stub of pencil and took out his notebook. 'Turn to a clean page and write down what I say.'

'I'm no good at spelling, sir,' she protested.

'Not to worry. Just write this down.' He read out the note, watching her pencil so he didn't go too fast. 'Lovely,' he said when they had finished. 'Well done. Thank you, Maisie.' His smile could have toasted bread and Maisie wafted down to the kitchen on wings of love.

Grand passed the notebook to Batchelor and Byng. 'See. The mistakes aren't anything like the ones on your note, Selwyn. She can't spell wife, true, and . . . well, I'm not sure what that word is . . . but she can spell beans, thousand and come. You see?'

Byng nodded reluctantly.

'So I think this is from the kidnappers and we have a chance to catch them.'

'But no police!' Byng was adamant.

'Why not? We don't have to worry about Emilia now, do we?' Batchelor was pragmatic but it was said kindly.

'No . . . but . . .'

'Don't worry,' Grand said. 'No police, but we will be there. We won't come with you so they will know we're there, but we'll hide somewhere nearby. How does that sound? Oh, and can you get ten thousand pounds?'

'I'm not paying them ten thousand pounds!' Byng was on his feet, a vein jumping in his forehead.

'No, of course not. But you need to go to the bank, make sure you are seen by as many people as possible, and draw it out. It will take them a while, so you won't be able to keep it secret anyway. Will you do that? We can keep you safe from having to hand it over.'

'I haven't had the trust money paid over, yet. Teddy and Micah . . .' he pulled up short.

'There's no need to tell us all your business, Selwyn,' Grand said, taking a swig of coffee. 'But if the long and the short of it is that you now have ten thousand at your disposal, then that will be fine and dandy, won't it? Do you want to meet here or at Durand's Wharf?'

'Er . . .' Byng felt he had been railroaded somehow, he wasn't sure how.

'I think the Wharf,' Batchelor said. 'You know it, of course? Timber importing place?'

Byng did.

'Shall we say a quarter to midnight. Mr Grand and I have a few errands to run first, but we'll be there, I promise.'

And with that, Mr Selwyn Byng, recent widower and permanent coward, had to be content.

EIGHTEEN

The wind off the river was chill and had the whiff of October in it that all the river's denizens had learned to dread. Under the scent of autumn leaves from the parks along its banks it was possible to discern the crack of frosty nights and the acid catch at the back of the throat that only comes from a couple of million chimneys belching the black smoke of cheap coal smouldering under a couple of million kettles and pans. Selwyn Byng clutched a large bag to his chest and burrowed his chin into his muffler. Nothing had been what anyone would describe as fun ever since Emilia had disappeared like a puff of thistledown between Eastbourne and London, but this night was the worst yet.

He was beginning to talk to himself. It was a habit which had worsened over the last weeks and he was trying to master it but even so, sometimes it just got the better of him. 'Where in God's name are those two idiots?' he asked himself through clenched teeth.

'Here we are,' a voice muttered in the dark. 'We've been here for the last half an hour, Selwyn. But don't mind us. It's just on midnight. If I were you, I would step out into the light, so that your hosts know you're here.'

'Don't leave me,' Byng whimpered.

'We won't.' This time it was Batchelor's voice and it held more irritation in it. 'Idiots don't do that kind of thing.'

Clutching his bag tighter, Byng stepped out of the shadow into the weak moonlight that flooded the flat area in front of the looming warehouse at his back. He strained his ears for any hint that he was not alone and after a few minutes, he was rewarded by the sound of a crunch of a leather-shod boot on gravel. Out of the gloom, a man appeared and he wasn't at all what Byng was expecting. Despite himself, and in common with almost everyone able to spare a copper or two, he was an avid reader of the *Illustrated Police News* and so he knew for certain that miscreants all had short chopped hair, a grizzled chin which stuck out a mile, far ahead at any rate of their severely receding forehead. In extreme cases, their knuckles almost dragged on the ground and their clothes were a ragbag of old jackets and trousers held up with string.

The man who finally stopped just an arm's length from Byng was of medium height but there was a hint of strength about the set of the shoulders and the breadth of the chest under the immaculately tailored charcoal grey suiting. His tie was in a perfect knot, clearly done by a valet; no one alive could tie anything that perfect in a mirror. His shoes shone with hours of burnishing with neat's-foot oil and a hot spoon; Jonathan Warren's blacking had never sullied their perfect surface. The man doffed his brushed beaver hat, revealing its bespoke leather and silk interior.

'Mr Byng?' His voice was mellow and modulated, no hint of the gutter to be heard.

'Er . . . yes.' Byng's grip on his valise loosened somewhat. This was a dream, surely. He looked vaguely around for the chicken which usually appeared at about this point but there was nothing. 'Did you send . . . was it you who sent . . .?' Somehow, the question sounded rather stupid. Of *course* this man didn't send an ill-spelled note made up of letters cut out of a newspaper!

'Well,' the gent sounded rather self-deprecating. 'Not *me*, exactly. It was Hamish.'

From the deeper shadows, an enormous tweed suit stepped out, encasing a giant of a man with a cigarette carelessly held between finger and thumb. Something about it suggested that not only was it something the suit's wearer enjoyed smoking, but that it could also be a handy weapon.

'Good evening, Mr Byng,' the giant said. 'Or,' he cocked an ear to listen out for distant chimes, 'could it be morning by now? Anyway, pleased to meet you.'

Byng gulped and grasped the money bag tightly again.

'Chilly tonight,' the first man remarked. 'Or at least, you seem to find it so, Mr Byng. You're shivering. Hamish. Warm Mr Byng up.'

Hamish took a long drag on his cigarette so the tip burned like lava from a new volcano and advanced on Byng.

'No, no need,' Byng whimpered. 'I'm not cold. I'm just a bit . . . nervous.'

'Nervous, Mr Byng? Whatever for?'

Byng, in the manner of a cornered rat, suddenly lost his temper. 'You get me down here in the dead of night,' he blustered, 'accusing me of all kinds of things. Extorting money. Beggaring me, to be frank. And you expect me to just smile and hand it over. Well, I won't. I just won't. I know you haven't got anything on me. There's nothing to have.'

'Oh, come now, Mr Byng.' Richard Knowes was nothing if not meticulous and he had been doing his homework. 'There's that little bit of fluff you kept down in Peckham.'

'Kept,' Byng said, triumphantly. '*Kept*. That's the main thing. I haven't seen Lucille in a year. And anyway, with my wife dead, who cares about Lucille?'

'Your father might.'

Byng shrugged.

'Your wife's trustees might.'

'It's nothing to do with them. And anyway, how did you find out about Lucille? No one knew about her. Certainly not Emilia, so even if you *did* have her, you couldn't have found out from her.'

'That's true,' Knowes said. 'But there's more than one way to skin a cat. What about your debts?'

'I don't owe a penny, anywhere.'

'Not *now* you don't,' Knowes agreed. 'But you did. And to a colleague of mine, Cauliflower-Ear O'Connor, one of the nastiest bookies in London. If you had wanted to gamble, Mr Byng, you should have gone somewhere reputable. Like to me, for instance.'

'A small wager, nothing more.' Byng was on the defensive, but still clutching his suitcase of money. 'And as you say, all paid off now. And again, Emilia knew nothing about it. She was in Eastbourne the whole time. You need to tell me something that only Emilia could know.'

Knowes was impressed. Worms could turn, he knew, but he had never actually witnessed it happening. 'Hamish,' he said over his shoulder. 'I think this is more of a cigar problem, don't you? Fire one up, there's a good chap. Now,' he turned back to Byng, 'you don't seem to fully understand the situation, Mr Byng. You see, I don't have to prove anything at all. Your wife is dead, true, and I am very sorry for that. I have spent a lifetime avoiding doing any harm to women. Hamish will bear me out . . .'

'Certainly will, boss. Always a proper gent, you are. And both the Mrs Knoweses would stand up in court to agree.'

'There you are,' Knowes said, 'never a truer word spoken. I don't like men who hurt women, but when they're dead, I suppose they're dead and that's all there is to it. Never mind, for anyone so inclined to part you from some more money, Mr Byng, there's still Lucille . . .'

'Lucille is old news,' Byng muttered.

'Perhaps so. But there'll be others. And we'll be watching, Mr Byng. It is my belief that you came here because you have secrets to keep. Otherwise, why would you? And I have found out two secrets without leaving my desk. So what others did your wife have under her pretty little bonnet?'

'None. My wife was a saint. She didn't have a bad bone in her body.'

'Rumour on the street, Mr Byng,' said Knowes, 'she discovered a few bad bones before she died. Medical examiner reckons she was at it like a weasel . . .' again, he turned to Hamish, 'it was "weasel" he said, wasn't it, Hamish?'

'I believe it was, boss,' said Hamish, between puffs on a large and dangerous-looking cigar.

'Like a weasel with whoever held her captive. Now, Mr Byng, at this point, I have to tell you, it wasn't me. Because the Mrs Knoweses keep me more than busy. But . . . well, science doesn't lie, Mr Byng, much to the chagrin of the criminal classes, or so I believe. So, who might that have been, do you reckon? Who could have got up the petticoats of your angelic Emilia? She was keen enough, goodness knows. I mean, she didn't take much persuading; she hadn't been kidnapped all that long. I've known it happen before, that I have. But it usually takes months. Years, even. But your Emilia – well! Days, if that.'

Behind the man, Hamish chuckled. 'Must have been a bit of a flighty piece, boss. I tell you who probably had her . . . hurr

hurr hurr.' Hamish gave a smoky laugh, 'it'd be Wang Wang, you know, that Chinese bloke in the Minories. Does a bit of white slaving but keeps the best uns for himself, they say. Not many as'd say no to him.' Hamish looked at Byng. 'On account of he's got a—'

'Come now, Hamish,' Knowes shushed him. 'Have some decency. Mr Byng doesn't want to hear that kind of thing. He doesn't want to hear his Emilia likened to a common trollop off the streets. He—'

Byng suddenly screamed and threw the bag at Knowes, catching him full in the face and knocking him temporarily off balance. 'You pigs!' he screamed. 'You're not fit to lace my Emilia's boots, let alone speak of her in this way. Whoever this man is, she wouldn't give him a second glance. She never had eyes for anyone but me, not from the moment we met. We were soulmates, do you hear me, soulmates.' He leaned over and grabbed the bag just before Hamish did.

Knowes brushed himself down and regained his poise in seconds. 'Don't take your eyes off that bag, Hamish,' he muttered. 'It's ten grand if it's a penny. Little twerp has actually brought the money. He's more of an idiot than we thought.'

Byng clutched the bag to his chest and crouched low, literally at bay. His eyes were wild and his mouth was working. 'My Emilia,' he said, through clenched teeth. 'My Emilia did *not* give herself to another. It was *me*, don't you see. It was *me!*' His eyes became vague, looking into far distant sunny uplands where only he and Emilia could go. 'We worked it all out, you see. She didn't know why, but she knew we were short of money all the while. She tried her best, little economies here and there. She even persuaded poor Molly to work for no wages until our ship came in. But then even she could see that it couldn't go on any further and that we would have to do something drastic.'

Deep in the shadows, Batchelor and Grand looked at each other; this plan was working better than they could have hoped. And Knowes and Hamish belonged on the stage; their double act would slay them down at the Elephant and Castle. Soon, they would have enough information to take to Bliss, though they knew it would be their word against Byng's; Knowes was not likely to go into Bliss's Abode willingly and there wasn't really any other method, when it came to Dick Knowes.

'So, she got off the train a few stations back down the line and I met her. We rented a little cottage in Hampton Wick and it was idyllic. It was like being on honeymoon, every day.' Even Hamish, not one of nature's sensitive souls, looked quite moved. 'Molly was there, to cook and keep house for us. Anyway, the rest you probably know.'

Knowes shrugged. He didn't know it all, by any means. He glanced across to where he knew Grand and Batchelor were hiding, a question in his eyes. Grand gestured for him to keep the conversation going. With a flash of inspiration, Batchelor had dashed off to find a policeman, any policeman, to hear what Byng had to say.

'I don't know everything, Mr Byng,' Knowes drawled. 'Even *I* don't know *everything*.'

'Well, we sent the letters. We had such fun. Emilia roared with laughter when we made up the spellings. Then, we found out that the trust fund couldn't be broached. Those mad old buffers Teddy and Micah had never told her that, just that she would get the lot when she was thirty-five. Thirty-five, I ask you! Her father was as mad as a tree before he died, or he wouldn't have pulled that kind of number out of the hat. We didn't even know about the trust until I had . . . until he had his accident.'

Grand's eyes widened. If he had had any sympathy for Byng and his plight before, he had none now.

'But surely you knew that there would be conditions?' Knowes was incredulous. There was nothing about tontines, trusts, escrow and other arcane financial shenanigans that he didn't know.

'Yes!' Byng spat. 'Yes, we knew about the age thing, but we didn't see why Teddy and Micah shouldn't be able to dip into it, let some free, so to speak, to help out. They *loved* Emilia. We thought they would . . . well,' his shoulders sagged, 'we thought they would just cough up the money.'

'But they didn't,' Knowes prompted.

'No. They didn't. They couldn't, as I see now. But I thought that they were being difficult. So, without telling Emilia, I . . .'

Byng dropped to his knees and howled the words to the indifferent London sky. 'I took Molly with me one morning, I told Emilia we were going marketing. And . . . and . . .'

Over in his shadowy corner, Grand heard footsteps and voices behind him and he ran to silence them. Batchelor had managed to find a bobby on his beat just up the road, but he had been difficult to convince. He kept his rattle in one hand and his truncheon in the other, ready for anything. His beat was a lonely one, and boring, so being accosted by a gentlemanly looking cove and told that a murderer was confessing not two streets away was hard to resist. On the other hand, he wasn't born yesterday, hence his high level of preparation.

Hamish and Knowes had known some bad people. They *were* some bad people. But even they were aghast at what they were hearing. The three men hidden in the dark lee of the warehouse could scarcely believe it either.

'I took her past the shops in the village, down to the river. I said we were getting some oysters from an old fisherman there. She was walking ahead of me. I . . . I strangled her from behind and cut off her finger.' The old Selwyn Byng, always ready to blame someone else, came to the fore. 'It was really difficult. You have no idea how hard it is to cut off someone's finger.'

Hamish and Knowes glanced at each other and shrugged.

The policeman did a double-take. 'Is that Dick Knowes?' he whispered.

'Best if you forget that bit when you put in your report,' Grand told him and the man nodded. No point in mixing with Dick Knowes unless you really had to.

'I had persuaded Emilia to remove her wedding ring – I told her I might have to send it to Teddy and Micah – and I forced it onto Molly's finger. I'd read all about the body parts some lunatic was leaving all over the Thames, and it occurred to me, if I cut off her hands and feet as well, to make it look more . . . how shall I put it, deranged? If cutting a finger off was hard, you wouldn't believe the difficulty with bigger bones. Then, I pushed her in the river.' He looked at Knowes, whose face was far from its unreadable self. Yes, he had done some terrible things, but only to people who deserved it. And he – yes, even the great and feared Richard Knowes – had often felt some measure of remorse. But this little rat seemed to be able to justify it all. 'It upset me,' Byng said. 'I wasn't right for days.'

Grand, who had come very close to Molly in the dark waters of the river, took a step forward. He didn't care what happened to him, but he would swing if necessary for the cold-hearted bastard.

'No, Matthew.' Batchelor grabbed his arm and held him back. 'Not yet. Wait.'

The beat bobby weighed in with his professional view. 'He ain't worth it, sir,' he said. 'We've got enough to hang him twice over.'

Grand stepped back, but his fists stayed clenched.

'And then,' Byng whined, 'it all started to go wrong. Grand and Batchelor poked their noses far further into it than I wanted them to go. I'd only gone to them to give the kidnapping some kind of verisimilitude. Going to the *actual* police would have been insane, but a pair of hopeless amateurs . . . perfect. If necessary, they would testify to my heartbreak and the hopelessness of my situation; that I had done all I could in the dreadful circumstances. They went round to the address I'd given that nosy old bat Auntie Jane.' He took on a singsong falsetto on the name and the men listening knew that he was mimicking his dead wife. Their stomachs turned over with revulsion. 'But I was ready for them. I knew it was empty, that's why I used that address. It's some stupid case of an unproved will, or something. Anyway, I went round to the agent and pretended to be a lawyer and they gave me the keys. People are just so stupid. I hired some furniture on sale or return, and a butler, some actor who needed a few extra pounds in his pocket. Grand and Batchelor, bunglers that they are, took so long about it that they were almost still there when the men came to fetch the furniture back. It was touch and go, I don't mind telling you.'

'It was, too,' Batchelor muttered. He still woke up sweating with the sound of the harness jingling in his ears.

'That actor would be a useful witness,' said the constable, promotion glittering above his head.

Grand rummaged in his pocket and passed over a slip of

paper. 'Here's his name and the address of his lodgings,' he murmured. 'We called on him at the theatre on the way here.'

The policeman had heard some harsh words about enquiry agents, but he couldn't help but be impressed. Of all the actors in London, how could they have possibly known which one it was?

'Emilia got difficult, though.' Byng whined like a toddler told he couldn't have a second helping of trifle. 'She wanted to know where Molly was, she wanted to go home. She was useless at cooking and we were living on bread and cheese. I couldn't afford another month in the cottage and we couldn't go back to the mews where we had been living. We'd been evicted from there while she was still in Eastbourne. So . . .' he slumped further so his head was on his knees. 'So . . .'

'So?' Knowes knew the score. He had often extracted information from people, though they were usually less forthcoming than Byng. He knew it was important to get every little detail; afterwards, when they calmed down and had a bewigged lawyer in tow, would be too late. 'Hamish.'

Hamish stepped forward and without preamble pressed the glowing end of his cigar to the exposed back of Byng's neck. The man writhed and screamed. 'There was no need for that!' he screamed. 'I'm telling you, aren't I? So . . . I killed Emilia. I waited until she was asleep. She had wanted to . . . you know . . . when we went to bed, so I did it for her, one last time.'

Knowes couldn't help a yelp of disgust.

'Well . . . it wasn't fair. I was tired. But I did it anyway. Then, I strangled her. She was asleep, though. She wouldn't have known anything about it.'

'That's it,' Grand said. 'That's just about enough. I'm going to kill the bastard.' He stepped out from the shadows and called. 'Byng. Byng, you monster. Come and take your medicine, like a man.'

Byng looked round, startled, and struggled to his feet and shambled over. 'Oh, Mr Grand,' he whimpered. 'Look what these men have done to me. Look.' He bent his head forward to show the burn. 'Is that a policeman? Arrest these men. They've been making me say all sorts of horrible things. I don't feel well. I feel sick.'

'So do we, sir,' said the constable, reaching for his notepad and pencil. 'I'm afraid I am going to have to arrest you for the murders of . . .'

'Arrest me?' Byng was outraged. 'Arrest *me*? What about arresting these four? They are in it together, I see it now. They have tried to extort ten thousand pounds from me, as well as assault my person.'

The policeman looked around mildly. 'What ten thousand pounds would that be, sir?'

'There,' Byng said. 'There, in that bag.'

The policeman raised his eyebrows. 'I see no bag, sir,' he said, calmly.

Byng spun on his heel and looked, aghast, at where the bag had been. The flagstones stretching down to the river were innocent of anything or anyone. The bag, Knowes and Hamish had all vanished as neatly as if they had never existed.

'But . . . but you must have seen those men,' he blustered. 'That huge one in the tweed suit. The one in the . . . The bag with . . .' He took the constable by the shoulders and shook him. 'Come on, man. You are a tool of justice. You must have seen them, surely.'

The bobby was not the quickest of thinkers, but he knew what was best for him. Ratting on Richard Knowes and the infamous Hamish was as good as breaking your own kneecaps and cutting out the middleman. He shook his head. 'No, sir. I just saw you, behaving rather strangely, if you don't mind my saying so, shouting and raving. You even went to the lengths of burning yourself with a cigar. Mr Grand, Mr Batchelor and I got quite concerned about you and called you over. That was when you made some rather strange remarks. Also, if you don't let go of me, I must add assaulting a police officer in the pursuance of his duty to the list of misdemeanours of which you stand accused.'

Grand leaned across to Batchelor. 'Good choice, James. When I think of all the others you could have chosen . . .'

Policemen they had known and come to despise wandered in a ragged line before their eyes.

'Yes, you're right,' Batchelor said, 'but it wasn't a choice so much as the only one available. Hold on, though, he's off!'

Byng, letting go of the policeman, had turned and was running for the edge of the dock. Slipping on the wet stones, he sped away, heading for the warehouse of Sillitoe, Byng and Son, which was within easy reach across a small culvert taking waste water from the road on the far side of the buildings.

'Don't let him get into his own warehouse,' Grand shouted. 'He'll easily lose us there. Spread out!' Batchelor and the bobby took the water's edge and Grand twisted to his left, hoping to head Byng off before he could jump the culvert.

Although Byng was not what could be called fit, he had the element of surprise and even more so when he suddenly swung back the way he had come and disappeared down the side of the warehouse of Durand's timber and disappeared into the dark. Grand was right behind him, so much so that it was easy for Byng to take him by surprise when he thundered up the alley into a dead end. As he shook his head to clear it, Byng stepped out from the alcove only he knew was there and grabbed Grand from behind in a choking hold across his throat.

'Not a word, you Yankee,' Byng said. Grand was outraged at the slur but couldn't say a word. He could hardly even breathe. 'Now, we are going to walk out of here, like gentlemen. Can you feel this?' Grand felt a knife prick him just above the waist. 'I may be just a timber merchant, but I know where a man keeps his kidneys. Try and cry out, I kill you. Struggle, I kill you. And when we are free and clear, well, I'll probably kill you. It won't bring me any pleasure. I quite like you, Mr Grand. But I don't see I'll have much choice. For now, we are going to take a walk round between these buildings, and I am going to let myself in to Sillitoe and Byng. Forget the son; father will have that painted out by close of business. I'm going to get us a carriage harnessed up and then I rather fancy a boat to France. What about you? Don't bother to nod. Just walk.'

Batchelor and the policeman had suddenly realized that there was no longer anyone to chase and they turned in time to see Byng and Grand sidle out from the side of the warehouse.

'Don't come any nearer,' Byng shouted, 'or he's a dead man. Stand back.' He brandished the knife, so they could see he meant business. 'Further. Further. That's it. Now, don't move and he'll be all right.' Then, whispered in Grand's ear, 'Perhaps.'

Grand's feet skittered on the cobbles. It was hard to keep his
footing on the slimy stones, without having to worry about
catching his next breath and keeping the knife away from his
kidney. He was an optimist by nature, but he was beginning to
think this might be his last ever walk. He wished it could have
been through a meadow of primroses with his best girl, a lark
singing its head off in the blue sky overhead, but perhaps this
end was pre-ordained when he started his career as an enquiry
agent. Lights were flashing behind his eyes and his chest hurt.
His legs were feeling rather weak and rubbery. In fact, his
thoughts tried to muster but he wasn't listening, in fact, it might
be simpler just to lie down and go to sleep.

His next breath was suddenly easier. The lights stopped but,
in the background, there was splashing and shouting. A hand,
small but hard and calloused, brushed the damp hair from his
brow. Soft lips kissed his cheek and warm salt tears washed his
face. He struggled to open his eyes, bruised and swollen from
the pressure on his throat. A face swam into focus.

'Maisie?' he rasped. 'Maisie? What are you doing here?'

She laughed when she saw he was alive, then cried some
more. 'I follows you sometimes, Mr Matthew, on my evening
off. I worries about you, you see. So, when you showed me
that note, I knew nothing good would come of it. That man's
a lunatic, Mrs Rackstraw says. So . . . I followed you. It wasn't
hard but I had to run sometimes, to keep up with the cab.'

'You ran after the cab?' Grand tried hard to swallow. His
throat felt as if it was on fire.

'Well, I can't afford to take one, not on my wages,' she said,
affronted.

'No, I see that, but . . . where's Mr Byng?'

'I pushed him in the culvert. He knocked his head, but Mr
James and that busy are getting him out.' Her face clouded over.
'Mrs Rackstraw ain't half going to be wild at me, Mr Matthew.
Can you have a word with her?' She looked so worried, he
couldn't help but try a small chuckle.

'Maisie,' he said, 'Maisie, Mrs Rackstraw won't ever shout
at you again, I promise.' They both knew that was a promise
no one could keep, but she knew he meant well, and that was
enough for her.

NINETEEN

The three of them wandered the bank of the river that October morning, the brown water more wreathed in mist than was usual for the time of the year.

'I read Constable Watkin's report,' Daddy Bliss said, his hands in his pockets, a wistful expression on his face. 'Pity you had to go out of Thames Division in this instance.'

'I thought you'd have been more concerned about our rather unconventional use of friend Knowes,' Batchelor said.

'That would be the friend Knowes who's not mentioned anywhere in the report?' Bliss checked.

'That's the one, but I'm guessing Byng will bring it up at his trial,' Grand muttered, 'muddying the waters, so to speak.'

'His brief won't use that,' Bliss assured him. 'He'd be laughed out of court.' He looked at the men on each side of him. 'Don't worry, gentlemen, I think I can assure you that Mr Byng will keep his rendezvous with old Calcraft.'

'I heard a rumour he's retiring any day,' Batchelor said. 'Hanging up his ropes, or whatever retired hangmen do.'

'Yes,' Bliss said. 'I heard that too. Let's hope he holds on for Byng, though, eh? One last bungle, for old times' sake? Nothing like slow strangulation to make the great British public think justice has been done. Tell me, what made you suspect Byng in the first place?'

'That business of the actor-butler,' Grand said, 'and the price tag still on that whatnot at his house. It was false, the whole thing. That and the fact that Mrs Rackstraw, our housekeeper, had him down for a lunatic from the very first day she clapped eyes on him.'

'I just don't think either of us thought that anybody could stoop so low,' Batchelor said. 'No wonder his old man couldn't stand him.'

'Hmm,' Bliss nodded. 'So, just to keep the record straight. We've got one count of impersonating a policeman,' he narrowed

his eyes at Batchelor, 'Sergeant Spinster. One count of co-
operating with a known felon, to whit, Richard Knowes and
the use of menaces to extract a confession. And I haven't even
started on . . . what's that?'

Whatever he was talking about and whoever he was talking
to, Daddy Bliss's eyes rarely left the surface of the water. All
his adult life, he had policed it, watched it, listened to it. More
than Mrs Bliss and the little Blisses, more than Bridie O'Hara
who might have been, it was the river Daddy Bliss loved.

Grand and Batchelor followed the man's pointing finger.
Bobbing out near the centre stream, rolling a little as the eddies
took it, was an arm. It was pale and sodden and very probably
came from a woman. Bliss looked up-river to where the bulk
of the *Royalist* rode at anchor. He could see the tiny figures
milling about on deck.

'Gosling!' he bellowed. 'Crossland! Brandon!' He paused.
'No, not you, Brandon! Get over here, now!'

He rolled up his jacket sleeve and grabbed an oar from a
skiff bobbing at the water's edge. 'Give me a hand, here, gents,'
he said to Grand and Batchelor. 'Gents?'

But the mist that was wreathing the riverbank, or perhaps two
clean pairs of heels, had turned the enquiry agents invisible.

AUTHOR'S NOTE

The Ring is based on the series of actual murders that took place along the Thames between 1873 and 1889. A total of eight women died. The case remains unsolved.